ASSIGNATION WITH DEATH

"Bondhe Amari, your life is claimed by Hoorka."
Amari crouched in the furthest corner of the room, cocooned in shadow, his back pressed tightly against the wall. Gyll could see the eyes, frightened, moving nervously. He began the ritual for a trapped victim.

"Prepare yourself, Amari kin-less. How do you want to meet the Hag?" He held out the capsule to Amari.

Amari looked sidewise at the capsule, his head half-turned from the Hoorka. Then something seemed to snap in Amari's eyes. He jerked upright, his hand clapped Gyll's away, and he screamed. Gyll reacted, powered by instinct and training, without thought. Gyll's dagger slashed forward, sheathing itself deep in Amari's midriff.

Amari gasped, a sound that turned to liquid gurgling. Pink foam flecked his lips. His knees buckled, and Gyll stepped back to let the body drop to the floor.

The Hoorka stared down at his hand. Amari's lifeblood stained him to the wrist.

Hag Death had come.

Bantam Science Fiction and Fantasy
Ask your bookseller for the books you have missed

DANCE OF THE HAG

Stephen Leigh

BANTAM BOOKS
TORONTO · NEW YORK · LONDON · SYDNEY

DANCE OF THE HAG
A Bantam Book / March 1983

ISBN 0-553-23034-4

Published simultaneously in the United States and Canada

Bantam Books are published by Bantam Books, Inc. Its trade-
mark, consisting of the words ''Bantam Books'' and the por-
trayal of a rooster, is Registered in U.S. Patent and Trademark
Office and in other countries. Marca Registrada. Bantam
Books, Inc., 666 Fifth Avenue, New York, New York 10103.

PRINTED IN THE UNITED STATES OF AMERICA

O   0 9 8 7 6 5 4 3 2 1

FOR JOHN MASSARELLA
—who made the dance begin,
and who never saw the first one

1

She had a name, but she would not let it enter her thoughts. It was archaic, a useless symbol of the past still clinging to her like an autumnal leaf, dead and lifeless—like an ippicator. Her existence belonged to the Dead now; the past was something she had forcibly torn from her mind. It had been a systematic pillaging, a harvest all of discarded chaff, pain and disappointment and too few joys—the onus of being lassari. Now she had no past to haunt her and no future to mock her with false hope. There was only the long and endless present and the companionship of her fellow Dead.

The Dead had no names and no kin. They were beyond the dull hurt of their lives. They had only themselves and the everpresent spectre of Hag Death, leading them on their procession to Her. They gave no notice to anyone else.

Yet tonight she could almost feel the brush of the Hag's talons against her skin. The presence stirred the air, made her forget the wall between herself and the world Neweden. She could smell the miasma of decay, the sweetness of rotting flesh. The presence moved with familiarity in the land.

As if it was very secure in its domain.

Close, very close. It was as if Hag Death mocked her with Her gap-toothed grin, as if—turning quickly, gasping—she would see Her and the end of this life would come.

There are always endings.

The Dead were encamped on the plain of Kotta. Someone had found the ambition to start a small fire: it threw a wavering circle of yellow warmth across the dry grass. There was little food to be had; those of the Dead that still had the desire to feed themselves were now huddled about the blazing sticks, silently eating. The woman who had sensed the presence shook her head at them, then turned outward to the plain once more, snuffling like an animal. Yes, it was there, mingling with the odor of burnt meat and unwashed bodies (for why should the Dead, who counted themselves beyond the ken of life, care for hygiene?). It was a spice smell and the cool sweetness of rich earth: the spoor of the Hag wafted to her, elusive, on the northern breeze. She shook her head, lashing her neck with stringy, grease-matted strands of hair as she strove to capture the essence moving over Neweden. She concentrated on feeling that ethereal world that lay, a gossamer veil, over reality. This was a meditation she practiced while marching with the Dead, during the long days while they chanted the eternal mantra. She often saw visions through the marches. Once, even the face of Hag Death had appeared to her, and she had trembled at the thought that the Hag had come at last to claim her.

No—she berated herself, pushing the thoughts away—*the Hag would come in Her own time.* Now she must get beyond the aching of her hard-callused feet, the itching of her flaking scalp, the hard knot of hunger in her belly.

Yes. The sense of presence was still there, but she despaired of its coming nearer. She tugged at the ragged tunic falling down one shoulder, sniffing. She hunkered down on the earth, grasping handfuls of dirt and letting it fall back through her fingers. She stared at the darkness beyond the fire.

A star moved in the sky, from east to west.

She knew, suddenly, that this would be a full night for Neweden, an evening of unrest. The Hag would see to that: She was full of cold mirth and an uncaring amusement. The woman found herself hoping that the presence would turn to her. Then, perhaps, Hag Death would embrace her at last. *The Hag would pull her to Her sagging breasts, drooping blue-veined over her stomach. She would suckle the bitter milk of those paps as the taloned hands of the Hag tore open her skin, as if it were the husk of some insect. The empty body, bloody, would be disdainfully cast aside for the maggots, and Hag Death would draw out her naked soul and place the morsel in Her broken mouth.*

To join with the All-Dead. To be, finally, at peace.

Letting the last of the dirt fall from her hand, she lay down on the high grass. Around her, the Dead—perhaps thirty of them in this group—slept or chanted or simply sat. The stars veiled themselves in cloud. Sleipnir, rising, colored the horizon with milky blue-white.

She wondered again at the Hag's presence. Who would She touch? Who were they?

The city of Remeale sat on the edge of the Kotta Plain, near Arrowhead Bay's triangular mouth. It was a mining town, a dirty and poor city perched wanly by the ravaged hills, a spectator to the exhumation of the earth's riches. Sectors of Remeale were legendary for their filth and anarchy—"a lassari from Remeale" was a vile description for any person on Neweden, a vivid insult even if somewhat of a cliché—and those sectors were noted for their ability to supply anything anyone might want of an illicit sort. By day, Remeale was merely shabby; at night, it took on a filthy animation.

Here, two shapes moved in the black night, cloaked with rough capes dyed matte ebony and gray.

In this burrough, dying buildings leaned drunkenly toward each other, at times meeting in a decaying embrace above the narrow streets, trapping foul darkness below. The walkways, littered with the detritus of humanity, weren't wide enough to allow a groundcar passage; at various places, a person walking would find himself crowded by the houses on either side or need to duck beneath an obstruction half-seen in the night. Even with the daylight, some part of the evening remained, darkening the area, making it a twilight landscape viewed through a dingy gel.

The two intruders came to a brief halt in a doorway. The smaller of the spectres leaned against a doorjamb that was many degrees from vertical.

"How close do you think we are, Ric?" The voice was a light contralto, pleasant even though roughened by whispering.

Light flared by the larger shape, which rapidly took on substance and form: a massive man enfolded in a cloak as dark as the streets around him, his face doubly hidden by a beard and longish blond hair glowing ruddily in the light of his handtorch. The light died as quickly as it had come, and he waited for his night vision to return.

"He's close, if the apprentices have done their work well—and remind me to tell Thane Mondom to repair this damned map. The light's gone out in it, and I don't like using the handtorch. We've still hours left to the contract, though. Dawn's at 5:56:40, and it's barely one at Underasgard."

"Good." Iduna sighed and pushed herself erect. "Let's move, then. I want some time to do other things before sleeping."

"Need a partner?"

"Certainly." She touched his arm briefly, a quick caress. 'Let's get this over with."

Masked again by night, the two Hoorka made their way down the tangle of streets, half-running and keeping to the sides of the walkways where shadows cloaked them. The Hoorka were rarely bothered by others, especially when on a contract with the

Hoorka armed and alert, but they wanted no interference tonight. They turned at a corner where a hoverlamp sputtered fitfully and cast a dancing illumination over a sated wirehead sprawled in the intersection, his open eyes glazed and unfocused. He moved fitfully, spastic, as the Hoorka slipped past him.

They went by a large house where some celebration was evidently in progress. The Hoorka could hear conversation, music, and—once—a scream that held genuine terror, a ululation of horror. D'Mannberg paused a moment, listening for the repetition of the scream, but Iduna touched him on the shoulder, shaking her head. They began moving once more into the maze of tiny streets and claustrophobic alleys.

It was only a few minutes before they came to a small square where the buildings leaned away from each other to form a marketplace. Empty stalls sat in disordered ranks around the area; a few hoverlamps bobbed in their holding fields, throwing erratic shadows about the houses bordering the square. The Hoorka paused in the dark mouth of an archway leading into the marketplace, searching for any movement before they entered—Hoorka had been killed on contract before; that knowledge bred caution where the assassins suspected traps. It was, after all, the victim's right to escape in any way he could. Dame Fate had no special dispensation for Hoorka, and Hag Death did not care who fell into Her maw. It was best to pray to She of the Five Limbs, the goddess of the extinct ippicators and patron of the Hoorka, and to be careful.

There was a man in the square.

They both saw him in the same instant. He sat on an overturned crate on the far side of the market, staring dully in their direction. The hoverlamps threw a gigantic shadow-parody of him on the wall behind. At the foot of darkness, he looked very small and fragile.

D'Mannberg squinted into the light. He nodded to Iduna and the two assassins walked slowly into the open space, drawing and activating their vibroblades. Their footsteps were loud in the night stillness, and the vibros gave forth a low humming that resonated and built, echoing from the buildings. The man made no move to flee from them. He watched the Hoorka approach, his face resigned and hopeless, his hands clenched between his knees. His head dropped slowly as they came nearer to him, as if he were unable to hold its weight any longer. By the time the Hoorka stood before him, he was in a huddled crouch. They knew he could feel their eyes on his back.

"Cade Gies, stand up." D'Mannberg's voice, though pitched

oftly, sounded loud in the square, deep and ritualistic. Iduna, eside him, looked briefly at the walls flanking the market. Jeads had begun to appear at a few of the windows, curious eople staring down at the tableau below them. It didn't matter. The spectators didn't look as if they intended to hinder the Hoorka in their task, and it was better entertainment than that offered in their holotanks.

Gies made no movement, still tucked against himself. D'Mannberg, glancing at his companion and the silent witnesses around them (lips drawn back from his teeth in a snarl of distaste at the watchers), put his hand on the man's shoulder. He felt Gies shudder at the touch and move away with a soft moan. The assassin tightened his grip on the cloth and pulled. Gies came stiffly to his feet, hands balled into impotent fists, his eyes closed and his head averted. He waited, a thin, soft wailing escaping his clenched teeth.

"Cade Gies, your life has been claimed by Hag Death. Dame Fate has severed the cords of your existence." D'Mannberg's words were brittle with ritual, but then they softened in pity/disgust as Gies suddenly jerked away from the Hoorka and doubled up, retching dryly. D'Mannberg stared down at the frightened man. "We're not monsters, Gies. You're a slave of the Hag, but we can make your passage to Her easier. It needn't be painful or frightful." His voice was a whisper, harsh in darkness. Gies did not reply. Still hunched over, he spat once, then again, wiping his mouth with the back of his hand. His breathing was rapid, wheezing from his lungs.

"Look at us, Cade." Iduna's velvet voice seemed to calm him. Gies stood, slowly, his gaze sweeping over the onlookers, now leaning on their elbows in the windows. His broken stare finally came to rest on the Hoorka. He saw two pairs of oddly sympathetic eyes. The rest of their faces were masked in their nightcloaks.

"Death comes to each of us," Iduna said. "Even as an off-worlder, you can understand that. Hag Death will have Her due. And we Hoorka are but instruments in Dame Fate's hands."

"They're not my gods." Gies's voice was a cracked whisper, his eyes as wild as an animal's, pleading with their moist softness.

"You're on Neweden, and those are the gods that rule here."

Gies shook his head. "I don't believe in gods."

"Then simply believe in death," d'Mannberg said. "You had your chance to escape us and you chose not to run—the apprentices explained your alternatives to you." D'Mannberg's voice struck at Gies as if it were a weapon. The man shuddered under the impact.

"You're going to murder me!" His last words were a frantic shout that echoed back to them from the surrounding walls.

"Not the Hoorka," d'Mannberg replied, very softly. "We're but weapons in another's hands. The guilt, if any, belongs to them."

"Who?" Gies demanded. His hands clutched at the assassin's nightcloak, and d'Mannberg backed away a step.

"I can't tell you."

"Tell me, if you have any compassion. I'm dead anyway— what difference would it make? Tell me, so that I can haunt her from my grave."

D'Mannberg glanced at Iduna, an exchange without words. "I don't know who signed the contract, Gies. I would tell you if I knew, but I don't. I'm sorry."

Gies swayed softly, as if he might fall. D'Mannberg reached out to steady the man. "I can't tell you," he continued, "but your kin will know. All Neweden will know. Our code commands that all successful contracts be made public. You can be assured of that."

"It's not *fair*!" He ended with a wail. A few more windows dilated to reveal new spectators.

"The Hag is never fair." Iduna held out her hand to Gies. The man looked down, as if expecting to see a vibro held there. But the palm held only a small gelatin capsule.

"Take it, Gies. It'll make your passage to the Hag enjoyable." Iduna waited as Gies reached out with a tentative forefinger to touch the capsule. He had small hands, dainty hands—he had not seen much labor. His fingertips trembled, and he hesitated, looking at d'Mannberg.

"Consider the alternatives, man. Would you rather I used my vibro?" He held the weapon out to Gies. Its angry snarl was frighteningly loud to the man. Gies, his lips tightly clamped, shook his head.

"It doesn't matter," he said. "Oldin—she wants Neweden, and she'll take it as she's taken everything else." He grasped the capsule gently between thumb and forefinger—always with that slight aura of the effete—and held it for a moment near his mouth. "She'll destroy you, too. You'll see."

With a convulsive movement quite unlike his normal demeanor, he tilted his head back and swallowed.

"Soon?" he asked.

D'Mannberg nodded.

The two Hoorka moved back from Gies as he sat on the crate once more. Gies stared at the assassins, blinking slowly. He grinned, abruptly, then giggled, a sound that, reverberating, became a full manic laugh. D'Mannberg glanced about the market: they were still watching, the silent ones, leaning forward now as if they wanted to be closer to the moment of this pathetic man's death, as if the Hag might momentarily become visible as She came to collect the proffered soul. D'Mannberg knew that this night would fill the next morning's conversations.

Gies was still laughing when his body found that it could no longer support itself. He fell backwards to the ground and rolled onto his side, his legs doubled up, fetal. He took a deep, rattling breath that began to dissolve into hilarity, then was suddenly still.

Silence wrapped the square as the Hoorka switched off their vibros.

Iduna took a spare nightcloak from her pouch, handed one end to d'Mannberg, and together they covered the body. The onlookers slowly began to withdraw, the windows going opaque as they returned to more private diversions. Distantly, they could hear a complaining voice and loud music beginning in midbar.

"At least this is over," d'Mannberg commented. He hefted the body of Gies across his shoulders, grunting with the weight.

He was wrong in that. It was just beginning.

"You're just reflecting your own doubts, Gyll. The meeting wasn't run that badly, no matter how you view it. Bachier's challenge couldn't have been anticipated. I thought Thane Mondom handled herself well."

"To a point, Cranmer. I saw her, I know what *I* would have done in her place, a few months ago. Bachier wouldn't have been cut by kin then. Gods, man, I have a good deal of affection for Mondom, both as a friend and a lover, but I can see that she shouldn't have been so abrupt with kin. They're all proud people. Leadership doesn't have to mean heavy-handedness."

"And it's always easier to criticize from the outside. Look, you're feeling an understandable loss of control since you abdicated in favor of Mondom. Couple that with the last several contracts you've worked and your, ahh, irritation..."

"Forget the last contracts. Just—*shh,* be still."

Ulthane Gyll and Cranmer were in the outer caverns of Underasgard, with the moon Sleipnir throwing cold light past the jagged mouth of the Hoorka-lair. Gyll, sitting slump-shouldered on a boulder, suddenly lurched erect and stared intently at a cave-rodent moving slowly across the broken floor. Cranmer, wrapped in a thick nightcloak, curled his lips, wrinkling his nose in distaste.

The rodent, a stalkpest—a furred body with patches of open sores (it had evidently been in a recent fight), a small head from which the thin whip of its eye-sensor sprouted, a lithe quickness when it moved—stopped, started, and crept forward again, always closer to Gyll. Underneath his nightcloak, Gyll fingered the hilt of his vibro as Cranmer glanced from stalkpest to assassin.

The stalkpest stood on its hind legs, the eye-sensor slashing like the tail of a nervous cat, then inched forward. Gyll lunged, the vibro hissing from its sheath already activated, the arm plunging down. The stalkpest keened in surprise and terror, the body convulsing against the weapon that pinned it to the ground, the claws skittering helplessly. Gyll flicked off his vibro and sheathed it. He prodded the body with a boot tip.

"One less to get into the stores," he said.

Cranmer, from his boulder seat, shivered. "The damn things give me chills. How can you stand to get near it?"

"A Neweden axiom, scholar—to kill with honor, you must always be near. Our Ulthane taught us that." The voice came from the darkness of the corridor leading back into the caverns. Gyll and Cranmer both turned to see Aldhelm regarding them. His nightcloak melded with the cavern's eternal gloom, but Sleipnir's glow played on his face—light eyes above the furrow of a scarred cheek. "Good evening, Ulthane, Sirrah Cranmer," Aldhelm said, nodding to each in turn. His gaze went to the bloody stalkpest. "Practicing, Ulthane?" A faint smile seemed to twist the ridge of the scar. "A pity our victims are rarely so easy."

Gyll felt a rising anger, fueled by the sarcasm he sensed in Aldhelm's voice. The last three contracts he had worked, the victim had escaped: Cranmer had mentioned it already this evening, and Gyll had been soured by the Hoorka Council earlier. Gyll had heard the whispers of his guild-kin. *Ulthane Gyll doesn't seem to care for the hunt any more—I was with him, and he didn't seem concerned, didn't have the sharpness he once had. He looks like he's brooding, lost. He's gotten out of shape—he doesn't work enough with long-vibro and foil. He thinks about the victims, wonders about their lives. He's depressed, moody. Ever since he named Mondom as Thane . . . By the code—Gyll's code—the victim must escape from time to time, but for the Hag to go hungry on three consecutive attempts:*

it could simply be Dame Fate's will, but the whispers and the well-meant jests from his kin hurt, made him narrow his eyes in irritation.

"You think I need the practice, Aldhelm? Is that your intimation? Because of the contracts?"

Aldhelm moved in darkness, frowning. Rock scraped rock under his feet. "I didn't say that, Ulthane."

"You didn't have to." Gyll swept his nightcloak over his shoulder. Moonlight glinted from the vibrohilt at his belt.

"Ulthane," Cranmer began from his seat, his voice uncertain. The short, thin man cleared his throat. "I think—"

"I was speaking to Aldhelm, scholar." Gyll did not look at Cranmer, but at the other Hoorka.

Aldhelm stared back. "When I failed *one* contract—yah, it was the Li-Gallant's and thus important, but you teach us that each contract is as important as the next—you gave me this." Aldhelm touched his cheek and the high ridge of the scar. "We all fail contracts, Ulthane. You set us up that way when you created Hoorka. It's what sets us apart. If your failures bother *you*, well, I think you need to shrive yourself, not be angry with kin." Aldhelm's face was set in careful stoicism, neither smile nor frown.

With the words, Gyll felt his anger cool. *Of all Hoorka-kin, he has the most right to taunt you, and he doesn't. You called him a friend once, after all.* But Aldhelm had opposed Gyll on the two contracts the Hoorka had worked for the Li-Gallant Vingi, both intended to kill the Li-Gallant's political rival, Gunnar. Aldhelm had twice felt the touch of Gyll's vibro, and whatever affection they had shared had gone with the blood. Gyll didn't apologize to Aldhelm, but nodded down at the stalkpest.

"Cranmer and I came out here to see if d'Mannberg and Iduna were back, and I happened to see the 'pest. It'll feed my bumblewort instead of raiding our grain." Gyll stopped, noticing the bulging pack under Aldhelm's nightcloak for the first time. "You're going out?"

Aldhelm stared at Gyll, defiance ready in his eyes. "Yah." For a moment, it seemed that he was not going to say more, but then he hefted the pack, adjusting it around his shoulders. "There's an Irastian smith in Sterka, visiting. He's reputed to be very good with blades. I'm taking a few things to show him, and I'm also going to see what he might have for sale." Aldhelm's affection for edged weapons was well known among Hoorka.

"You've gotten Thane Mondom's permission?"

"After the uproar during Council last night? We both saw the blood from Bachier's wound, Ulthane—and I'm not saying it wasn't what he deserved for arguing with the Thane. But I'm not going to risk my own skin by leaving Underasgard without telling her first."

"I thought she had sufficient reasons for making the ruling," Cranmer said. He had wrapped the cloak more tightly around him; the offworld scholar had never gotten used to the cooler Neweden climate. "With the reports of lassari attacks on lone guilded kin, and Eorl being killed in an unprovoked assault, it makes sense to know where all Hoorka are."

Aldhelm nodded. "I realize that. You don't have to lecture me, scholar."

Though the man's reproof was gentle, Gyll's irritation rose once more; he was silent a moment, forcing it down with an effort. *So quick to anger of late—calm down, old man.* "Go on, then. But be careful, Aldhelm. The kin can't afford to lose you."

"I'm always careful, Ulthane. And I'm also very good with my weapons—I'd worry about the lassari, not me."

Gyll watched as Aldhelm strode past him to the cavern mouth. Gulltopp had risen—its crescent grinned below that of Sleipnir. Aldhelm was briefly a silhouette against the backdrop of night sky (twinned shadow dark on the jumbled rocks of Underasgard), and then he moved on into the night.

Carefully, Gyll picked up the stalkpest in a fold of his nightcloak. "For the wort," he told Cranmer.

"Aldhelm seemed angry." Underneath cloth, Cranmer hugged himself.

"He's always angry," Gyll said. He stared past the cavern mouth to the dawnrock standing lonesome in the clearing and the newly clothed fingers of the trees beyond. "It hasn't killed him yet."

The grounds outside Gunnar's window lay hushed in twilight, which was quickly arranging itself in the darker shades of full night. Sleipnir was up, Gulltopp was rising. Gunnar stood before his window for a long minute, staring at the landscape that surrounded his guildhouse, then he touched the contact that opaqued the glass. A wash of purplish black swirled in the panes; then the tendrils met, snaking about each other, swelling until all was black. Gunnar turned back into his room.

He was not feeling well tonight. A vague boiling churned in his gut and a sour taste lurked in the back of his throat—though, he mused, one might expect such reaction after the evening's dinner. De Vegnes had been the cook for the night; his tastes ran to the unusual, the exotic, the highly spiced. Such fare tended to unsettle the stomachs of guild-kin used to a blander and more provincial menu. But if he wanted Potok to be able to speak before the Assembly next week, he would have to ignore the moaning of his stomach and work. Gunnar shook his head: Potok was an excellent speaker and a charismatic personality, but he needed to be fed the words he regurgitated. He was never able to create them himself.

The Muse of Speech was resting this evening. Even Gunnar, usually quick and facile, couldn't find the words he needed— every phrase that appeared in the terminal of his desk seemed clumsy, falling over itself with pretentiousness. Gunnar clutched his complaining stomach, grimacing. He finally sighed in resignation and reached for the wooden box that sat on one corner of the desk. He opened the malawood lid, taking out the black silk that held his Tarot. He toyed with the cards, turning them in his thin hands and leaning back in his floater. He riffled the deck, though his mind was still entangled in the forest of Potok's speech. He thought—as he did every time he handled the cards—that he would have to have them reproduced soon. They were simply too old and fragile for his constant handling. The trader from whom he'd purchased the cards claimed that they came from Terra herself. Extravagant tales of their lineage aside, the cards were ancient in appearance if not in fact: they were printed on cardboard, the image inked on the surface, two-dimensional. The corners were soft, bent, dog-eared with use, and one of the cards—the knight of swords—had once been folded in half.

Abandoning all hope of finding an opening for Potok's speech, Gunnar spread the cards face down on his desk and plucked a card from the array.

The Tower: an edifice crumbled to dust in the midst of a storm, while figures plunged to their deaths from the ramparts. An eye veiled in clouds watched impassively from above. Gunnar shook his head once more, his narrow face pinched in irritation. The card was ill-omened, not that Gunnar professed a belief in the card's ability to predict events. His attitude was more that of an interested skeptic, though he did feel that a person of some power had once possessed the cards, and that this imagined person had been able to use them to peer murkily into the many possible branches of the future. For his own part, he doubted that Dame Fate would be willing to reveal Her whims so easily. There were times: more than once he had thought he could discern a pattern to the cards that had fallen into a reading, some cohesiveness that suggested a single course of events.

The Tower, then: danger, destruction of plans, ruin. Gunnar tossed aside the card and pulled another from the pile without looking at its face. He held the card in his hand for a long moment, his eyebrows lowered in concentration, studying the intricate scrollwork on the back. The Sun, he guessed.

The Devil. Fate, blind impulse, a secret plan about to be executed: from the card's face, a horned goat stared at him balefully, a sceptre before it, and figures below the animal joined in mystic symbols.

"Well, then I'm to be damned and double-damned," he muttered. He threw the card down.

"Light," he said, and the room brightened in response to his command, the hoverlamps in each corner irising open. "Enough." Gunnar leaned forward, gently moved the cards to one side, and touched the metal circle of a contact on the desk's surface.

He leaned back once more, hands behind his head, eyes closed.

"Some notes for you, Potok. Though I think I might end this by telling you not to listen—I think de Vegnes's supper has ruined my sense of composition.

"Point One: that Oldin woman insists that our guild will figure prominently in her plans, though she's yet to give me any indication of what that might mean. She smiles when she says it, and she has a predatory smile. And she's also as closemouthed about her 'plans' as a puffindle. I think we might do well to find out more about her and the Families—she's only been here a few months, but there's been more disruption around Sterka in those months than in the last five standards. There might be a file on the Family Oldin in the Alliance Center. An offworlder isn't going to react as will those of us born to Neweden, and we can't expect her to have our best interests in mind. We need to know which way she'll jump if we push. By all means, bear in mind that you can't trust her—she's an avaricious bitch and she'll go whichever way promises her the most, and I know she's had meetings with the Li-Gallant as well. We have to be in a good position to promise her more, or she may start dealing with the other side. Butter up that tongue of yours, kin-brother. I expect miracles of it."

(His eyes shut, his back to the window, Gunnar did not see the darkness swirl or the stars become visible through the now clear pane. Nor did he see the apparition that appeared there: the head and shoulders of a person wearing a light-shunter. His/her features were torn and scrambled, waves of pulsing shadow moving erratically. Dark against blackness, the head turned and fixed upon Gunnar.)

"I'm going to work on your speech tomorrow." Gunnar stretched his legs out beneath his desk—a joint cracked loudly. "We have to stress the fact that our guild has gained in strength in the last several months. I actually think that I have the Hoorka to thank for that, having failed to kill me twice. It certainly put us in a good light with the other guilds. We'll cite all the economic woes that Vingi's rule-guild is causing. And I'll hit hard on the ippicator smuggling and the lassari troubles—that's Neweden's lifeblood. I expect you to have them shouting by the finish, so we can call for a vote of confidence in the Assembly. We'll lose, but it'll give an indication of the rate of erosion in support for the Li-Gallant, and it might just throw a scare into Vingi. If we can force him into an open election . . ." Gunnar's voice trailed off. His eyes opened, questioningly. He sensed something *wrong* with his room, though he could see nothing out of place. He started to turn in his floater, to rise.

He had only a brief second to glimpse the night-veiled face at the window before the soundless blast of a render tore the substance of the glass into dust and then struck him. His face contorted in agony so intense it did not truly register as pain. The render shredded the fabric of his chest, the living cells ruptured and smashed. Gunnar fell backwards over his desk, his flailing arms scattering the cards of his Tarot. The body, unwilling to admit the reality of its death, jerked spasmodically, then finally lay still.

The face at the window (an elusive and vague outline, a monstrosity of fluid shape) stared into the room for a few long seconds before dropping from sight.

Alarms, far too late to help Gunnar, wailed through the house.

Morning.
The sunstar lathed the Kotta Plain with heat and light. The silent call of dawn woke the small encampment of Dead. Drowsily, they rose at the light's beckoning, gathering their chimes and censers and bells. Someone—an emaciated young man, the filth of the five day journey across the plain on his body and a scraggled, matted beard of indeterminate age masking lips cracked bloody with heat—began a plainchant, a dirge of greetings to the Hag. The

morning offering to their patron rose from the several throats to be snatched away by a westerly breeze.

They readied for the day's march. Though no one spoke to another—conversation was also a thing of life—they knew that they would reach Remeale before the sunstar set again, and perhaps the Hag awaited some of them there. If not, they would seek Her beyond. It was a simple axiom: the encounter with the Hag was inevitable. Until that time, the Dead paid no attention to those that still sought their living dreams on Neweden.

Even the living would one day find the Hag waiting for them.

They were standing now, waiting for one of their number to take the initiative and begin the march. A fume of incense wafted ahead of them, and they were now assembled in ragged order. The chant wavered, then altered itself. It had been noticed that one of their number lay still and unmoving in the grass—a woman, dressed in a soiled, torn tunic. She had been with them for some time, and the Hag had come to her during the long night. They chanted their praise to the Hag. Still singing, the Dead began the slow, inexorable parade to nowhere, leaving the body on the grass of Kotta Plain.

When the noise of their passage had subsided into a faint treble chiming (the Dead now dark specks wavering in the heat of the horizon), the carrion eaters came. They padded toward the abandoned campsite and the burnt circle of grass, moving with habitual caution, stopping every few seconds to sniff the air which reeked of human spoor.

They found the gift that had been left them. If they praised any god for the bounty, they did not say.

They merely feasted.

2

Excerpt from the acousidots of Sondall-Cadhurst Cranmer, taken from the notes of his stay with the Hoorka assassins of Neweden. The access to these notes are with the kind permission of the Niffleheim University Archives and the Family Cranmer.

EXCERPT FROM THE DOT OF 2.27.216:

"I'd thought that the Thane—no, dammit, Gyll isn't Thane anymore; I'll learn that one day soon—I'd thought that *Ul*thane

Gyll had managed to stagger toward some even keel with the Hoorka, but that optimism might have been premature. It's partially his own fault, I admit, and he'd probably admit it also: his ambitions for Hoorka, to see them implanted offworld and escape the bounds of Neweden, are likely to lead to problems. And despite his resignation and the conferral of power to Mondom, I suspect that Gyll still tries to guide the Hoorka through her, thus removing the guilt of failure by one place.

"No, that's unfair as hell to Mondom... Gyll is probably learning that if he wanted to use her as a figurehead, she will not play that game with him. She's a strong-willed person in her own right; I hope I'm wrong, but I expect the two to come to some confrontation over that.

"The Hoorka are still not politically stable. Certainly the Li-Gallant Vingi holds a grudge against them, as it's an ill-kept secret that it was *his* contract for Gunnar's death that was twice failed. Or, as Gyll would probably say: 'Gunnar was blessed by Dame Fate.' Since the Li-Gallant holds the reins of power on Neweden, the Hoorka are not going to be given any concessions in their quest to become independent of Neweden, though Gunnar's rule-guild is gaining in support, by all indications I've seen. The problem that's making all that significant is the caste-bound social system of this world. In time, there might have been a slow, natural progression away from the idea of guild-kinship, but the Alliance has put too great a strain on the structure—cracks are beginning to appear, for Neweden finds itself no longer alone. In particular, the lassari are responding to this and becoming militant, no longer content to accept their role as the dregs of Neweden society.

"Now if I can remember to correlate and substantiate all this in the eventual paper..."

(Here there is the sound of glass against glass and liquid being poured. The transcriber was turned off; when the recording resumes, the time-tone indicates that it is a few hours later. Cranmer's speech is noticeably slower and muffled.)

"The, ahh, social structure here hasn't been subjected to outside influences in centuries: the planet was only on the outer fringes of the Huardian Empire and never knew the yoke of that Tyrant's oppressions; before that is the long darkness of the Interregnum, with only a modicum of contact from the Trading Families. And Neweden was settled only after the First Empire fell apart—that's *your* area of expertise, Bursarius—yah, I know you'll listen to this when I ship it back to Niffleheim, and I'm not going to meddle with that part of history.

"A point. Is there any significance to the fact that Neweden was settled not by a normal outward push of humanity, but by a group of exiled bondsmen?

"Wandering again . . . I'm glad I'm the only one that has to listen to these dots, and I apologize to my future self for all the maunderings. And of course to you, Bursarius. You still there?

"Umm . . . I know I wanted to say something else. Oh—the Hoorka code still bothers me, despite all of Gyll's rationalizing. It sets them apart from the common criminals and makes them viable in Neweden society, but it also makes them susceptible to damage from outside change. When Neweden society eventually shifts, as it's going to, I'm afraid the Hoorka will find themselves just one of the corpses in the pile.

"By all the gods, that's a gory image there. Too much binda juice again . . ."

(Here there is the sound of Cranmer drinking, followed by another refilling of his glass. At that point, the transcriber was shut off once more.)

M'Dame Tha. d'Embry, Alliance Regent for the world Neweden, was not pleased with the way the day had gone thus far. She'd awakened to a dismal rain that left the sky a uniform, wan gray. There was also a constriction in her chest that made breathing difficult until she grudgingly let the autodoc in her room minister to her for a few minutes. Her left arm still felt the prick of the unit's sensors, and the constriction, while lessened, was still there, a faint shallowness of breath when she exerted herself. And the rain had not stopped when she'd reached her austere offices in Diplo Center. Outside her window, the ranks of clouds sat unbroken across the sky, and water pooled on the flat expanse of Sterka Port.

The news, when she'd asked Stanee for her report of the night, had not been encouraging: Gunnar had been killed, assassinated by an unknown assailant in his own guild-house. She'd drawn back from her viewer in genuine shock. Murder, the cowardly slaying of someone without declaration of bloodfeud, was a very rare occurrence on this world. It was far too easy to gain satisfaction through duel. And Gunnar's rule-guild was second in power only to that of the Li-Gallant Vingi. It had been reputed that Gunnar would one day wear the robe of the

Li-Gallant; it could not happen now. D'Embry decided she would not like to see this morning's Assembly meeting.

A dim suspicion formed in her mind. "Stanee, is there any indication that the Li-Gallant might have been involved in the murder?"

The face in the viewscreen—amber hair short at the sides and cascading unshorn down the back, lips and earlobes and eyelids touched with shimmering lapis lazuli; all the latest fashion done correctly but without dimming the counter impact of a plain face—frowned below d'Embry's field of view. "No, m'Dame, though let me check with Intelligence." A moment's pause, then Stanee looked up once more. "By all reports, all of the Li-Gallant's guard force is accounted for last evening; the Domoraj had some festivity. Unless Vingi used a hireling, maybe a lassari . . ."

D'Embry cut off her speculations with a wave of her veined hand. "No, I doubt it. Let it go, let it go."

"Will there be anything else, m'Dame?"

D'Embry ran a hand through dry, whitened hair, glancing sourly out the window to the damp morning. "No. You may return to your other duties."

"Thank you, m'Dame. Oh, Karl's asked me to remind you that Kaethe Oldin of the Trading Families has entered the Center. You'd asked to see her today. Did you want her sent up immediately?"

"Shit," d'Embry said, loudly, then smiled at the shock Stanee tried unsuccessfully to mask. "Surely, child, you didn't think we relics lack the words to utter a curse?"

A tentative grin.

"Send her in, Stanee. I wish I could avoid it today, but why ruin a perfectly awful morning." She sighed, then frowned as a twinge of pain accompanied her next inhalation. "That's all." She reached out with a quick gesture. The screen flickered and went dark, receding into the floor. D'Embry sat back, gingerly testing her breathing and awaiting Oldin's entrance.

Kaethe Oldin was tall and rather too heavy for the standards of Alliance beauty—the legacy of low-gravity life. Yet she carried it well. Her demeanor spoke of confidence in her appearance. The face was angular, a denial of the body's weight. Above high cheekbones, her eyes were large, dark, and impressive. The woman evidently knew the impression they made, for her eyebrows were gilt, drawing immediate attention to the walnut pupils below. The stamp of FitzEvard Oldin, head of the Oldin conglomerate, was in his granddaughter. Her attitude told d'Embry more than she wished to know—Oldin strode into the Regent's office with no hint of timidity, nor did her gaze move from the Regent to the soundsculpture in a corner of the room or the animo-painting on one wall; her entire presence exuded purpose. When she stood before d'Embry's desk, it was with one hand on her hip, the other thrust into the pocket of her pants.

"M'Dame Oldin, the Alliance is always pleased to welcome a member of the Trading Families." The words came fluidly from her, but the Regent's intonation was deliberately cold and removed. *It's so easy to fall into after all the standards of practice—that aloof Diplo manner. It's been so long that it sometimes becomes the reality and not the mask. And it's far too late for me to change.* "I once knew your grandfather. You remind me of him."

Oldin flicked her gaze over d'Embry, and the Regent felt as if she'd been dissected, judged, and dismissed: yes, her grandfather's legacy. He'd had the same disdain for the Alliance, the same subliminal declaration of challenge. D'Embry didn't find the realization particularly satisfying.

"Yah, he'd mentioned that you had banned him from Crowley's World after a disagreement over trading rights. He said to give you his regards, Regent." Oldin's voice was bitter honey; a slow, pleasant alto that hid all the meaning behind her words. With her attitude, with her tone, Oldin reminded d'Embry that the Trading Families were not part of the Alliance, that, at best, the two factions enjoyed an uneasy truce.

"I hope you didn't find my request inconvenient."

"It wasn't particularly convenient, Regent—I've duties aboard *Peregrine*. But the Alliance rules here, doesn't it?" Oldin smiled.

"Rule is a poor word, m'Dame. The Alliance is more flexible than that. We oversee, advise, or leave a world as it wishes." D'Embry folded her hands on her desk—fingers tinted yellow-orange with bodypaint—and allowed herself to sit back in her floater. "Would you like to sit?" She touched a stud on her desk, and a hump-chair extruded itself from the carpet.

"I'll stand if you don't mind, Regent." Oldin glanced at the chair, then back to the older woman. Again a slight smile touched the edges of her mouth.

Bitch. Like FitzEvard, yah. "As you wish." D'Embry shrugged. "And since this *is* an inconvenience to you, I'll be brief and frank." Deliberately, she stared at Oldin, meeting her dark eyes. "As a matter of course, I receive all Hoorka contracts here, since

hey've applied for and been granted temporary offworld visas.
Your name was on the contract the assassins worked last night.''

"Everyone knows that, Regent. The body of Gies was given
to me at my shuttle on the Port. The Hoorka made no secret of
that—it's part of their code, is it not?" Her gilt eyebrows flashed
reflected light, but she did not blink or look away.

"Cade Gies was an Alliance citizen and an offworlder to
Neweden." D'Embry's voice held a cold edge; she pulled her
gaze away in anger, glancing at her window. Rain sheeted down
the glass. When she looked back, Oldin was examining her
hands, unconcernedly; long, thick fingers, broken nails.

"Gies *was* an Alliance citizen," Oldin replied, emphasizing
the past tense with a nod. She shoved a hand back in her pocket,
put the other on her hip. "And I'm of the Families, and *your*
allegiance is to Niffleheim. But we're all on Neweden. It seemed
fitting that I, ahh, deal with our conflict, Gies and I, in Neweden
manner. That's the Trader way, Regent. When I've dealt with
aliens, I've tried to adopt at least a superficial gloss of their
customs. The Alliance would not understand that." D'Embry
opened her mouth at the unsubtle hint of Alliance xenophobia,
but let the woman finish. "I wanted to see the Hoorka work, in
any case. They're an interesting group, don't you think?"
Oldin's voice was casual, lazy.

"On other worlds of the Alliance, a 'conflict' doesn't have to
end in death. Gies wasn't a physical man nor was he easily given
to entering arguments. I knew the man slightly, m'Dame Oldin,
and I'd be curious as to the nature of your altercation."

D'Embry's voice had risen and she found herself sitting
forward in her chair, her back erect. The chest pain of the
morning returned, suddenly, and she found it difficult to take a
deep breath. She forced herself to relax. *Be calm, old woman.
You're giving her exactly the reaction she wants.*

Oldin watched the Regent. She shifted her weight from one
foot to another, staring as the Regent made an effort to control
her pique. "There's nothing you can do about it, Regent. I
violated no laws, and Cade Gies was given every opportunity
that would have been given any Neweden kin—or that *you're*
going to give other Alliance citizens by allowing the Hoorka
offworld work. Are you going to inquire into the disputes for
every Hoorka contract? The argument between Gies and myself
is my own business—I won't bother you in your areas of
authority; please give me the same consideration. I'm here to sell

my stock, nothing else.'' Oldin paused. ''With all due respect, Regent.''

''All of Neweden falls under my authority, m'Dame.''

''It must be a heavy burden.'' Oldin's voice was just shy of open sarcasm, but her eyes danced under the golden eyebrows. ''If there's nothing else to discuss, Regent, I do have work on *Peregrine*.''

As Oldin began to turn (the stocky body eclipsing the rain-smeared window), d'Embry stopped her with a tapping of fingers on wood. ''Trader, Neweden is not an open port. You'll abide by all the regulations and restrictions here. I can assure you that I'll be watching you.''

Oldin spoke over her shoulder without looking back at the Regent. ''That's as Grandsire Oldin said it would be. I can quote verbatim the text of the Families-Alliance Pact—all of the Oldins can. It was drummed into our heads very early. I *know* the rules of this game, Regent.'' And she walked away with a casual, quick stride, barely giving the door time to dilate.

D'Embry, after the door had shut once again, thumped her fist against the desk. ''*Games!*'' she shouted. ''The woman speaks of *games!*''

''This is no longer a game, Li-Gallant—it has happened too often for us to remain complacent. The facts are known to all of you: a Hoorka contract was signed for the death of Gunnar. Twice, he escaped the assassins. Ricia Cuscratti, the betrothed of Gunnar, was slain by as-yet unknown assailants. Now Gunnar himself has been shamelessly murdered, a deed without honor done in a most cowardly manner. Is there anyone here that wonders why all my kin cry out for the blood that is our due?''

Potok stood in the Assembly Hall, resplendent in the shimmering turquoise robe of the rule-guild. The sleeves of the robe were ripped and tattered: the sign of his grief. The seven windows of the dome above him, each rendered by a rival artisan's guild, were dull with rain, the colored, shifting glasses wavering with collected water. The sunstar hid behind shifting clouds, unwilling to illuminate the murals. Potok flung his arms wide, displaying his raveled, savaged robe.

The Assembly was unusually quiet. Normally the representatives of the various rule-guilds heckled and insulted one another, interrupting the order of business. But now the echoes of Potok's stentorian voice died unchallenged in the vast chamber as the representatives stared at him, afraid to break that silence: the

death of Gunnar had shaken them all, for it violated the founda-
tions of Neweden. If Gunnar could be killed in this manner, what
protected their own selves?—the thought, uneasy, ran through all
their minds.

"There is a vile cancer gnawing at the vitals of our society."
Potok let his voice drop into a rasping half-whisper. It pulled the
Assembly forward in their seats, made their eyes squint in
concentration as they strained to hear him. Again, Potok found
himself wishing he had Gunnar's gift for words—this speech had
been written by de Vegnes, and Potok could sense that, cliché
ridden, it lacked the fury the subject should have possessed. *My
voice of fire and steel,* Gunnar had once said, referring to Potok.
But now that voice was deprived of the mind behind the words,
shorn of substance.

Still, it could have its effect.

"There are those among us that would drag Neweden down
into chaos, would destroy all that guilded kin have striven to
create. My fellows, Neweden has at its core the idea of honor
and truth. We do not hide behind our hatreds or our loves. Yet
Gunnar has been taken from us, taken by a dishonorable act. It
insults us, it laughs at us. No matter how high or powerful, if we
wish to keep Neweden as it should be, we must find that
diseased part and *cast it out!*"

His voice had risen to a thundering crescendo. He spoke with
a grimace of rage; a fisted hand struck his palm with fury. He
waited, but no one dared to mar the quiet. To the rear of the hall,
someone muffled a cough with a hand.

"My guild-kin mourn. We weep. We are lost in sorrow. Our
sadness is greater than any words I can speak. Gunnar was
guild-father to us all. He cannot be replaced. But he may rest in
the assurance that he will be revenged. I vow now that he will be
given a companion for Hag Death. My guild declares bloodfeud.
When this coward's name is known, we demand our satisfaction.
Give him to us, as you would a common lassari.

"We cannot be comforted, we cannot be placated. We demand"—a pause—"that the government of Neweden extend all
its powers to find the killer of Gunnar. This unknown person
struck not only at Gunnar, but at each and every one of us. He
struck at the heart of Neweden, and Neweden must show her
anger." Potok slumped forward suddenly, as if weary. His voice
was a harsh whisper. "I can say no more to you."

Now he sat, his arms dropping to his sides as the sunstar slid
from behind a cloud momentarily, lighting the dome with brief

shafts of colored light. The first tentative waves of applause
broke, then became a flood as the rest of the Assembly, in a rare
showing of mutual support, acted as one.

(De Vegnes leaned forward toward Potok, sitting stolid and
solemn as the ovation continued. "That was a nice touch,
waiting for that rift in the clouds," he whispered. "I noticed you
watching for it. Good timing, Potok." Potok did not reply, but
the faint hint of a smile raised the corner of his mouth.)

The applause cheered him. Even the Li-Gallant, who had little
affection for Potok and his rule-guild, found it politically advis-
able to force his massive bulk from his floater on the dais and
add to the storming of hands. When the clamor began to show
signs of abating, he sat quickly and gaveled for attention, the
amplified thud of wood on wood sharp in their ears.

"The Assembly is grateful for your words and sympathetic to
your feelings, as you must know, Representative Potok." Vingi's
voice was ponderous, as heavy as the frame from which it
emerged. Corpulent, huge, the Li-Gallant fingered his several
chins as his rings flashed light. "You may rest assured that my
guard force will do everything in its power to find this person. I
will command the Domoraj to begin immediately. Gunnar will
not go to Hag Death unattended. We've always had the greatest
respect for him." Vingi folded his thick hands on the desk before
him, staring down at the Assembly.

Potok exhaled noisily, a sarcasm that only de Vegnes, beside
Potok, could hear. Nodding at the Li-Gallant, Potok whispered
sidewise to his kin-brother: "They'll probably be just as effective
in this as they were when he vowed to find Ricia's killers." The
murderers, who had slain her when Gunnar was first involved in
a Hoorka contract, had never been apprehended. "I suppose I
have to be polite, though."

Potok stood once more, bowing slightly to the Li-Gallant as
etiquette required. "We extend our thanks, Li-Gallant. The skills
of your Domoraj and his force are well documented." *Let him
chew on that and see if it adds up to a compliment.* "My kin and
I will endeavor to find this dungheap of a person as well. The
formal declaration of bloodfeud will be posted before the Assembly tomorrow—a blank certificate until we have a name. We
ask also that a formal day of mourning be declared for all
Neweden, an official recognition of all that Gunnar has done for
this world. It seems appropriate."

Now, for the first time since Potok had begun speaking,
Vingi's face revealed his quick irritation, his mask of sympathet-

ic attention slipping. A scowl bared his teeth. His fingers clenched once and he moved back in his floater, the chair dipping in the holding field as his bulk shifted. It was only a moment, then his face took on once more the aspect of intent seriousness. His voice, when he replied, was as soft as fur.

"It's unfortunate that such an action is not within this Assembly's province. We've no machinery to set such a day aside—we can ask that all guilded kin abide by our wish, but it is a matter of their own discretion. Beyond that"—he raised his arms in a shrug—"we have no power."

Potok flashed anger. His voice, a whip, lashed at the Li-Gallant. "Do you say, Li-Gallant, that you simply don't wish the Assembly to make such a motion? All we ask for is the gesture. The guilds will always act as they wish."

"We'll give all that's within our power." Vingi nodded to Potok, his trebled chin waggling.

"And that is nothing."

"This is an Assembly of the rule-guilds of Neweden, man. I understand your grief and sympathize with your great loss, but we have other duties here. Would Gunnar have wished us to stay idle?"

"You will not make the motion?"

"We can't walk away from the responsibilities we have for the death of one man."

"And what is more important than *your* life, Li-Gallant?"

Vingi smiled. In him, it was not a gesture of mirth. "We ignore a great many insults when in session, Representative, and your sorrow must be taken into account. But I won't ignore covert threats. Withdraw your words."

"Will you make the motion?"

Potok stood defiant, hands on hips, the tattered sleeves visible to all. Vingi stared at the man. Neither moved, neither spoke.

The Vingi sighed. "With the understanding that this will be entirely voluntary to all guilds, I make the motion. I'll have the clerk draw up a proclamation and have it posted. It will be by order of the Li-Gallant, and I'll not call for a vote on this. Are there objections?"

Silence.

"And for your part, Potok?" Vingi scowled down at the man.

Potok, hiding his satisfaction, bowed deeply to the Li-Gallant. "I spoke far too hastily, I'm afraid. I hope that you realize that my mind is addled by grief, and forgive me." Then, under his breath: "You slimy bastard."

Only de Vegnes heard.

* * *

Mondom was a warm softness beside him. Gyll still breathed heavily from their lovemaking, sweat cool on his chest. She cuddled into the curve of his arm, resting a moment, then—with a low growl of mock anger—turned to nip the flesh of his shoulder with strong teeth.

"By the Hag's left teat—" Gyll slid away from her, rubbing his shoulder as the bedfield rippled around them. On his flesh, the impression of her teeth showed white, fading slowly to a dull red. "That *hurt*. What did I do—or didn't I do—to deserve that?" His face was creased in overdone bemusement, the lines about his eyes deepening.

He was answered by an unrepentant giggle. "*That*," she said, very deliberately, "was for your lack of support during the council meeting last night. A little help from you"—she held thumb and forefinger a centimeter apart—"and Bachier wouldn't have made that firm a challenge. You know as well as I do that he was just testing me."

"You have to pass such tests yourself."

"This one wasn't necessary."

She knelt on the bed, her head slightly tilted, her short hair tousled. Gyll could see the yellow-brown mark of a bruise on her left thigh, a reminder of the fight with Bachier.

"Is this what you think of when we're making love?" Gyll tried to turn the subject, discomfited by her sudden seriousness.

If he expected an apology, he was disappointed. "Yes," she said. Then, as if to take the sting away, she shook her head, grimacing. "No, not entirely. I'm sorry, Gyll. But if I can't expect support from my favorite lover . . ." She shrugged, turning her head away.

"I didn't agree with you. It was that simple. Why should the guild-kin need the Thane's permission to go into Sterka when they have no other duties to perform in Underasgard? *I* never requested—"

"Perhaps you should have," she interrupted, turning back to him. She uncrossed muscular legs, sitting with hands on knees. Her dark eyes challenged him, her chin held upward defiantly.

He reached out for her with a hand. "Mondom," he began.

She backed away, swiveling from the bedfield with a lithe movement. She went across the room to the floater that held the disorganized pile of their clothing, pulling her tunic from underneath the tangled heap. As Gyll watched silently, she straightened the garment, pulling the sleeves out.

"Gyll," she said, "there wasn't any resentment of the Hoorka until we failed to kill Gunnar. That made us look as if we'd allied ourselves with his rule-guild. That's when all this started."

"Neweden knows the code—" he began as she raised her arms, pulling the tunic over her head. Then she stopped, her head just emerging from the cloth.

"Yah, by the code, some of the victims must escape. But Gunnar was important, a rival to the Li-Gallant. I can understand the reasoning the guilded kin followed. If I were outside the Hoorka, I might wonder myself. Certainly Aldhelm thinks we acted wrong." She tugged the cloth down, pulling it over her small breasts and shaking her head to free her hair from the high collar. "And then Eorl was killed by lassari, or so we both think. We've yet to avenge his death. He still stands alone before the Hag. The Hoorka can't afford any more Eorls."

"And your ruling will prevent that?"

One corner of her mouth lifted: irritation. "Must we argue this again?"

No. How many mistakes did you make as Thane yourself, how many arbitrary decisions made simply because something had to be done, right or wrong? You made yourself resign because of those uncertainties . . . But his pride had already spoken for him. "You began the argument." He didn't like his voice. It sounded petulant, weak.

She turned away from him with a raising of thick eyebrows. She pulled the loose trousers of the guild uniform from the clothing (the rest going haphazardly to the stones of the floor) and sat on the floater. From across the room, Gyll could feel the chill of her displeasure.

"If I began it, then let me continue a bit," she said finally. "There are other things that hurt Hoorka, more than any ruling I've ever made. You, Gyll, as an example. You've been involved in three consecutive failed contracts, you who created the Hoorka, who should be a model to them. Your partners in all the cases have indicated that you lacked spirit, that you were slow and seemed uncomfortable."

She could see that her words hurt him. He closed his eyes, as if to deny her existence, but the words still bludgeoned him. With an abrupt movement, a grunt of effort, he sat on the edge of the bedfield. He made a conscious effort to pull his stomach taut, and the unbidden vanity made him angry with himself and, more, disturbed that it was necessary.

"Mondom," he said. "I think—"

She glanced toward him, her trousers halfway up her thighs, hiding the mottled bruise. She stopped, glaring at him. "You're getting flabby, Gyll. Your muscle tone is deteriorating, and you don't seem to care. You move about as if half somewhere else. You spend too much time inside your head. What's the matter with you?"

He ignored her. "This all started playfully, Mondom. We were joking with one another, laughing. I didn't mean to hurt you, and I didn't want us to start sniping at one another."

"It was you as much as me."

"I'm sorry for that." He ventured a half-smile. *Please, let's forget this. I don't want to think about it—it haunts me too much already.* "You don't have to leave yet. And besides, these are *your* chambers. I should be the one to depart, tossed aside." He rubbed the gray fur of his chest with one hand. He lowered his head, looking at Mondom from under the ridges of his eyes. "I'd like you to stay." Softly.

Mondom shook her head, eyes closed and head raised. She inhaled deeply, through her nose, then let the air escape in a slow sigh. She stood, the pants falling to the ground around her ankles. She kicked them aside, pulling the tunic over her head once more.

"Do I have an apology, Gyll?" She waited by the floater, hands on hips, just out of his reach. Her nakedness taunted him: the darkness between her thighs, the gold-brown areolas of boyish breasts.

"I never meant to hurt you—and I'm always sorry when I do."

"You bastard," she said. But there was a hint of a smile. She came to him; her lips on his, her tongue thrusting into his mouth, and her hands moving low on his body. Gyll tried to respond, but the argument, the recent lovemaking, his tiredness: all defeated him. Mondom finally rolled away from him, and he reached out to touch her, beginning another apology.

The bell to the room's holotank chimed, a soft insistence. "Damn," Gyll said. Mondom gave him a glance he could not decipher, then called out loudly into the darkened room. "Yah?"

"Thane Mondom?"

"Speaking."

"This is McWilms. I was listening to a holocast from Sterka. There's news you should hear."

Mondom sat, leaving Gyll's side suddenly cold. "I'm listening. What is it, McWilms?"

McWilms said it very simply, and its implications were more intense for the simplicity.

"Gunnar's been killed."

3

Two rooms, a study in contrasts . . .

. . . Gyll's room, in the labyrinth of Underasgard, was a bare cavern, the walls unadorned dry rock—brown-gray with runneled streaks of some orangish mineral. His few furnishings were scattered about it in no discernable pattern: a bedfield, a floater sitting before a small metal desk at an oblique angle to the wall, a privacy screen in one corner that hid his rack of clothing, and a small wooden table on which sat a cage. The cage shimmered— scarlet lines indicating the perimeters of the field that enclosed a small animal. Gyll stood before the cage, looking down at the bumblewort. It mewled up to him with its small, triangular head and limped to the side of the cage, the large soft pads of its feet still cracked and lined with dark brown—dried blood where the rocks of the hills had torn its tender, unprotected skin. The fur on its soft shell was matted and dull. The wort moved slowly, breathing too quickly, illness showing in its dull gray eyes and the cough as it stopped—half-falling—to sit and stare up at him. Gyll shook his head, reaching down to scratch behind the large oval ears. The wort had been moving better yesterday.

"Why don't you get over this?" he asked it softly, with just the slightest hint of an echo from the bare walls. "If you want to die, you little bastard, you're going to have to do it yourself. I won't help you."

He stood there for long minutes, staring down at the wort without seeing it, petting the animal absently.

. . . Vingi's room echoed wealth. It was large, the walls soft and pliant with hangings that varied their patterns, the warp and woof fluid. His long desk dominated the room, placed carefully where a visitor would see it first. Its high polish mirrored the room in reverse. Only the inset screens of the Li-Gallant's com-link interrupted that brilliance: no papers cluttered the surface, no stray verticals stopped the eye. The shape of the room—a parallelogram—the arrangement of the furniture, even

the programmed movements of the hangings, all channeled the
gaze to the Li-Gallant.

He sat and watched his com-link, a wash of green from the
unit casting its hue over his face, illuminating it from beneath.
Vingi grinned his corpulent grin. The screen flickered with the
evening's news bulletins, all full of Gunnar's death and its
import to Neweden.

The Li-Gallant sighed, sinking back into the pliant grasp of his
floater. "Nisa," he said.

The light from the 'link went green to blue. "Li-Gallant?"

"Have the kitchens send me a small glass of brandy—the
bottle of Neasonier from Longago."

"As you wish."

"And make damned sure the lackey doesn't sample it himself.
Tell him I *know* the level of that bottle and I expect to find it
lower only by my glassful. Have him bring it immediately. Off."

The glow from the 'link died. The Li-Gallant put thick hands
behind his head. He closed his eyes.

Gyll was both hot and uncomfortable. The Hoorka had gathered
in the cavern they used for meetings, and the coolness of
Underasgard was tempered by the warmth of their bodies. The
nightcloak Gyll wore chafed his neck. He cursed the impulse that
had caused him to choose the new one over the bedraggled but
soft old cloak. Nor could he seem to find a comfortable position
in his chair. Even the mead set before him by a dutiful apprentice
was warmer than he liked it. Gyll wanted nothing more than the
oblivious comfort of sleep.

It didn't appear that sleep was something he would gain soon.

The Hoorka had been called together by Thane Mondom. The
several elders of the guild sat around a battered wooden table
marred with the rings of forgotten drinks. Hoverlamps threw
erratic shadows over them. In one corner, Cranmer fiddled with
his recording gear, a look of dissatisfied ire on his thin face. The
rest of the guild-kin sat on the broken rock around the room,
making themselves as comfortable as they could. Around Gyll, a
score of unrelated conversations fought each other. He shook his
head but could not blame them—the news had caused a flurry of
speculation.

Only Aldhelm seemed solemnly quiet. Unlike the others,
seated in rude chairs around the table or slouched about the
room, he stood against the rock wall of the entrance, his light
eyes glancing from one to the other but always seeming to avoid

Gyll. His long arms were crossed before his chest, the taut muscles of his forearms standing out in high relief. A gloomy air hung about him, a pall that ignored the brightness of the hoverlamps.

Thane Mondom entered last. She nodded to Aldhelm as she entered and strode quickly to her seat at the head of the table—with a smile to Gyll in the process. She waited for the talk to quiet.

"I won't bother with normal procedure here," she said when all faces had turned toward her. "We all have heard the news by now, and Gunnar's death may have problems for Hoorka, if it has the import I believe it will have." She swept her nightcloak over one shoulder, moving in her seat. Her forehead was glossed with perspiration. *Simply the walk, or is she that nervous?* Gyll wondered. "I'll let Aldhelm speak now, as he's been in Sterka and has felt the mood there."

Mondom waved a hand to Aldhelm, who pushed himself from the wall with his shoulders. His hands dropped to his sides. "It's simple enough, Thane," he said. "I heard the news while in the city, and I stayed there long enough to find out what I could, since it seemed to be important to Hoorka." He paused. Gyll saw his hands clench once, then relax. "I'll tell you what little I've garnered. Gunnar was killed by an unknown assailant. The weapon was, by the description I've heard, probably a render. He or she was also very good—from what I was told, the butler posts around Gunnar's grounds did not sound an intrusion alarm, nor did their equipment have any image of the assassin. There have been no bloodfeuds filed against Gunnar or his guild, and he wasn't given a chance to defend himself honorably. It was a shameful murder. And the rumors have already begun. One of them in particular worries me. It's not a pleasant thought, my kin, but the speculations include the Hoorka."

From the table, the deep voice of d'Mannberg dominated the room. "That only makes sense, since the Hoorka failed twice in the contracts with Gunnar. What did you expect them to think, man?"

Aldhelm's face went stony, his jaw clenching, the scar light on his cheek. When he replied, his voice was cool with careful politeness. "What I think isn't important here. I'm concerned with what these rumors mean for us."

Mondom spoke. "What do they say, Aldhelm?" Her fingertips drummed the tabletop, an impatient rythym.

He spread his hands wide. "I heard it said that the Hoorka

were embarrassed by Gunnar's double escapes and that to redeem our gods' favor, we killed Gunnar. And it was also whispered that perhaps we had done this to regain favor with the Li-Gallant.''

Gyll shook his head. "No," he said. "I can't believe Neweden would believe such a thing. The Hoorka code is our shield, and we've never been accused of breaking it—if anyone believes we'd abandon it, how are they to place trust in Hoorka?"

Aldhelm shrugged. "Maybe they don't. Maybe we don't give them enough reason to trust us, and give too much leeway to Dame Fate on our contracts."

"If we guaranteed success, we'd be no better than common lassari. I made the code to give us kinship, Aldhelm."

"Gunnar is not the only failed contract we've had recently, Ulthane Gyll. *You*"—with just the faintest emphasis on the word—"should be aware of that."

A frigid rage stabbed through Gyll's composure. The hand went unbidden to his vibrohilt while the other grasped the arm of his chair with knuckles gone white. *You're a failed kin. Three times; not the victim's doing, but your own incompetence.* His own guilt echoed Aldhelm's words, amplifying them and feeding his anger. He spat out his words. "We've had this argument before, Aldhelm, when I was Thane. We're *not* mere assassins— we're instruments in the hands of Dame Fate. Anyone can kill, anyone can do the dishonorable and hire a lassari to do the cowardly deed. We give the option of death *with* honor to both victim and signer. Some must escape, those lucky or fit enough to survive. It will stay that way."

Aldhelm stared down at Gyll, looking significantly at the Ulthane's knife hand. "Survival cuts both ways, Ulthane Gyll. Sometimes to survive, one must change. I'm not afraid of change, and I suspect that the Li-Gallant will now be less likely to harass us."

"We *do not* change, Aldhelm!" Gyll shouted.

"Kin-brothers, please . . ." Mondom began to speak, softly, but Gyll interrupted her.

"I'll not have the Hoorka a guild that alters itself at a whim. By all the gods, I've finally got us offworld, made d'Embry and her damned Alliance acknowledge us."

"Be silent!" Mondom pushed herself away from the table with her hands, standing abruptly. Her chair overturned behind her—the clatter of wood on rock was loud in the cavern. "Children," she hissed, her eyes narrowed, "the Hoorka have

more important business to discuss than your Hag-damned differences. The practice floor is open—afterward—for a duel, if
that's the only satisfaction the two of you will take. But, by She
of the Five, we'll keep this discussion germane to Gunnar's
death or I'll have both of you doing apprentice work tomorrow.
Gyll, *I am Thane*. Remember that, and let me run this meeting.''

Silence. Before her anger-sparked gaze, both Gyll and Aldhelm
bowed, first to Thane Mondom, then, with a certain stiffness, to
each other.

''Better,'' Mondom said. ''Better.'' Behind her, an apprentice
moved from the shadows to pick up her chair from the ground
and replace it at the table. Mondom sat, her hands folded in front
of her. ''Aldhelm, what's the mood in Sterka?''

Gyll watched, still angry, as Aldhelm strode to the end of the
long table and leaned down, supporting himself, his fists on the
rough top. ''Bad. Confused. Angry. Very ugly for Hoorka. I
could feel the hostility and hear the murmuring behind my back.
I stopped in at a tavern to hear more, and only hesitantly did I
get served, with the barest politeness due to a guilded kin.''

''Were you threatened?''

A look of scorn. ''Not by the barkeep. The guilded kin won't
risk a bloodfeud with Hoorka, not yet. And lassari give me a
wide berth.''

Mondom frowned. ''I'd remind you that Eorl was Hoorka,
and lassari killed him, neh?'' She cocked her head in question,
one eyebrow raised.

Aldhelm straightened, his nightcloak falling around his body.
He nodded to Mondom. ''You've made your point, Thane.
Forgive me for my presumption.''

Gyll watched as Aldhelm went back to his station by the
entrance, his movements precise and easy. *Is that why we could
never stay close? He's so stoic, so graceful, so confident and
self-assured —what I've always pretended to be. Is it envy that
causes me to dislike him, or is he truly as dangerous to Hoorka
as I think?*

From further down the table, another of the Hoorka—Sartas—
spoke. ''My bet is that the Li-Gallant is ultimately responsible
for this. That man's a shameless coward, a disgrace to guilded
kin.'' A murmur of agreement came from the others. ''Who has
better reason to want Gunnar dead?''

''I don't know that even the Li-Gallant would be that foolish,
Sartas,'' Mondom said.

Gyll nodded his agreement. ''Gunnar's rule-guild may well

benefit from Gunnar's death in this matter, Thane. I don't credit
the Li-Gallant with great intelligence, but he has the craftiness
and the sense to have kept most of his power for years. He
wouldn't undermine his own position. It's possible, I suppose,
but . . ."

Sartas drank from the mug in front of him. Then he thumped
the drink back down. "Still, you have to admit that Gunnar's
death would give him great pleasure. He's attempted this three
times before, twice with us and once on his own. Vingi wanted
Gunnar dead." His long olive-tan face turned from Gyll to
Mondom.

Gyll shook his head. He glanced back at Aldhelm. The man
stood, leaning back against the wall, arms akimbo under his
cloak and his attention on Gyll. Yet—Gyll didn't know why,
perhaps something in the man's easy stance, his seeming
nonchalance—the glimmering of a faint suspicion came to Gyll:
it had been Aldhelm who had advocated the alteration of the
code during the last contract on Gunnar, and it had been on that
contract that Aldhelm and Gyll had experienced the final confrontation which had driven a wedge between their friendship.
And it had been Aldhelm that had failed in that first contract—
and he had felt Gyll's knife for that failure. Aldhelm was a good
assassin, good enough to have evaded any safeguards that
Gunnar could have set around his guildhouse.

Gyll remembered the pack Aldhelm had when he'd gone out
the night before. It was easily large enough to have held a
render, and there was one in the Hoorka armory.

*No, you old fool, you're letting your paranoia and dislike play
games with your common sense. Surely Aldhelm wouldn't do
such a thing.* But he fell silent, and he looked at Aldhelm with a
new intensity.

Mondom had begun speaking during his musings. ". . . This is
all the more reason to continue with the ruling made last
meeting. No kin will go into Sterka without my knowledge and
permission. And you might do well to be sure that you have a
companion, since all the attacks have been on lone Hoorka.
You're all well trained, but training means nothing to ambush or
overwhelming numbers." Mondom glanced at Aldhelm. "We
keep the code strictly. We perform as we're supposed to. And we
should make every attempt to do well—that would do the most
to allay suspicions." She waited; a breath. Someone coughed in
shadow. Cloth rustled against stone.

"We have a contract for tonight," she continued. Gyll, torn

from his inward contemplation, sat up sharply: he was next in the rotation. "It will begin, at least, in Sterka, so Vingi and those that speak against Hoorka will be watching. I can't stress its importance enough, in light of what Aldhelm has told us."

Gyll knew that she was well aware of the rotation schedule, but she would not look at him. He fidgeted, wondering why she wouldn't meet his eyes.

"Who works tonight?" d'Mannberg asked.

"I." Sartas, from his seat, his dark eyes alight.

"And I," Gyll said softly.

"Ulthane Gyll." Mondom turned to him now, one hand stroking her forehead as if in concentration. Her hand threw deep shadows over her eyes. "I have need of someone to meet Kaethe Oldin tonight. The woman owes us payment for last night's contract. I'd like you to go. She's an offworlder and of the Families, and I'd like to represent us with someone more than an apprentice." She spoke too hurriedly, as if anticipating his anger.

There was silence when she finished. Gyll looked down at his mug, his hands around it, the fingers stroking the ceramic smoothness. "I work tonight, Thane," he said. His voice was low, his eyes still fixed on the mug. He waited. *Don't force this, Mondom.*

"Gyll," she began.

He broke in, glaring at her. "Thane, don't say it. I will work tonight."

She did not look away. Her words were suddenly cold with distance. "I'll consider your feelings, Ulthane."

He allowed himself to relax slightly. "I thank you for that."

"Beyond that, I make no promises."

That was all she would say.

The radiance of a captured sun blazed about her, cloaking her naked body in bronze. She stretched out her arms to embrace the glow, basking in its warmth and feeling it, a thousand fingers, on her skin. She sighed, she squirmed in immodest delight.

"You keep using that and your skin'll look like a lizard's."

Kaethe laughed from within her bath of light. She reached out and touched one of the four metallic posts that surrounded her. The throbbing aura began to die as the posts receded into the carpeting of the floor. "You're too sour, Helgin. You make up in foulness what you lack in height."

"Wisdom from the bitch?" Helgin, a Motsognir Dwarf,

scowled up at Oldin, staring at her with eyes the color of smoke, his gaze unremittingly critical as it moved from crown to feet. She endured his inspection, smiling. "You're ten kilos too fat for Neweden—if you didn't choose your clothes carefully, you'd never get a second glance. And the Battier Radiance hasn't made a damned bit of difference. It's a passing fad for the stupid and gullible. That skin's destined to get old just like the rest of you."

"I'll shrivel up and look like a Motsognir?"

"I'm as human as you."

"So you claim." She laughed. Bending at the waist, she touched the Motsognir's head with cool lips. "Where would I be without your pessimism, Helgin?"

Helgin backed away from Oldin, two quick steps. She grinned down at him, and he turned his head to spit on the rug of the compartment. "You'd still be your grandsire's whore, spreading your legs for his captains."

Kaethe pursed her lips. "So touchy," she said, as if to an unseen observer. She walked away with her long-legged stride; in the reduced gravity, she seemed to glide. The room was large, by ship standards, as comfortable as her rooms at OldinHome. Deep, soft rugs covered the plating of the floor in subtle earth hues, the deck itself sculpted into irregular hills and valleys— there was no need for other furniture here. The only reminder that Kaethe was on a ship rather than planetbound was a circular viewport that covered most of the ceiling. There, in a sea of darkness flecked with star-foam, Neweden floated, attended by its two moons, Sleipnir and Gulltopp. In this, her refuge, music would come at Kaethe's bidding, the walls would shift, the lighting would respond to her moods; here, she had no pretensions, and here she allowed few visitors. The crew, most of her staff, prospective buyers of the goods stored in *Peregrine*'s vast holds: these she would see in the ostentatiously gothic office, two decks below.

Kaethe stretched, yawning, and turned. Abruptly, she sat, lounging back against a carpeted hillock. Helgin followed her graceful movements, glowering at her. He had the typical build of the Motsognir Dwarves, that half-mythical race wandering the frontiers of human space (and, it is rumored, far beyond) since the Interregnum, when the First Empire died and left humanity in darkness. An experiment in genetic manipulation, they had been bred for the heavy planets. The Motsognir were nearly as broad as they were tall, standing about a meter in height, with thick-bunched muscles. Their strength was legendary, as was their vile temperament. The Motsognir, by preference, tended to stay with their own; to see one was something to tell one's children.

"Your trouble is that you're too sure of yourself. What are you going to do when you fail?" Helgin was as hirsute as the rest of his kind. He tugged on the full beard that masked his large mouth.

"I don't plan on failing." Kaethe closed her eyes, relaxing. Stretching out her legs, she hugged herself, then let her arms go to her sides. "I don't care how much you scoff, Helgin—the Battier makes me feel regenerated and alive, and you saw that it worked for the Nassaie."

"The Nassaie are avian, not human. You heard what Nest-Tender said. He didn't think the Battier would work for us, and wouldn't guarantee there'd be no side effects."

"But we've sold 'em."

"Fools will buy anything," Helgin grumbled, a voice like rock scraping rock.

"Don't be so damned tiresome, Motsognir. Maybe the Battier could give you a little height—then you wouldn't have to worry about knocking your teeth out on somebody's knee," she said sweetly.

"I'd bet on my teeth before your knee, Oldin."

A smile. Eyes still closed, she waved a lazy hand toward him. "Did you send someone to get the geological reports Gies left with Renard?"

"I did."

"Good. I'll want to see it in a few hours. Now that Gunnar is dead, we make the shift toward Vingi—and the Hoorka still intrigue me." She rolled to her side. Kaethe glanced at the Motsognir, standing—thick legs well apart, arms folded across his broad chest—near the door. "I read the profiles on their leaders. You might commend whoever got them for you—quite good. Gyll Hermond is no longer Thane?"

"No, but I suspect that he's still their guiding force. They are his creation."

"I want to meet him then. Get him here."

"You have the most gentle way of making a request."

"Yah. But you'll do it, won't you." The last was a statement, not a question. Her face, for all its smiling, held little amusement. She seemed more tired than anything. "And soon, Helgin." Kaethe lay again on her back. "And have Renard told that I want another report soon. He's had enough time to give us an update."

In self-imposed darkness, she listened to the Motsognir: a
harsh breath, the beginning of another retort, then a guttural
obscenity. Helgin's heavy stride hushed on carpet—even in the
light gravity, he sounded ponderous—and the door slid open with
a hiss.

"Helgin."

She could feel his eyes on her.

"When you've made the calls, find me a lover," she said.
"And make sure he's tall."

Helgin snorted derision. "You need to become more self-
reliant." The door shut behind him with the sound of serpents.
Kaethe laughed.

She opened her eyes. Above her, Neweden basked in the
radiance of the sunstar. She stared at the world.

The Domoraj Sucai could barely hear Vingi's whining mum-
ble. He scowled in irritation, trying to pierce the auditory murk
that fouled his ears. Snatches of song clutched at the Li-Gallant's
words; his own thoughts, thundering, drowned them.

Vingi himself seemed to be encapsuled in a shifting cage of
sapphire flame that, gelatinous, moved about him slowly. The
Li-Gallant's desk rolled like the open sea, but Vingi did not
seem to notice. The Domoraj thought that peculiar but decided
not to mention it. *Why bother? The Li-Gallant, dear bastard that
he is and putting bread in all the kin's mouths, should be
allowed his whims. Quiet, quiet; what is he saying?*

Ignoring the muted orchestrion that insisted on playing in the
back of his skull, the Domoraj—head of Vingi's guard—cocked
his head with intense concentration.

". . . to my attention that you've, well, taken up some odious
habits, Sucai," Vingi said. "I've been told you've used lujisa,
other drugs—man, how do you expect to guide my guards in this
state?"

I don't. I don't want to. Then: *Did I speak that aloud? No,
he's still talking. The flames around him are larger now. How
can he not feel the heat?*

". . . understand why this sudden sloth, this abuse. What's
going on inside your head, kin-brother? You were my most
trusted captain, one with whom I could be honest . . ."

*Inside my head? Listen: There is a trumpet sounding like
green-white shards of ice, and a crystalline note that smells of
spices. You hear velvet or taste fire. I don't have to think of the*

disgrace you—no, there is the smell of silken cloth against my kin.

". . . since the lassari I had you hire to kill Gunnar a half-standard ago failed. I've grieved over that decision a hundred times, Sucai, believe me. I know it caused you considerable pain to send a shameful lassari rather than declaring bloodfeud. But the Li-Gallant must always hold a larger view. It was for the good of Neweden—it gives you no disgrace. Believe that, Domoraj—you should feel no shame."

Shame is a ruby spear. It slices through you and you can't see the lifeblood on the stone. It stays, gigging you wherever you move, and you can't tear it out.

". . . and any dishonor should fall to me. Not you. You were following your kin-lord's orders, as any dutiful kin-brother would. When you reported the failure, I was *glad* the attempt had failed. Do you wish time to think this through, Sucai? Do you wish my help? I could set up an erasal at Diplo Center—d'Embry would do that for me, and the Alliance has an excellent psych unit. Answer me, Domoraj, please."

Sucai struggled to pierce the fog in his head, the hues and tints that chased each other behind his eyes. He spoke, hesitantly, his voice a harsh whisper, his fingers knotting and moving in his lap as he sat before the Li-Gallant.

"I . . . forgive me, Li-Gallant, but I feel . . . disgraced. You've brought shame to me . . . I'm sorry, I wasn't ready when you called for me today . . . I was the instrument of shame." *The ruby spear.* "I've tried . . . a few times since, to talk with . . . our gods. They—" Sucai stumbled over the words, his tongue moving, his face contorted as if he were about to weep. "They . . . don't answer me."

Vingi was speaking again, but the Domoraj could not hear him. A wind like emeralds whispered in his ears, twisting around the ruby spear that impaled his chest and pulling so that the weapon wrenched inside him. He shook his head and the storm abated, moving away. Sucai stared at Vingi and saw that a forest of dark towers had sprung up around the Li-Gallant, each with a scarlet light on its craggy summit. ". . . an erasal whether you wish it or not. As the kin-lord, I command it. You're of no use to me in this state, Domoraj. That, above all, should bring you the most shame."

The spear . . .

"Go and rest. Tell Domo d'Meila to come here at once. He'll be in charge during your absence."

Sucai sat for a moment as the slow realization that he had been
dismissed filtered into his consciousness. Vingi, his face like
melted ire, gazed back at him. The baleful, laughing eyes of the
dark towers about the Li-Gallant surged, flaming about Vingi
without harming him, cold. The Domoraj lurched to his feet,
nodding in salutation and wonder. He turned to leave, as Vingi,
fluid, became tall, thinner.

The carpet whispered quiet insults under Sucai's feet. The
door showered him with warm mockings. The air, shrieking, bit
into him with a thousand small teeth.

4

*An excerpt from the acousidots of Sondall-Cadhurst Cranmer.
This is an early transcription, dating from the time well before
Mondom became Thane, long before the term "Hoorka" would
become a curse throughout the Alliance. It is best to remember
that Cranmer was neither a technician nor a fighter, that his views
on things military were those of a sheltered layman. Cranmer
had never taken a life.*

EXCERPT FROM THE DOT OF 8.19.214:

A rustling of paper.

"Here, Mondom. These are the specifications I was talking
about—I had the Diplo librarian dig them out of the Center files.
The holocube'll give you an indication of what the damn thing
looks like—that's somebody's hand by the stock, so you'll get
the sense of scale."

"Sond, did you see how *heavy* this is?" (Her voice holds an
obvious amusement—laughter is near the surface of her words.)

"It's no heavier than a long-maser, Mondom; I checked. The
Alliance uses LMs as standard equipment."

"And they also use powered suits. This would weigh down a
Hoorka."

"Perhaps, but look at the advantages. You sight through this,
and when the trigger is depressed, the weapon uses a rangefinder
coupled with the heat-seeker to determine distance—you can also
override the automatics if you need to. A beam's generated in
both spire-chambers—here—and the two beams fuse at the
indicated distance. All the destructive power is generated there,

ince each of the beams by itself is harmless. You can fire
lirectly through your own people and not worry. The range is
;ood, too, and a bodyshield won't keep this one out if it's tuned
inely enough.''

"Sond—"

"No, let me finish, m'Dame. I may be a scrawny little
lesthete to your eyes, but damn it, I can see applications here. If
'ou were within sight of your victim, you could use this and be
;ertain of a kill.''

"Sond, that's just the point. The whole thrust of the Thane's
:ode is that the victim is always given a proper chance to
:scape—we never overbalance the odds. This gadget might be as
:ffective as you claim; if it is, it's *too* effective. You misunder-
;tand Neweden ethics, but then you haven't been here long.
There's too much honor involved in a bloodfeud—it's a very
)ersonal thing.''

"That's just what you Hoorka circumvent: the personal con-
act of a person with the one he wants to kill.''

"That's why you see us using a variant on a blade so often. To
Neweden, killing is, as I said, a thing of honor, an individual
natter. To be truly honorable, you have to be closely involved in
he other's death: you never strike without warning, and your
:nemy must have the same chance as you. You have to under-
;tand the finality of death, how much pain is involved. This toy
)f yours—well, the more impersonal and distant the call to Hag
Death is, the more unlikely you are to hold back. Killing
)ecomes too common and easy a solution. You have to see the
)lood, Sond, watch the blade sink into flesh, hear the grunt of
)ain, and feel the life flow away into the Hag's claws. . . . Many
)eople won't do that, and that's good.''

"Yah, I understand that point—mind you, I don't necessarily
agree with it, but I understand what you're saying. That's still
:xactly what you Hoorka allow. You're a means of depersonalizing
:ombat, of making killing distant and secondhand.''

"Which is why we won't guarantee the death of a contracted
victim. It *would* make it too easy, and we'd insult both the honor
of the signer and their gods. It's also why we give the body of
the victim—if there is one—to the contractor and make his name
a matter of public record. Then he sees the results of his actions
and receives the consequences. We're not murderers, just weapons.''

"Yah, yah, I've talked to the Thane and received the same
lecture.''

(Mondom laughs again.) "Well, if you show him these plans
you'll hear it one more time."

(Here there is the sound of paper being torn.) "Then I'll save
my ears."

The last three times you have not killed—the thought nagged
at him as Gyll stared at the panting bumblewort. He'd come back
from the meeting to find the wort on its side, moving feebly, the
fog-gray eyes moving dully as it stared up at him. He'd forced it
to drink some water, watched it lap halfheartedly at the offering.

"You should put the poor thing out of its misery, Gyll."

Startled, he turned from the wort to see Mondom leaning
against the doorjamb, her nightcloak swept over one shoulder.
He found that her presence made the tension return, and he made
an effort to appear relaxed, stroking the wort. He wondered if he
fooled her.

"You surprised me," he said. "I thought I'd let the door
shut." Under his hand, the wort chirruped plaintively; he made
his caress softer, slower. The snub nose came up and nuzzled his
hand wetly. From the mouth, the slender whip of its tongue
rasped around his forefinger, tugged once, then released.

Gyll shook his head. "Come in, Mondom." He still looked
down at the wort. "I assume you've come about the contract."

"Yah." She nodded, pushing herself erect with a quick motion. She went to the floater that sat by his bed.

Gyll was silent, observing her. In the months since he'd given
her the title of Hoorka-thane, she'd changed. She smiled less,
she laughed less; an aura of moodiness enveloped her in a smoky
embrace. He felt responsible and slightly guilty—it was his
burden that she'd assumed, because he no longer wanted the
problems of leadership. He'd given it to her, and it had sunk its
talons deep in her soul.

He stroked the wort a last time, scratching under the delicate
skin of the earflaps, and sat on the bed. Mondom watched him
with dark, veiled eyes, her face carefully arranged and neutral.

That hurt worse than anything she might have said.

"How's the wort?" she asked at last. They both knew it for
the avoidance it was, and Gyll found it difficult not to lash out at
her circumspection. He began to speak, harshly, then swallowed
his irritation with a visible effort.

"No better. I doubt that it'll live much longer—its ancestors
may have been able to fend for themselves, but we've bred the
worts into something that can't be undomesticated and wild. I'm

surprised this one's lived as long as it has, since it had to have been abandoned in Sterka. It keeps fighting." He stared at her, waiting.

Mondom nodded. Her lips tightened once, parting with an intake of breath as she started to speak. She glanced at the wort's cage, as if unwilling to meet Gyll's eyes. He made no effort to make it easier for her. He waited, belligerently silent.

"You know what I'm going to say." Eyes the color of old, much-polished wood: they accused him.

"I suspect—but you're going to have to say it, Mondom." He shrugged. "I'll tell you that your logic is wrong, though. Yah, I've failed on the last three contracts I've worked. It happens—it *has* to happen. By the code—*my* code—the Hoorka must give the victim a chance to live. If they stay alive, then the Dame wants them to do so. They deserve life. If not—then let them join the ippicators in death and dance with the five-legged beasts before the Hag."

"That's very poetic, love, but it's not all of it." She shook her head, the short, dark hair moving.

Gyll raised an eyebrow in question, making the creases in his lined forehead deeper, and running a hand through his graying hair. He looked down at himself and pulled his stomach in.

She was still not looking at him. Her fingers plucked imaginary lint from the black and gray cloth of her sleeve. "I've talked to the kin that worked those contracts with you, Gyll. They all told me that you seemed listless, unenthusiastic. You seemed to be going through the motions. And they said you complained of tiredness . . ." She glanced up, her mouth a grimace of censure. "I think that you're questioning yourself—whether you still believe in Hoorka."

"I *made* Hoorka." He felt his voice rising with emotion, but it was not anger—his cry was more that of denial than ire. "By She of the Five, Mondom, I've given more to Hoorka than anyone. How can you question me?"

"You gave up the title of Thane—because you felt yourself to be no longer effective in that role. You can't deny that; you've admitted it to me." Her gaze held him, a vise of accusation. "Now you've failed your last contracts in a sluggish manner. I have to wonder at that, Gyll, and make some kind of judgment."

Now her voice softened. Her back, which had been rigidly straight, relaxed, and she slouched back in the floater. "There's nothing wrong in that, Gyll. I can understand, and there's much you can teach the apprentices, if you don't desire more. You don't have to stay in the rotation if you don't wish to do so. Hoorka have retired: Felling, Brugal, Hrolf . . ."

"No," he said. Very simply. Quietly.

"Is that your pride speaking, or do you really feel that strongly about this?"

"*Damn* your implications, Mondom!" Gyll shouted. The wort cried in sudden fright, and Gyll rose to his feet, stalking over to the animal's cage. "I was trained to this from the beginning by my true-father, who didn't have the sense to see what those skills could mean to Neweden *if* tempered with discipline, and it was *me* that set up those disciplines and gave the training. You've no right to question my abilities, not even as Thane. I'm as good as any of the Hoorka, my age or mental state regardless. I'll prove that on the practice floor if you insist. I'll challenge you or any of the kin—first blood."

Mondom was calm, staring at Gyll as if his rage rendered his soul transparent. "Your abilities are not in question."

Gyll shook his head in mute denial, muttering an inward oath but not knowing whom he cursed. "I demand, as kin, to take my place tonight," he said. "I'll consider it an insult to be replaced." His stance was as much a challenge as his words: feet well apart, hands on hips.

There was silence as Mondom regarded him. They locked gazes.

Mondom glanced away, shaking her head once more.

"As you wish, Gyll. I won't fight you in *this*"—with a slight accentuation—"but . . ." She caught her lower lip between her teeth, breathing once. "I am Thane, Gyll. I love Hoorka as much as you, and you've made it my duty to see to our kin's welfare. If that means going against you, I will. I won't enjoy it . . ." She stood, stretching. "I'd do this much for any of the kin. Come to the entrance in an hour. Your gear will be waiting."

She walked over to where Gyll stood, staying a careful handsbreadth from him, and glanced down at the sickly wort. "You shouldn't let it suffer like that, Gyll. You should kill it."

She began to move toward the door. Gyll called after her. "Mondom."

She turned.

"Thank you," he said.

She didn't smile. "I knew you'd say what you did. I've talked to Sartas. He's grudgingly let me change the rotation. I've given you a new partner for tonight. You'll work with Aldhelm."

And she was gone.

*   *   *

He would have chosen another partner for the contract, had the choice been his and not Mondom's.

Aldhelm was waiting with bland patience when Gyll finally arrived at the entrance to Underasgard, the Hoorka-lair. A small group of the kin were standing with him, jesting with the apprentices, their voices a loud echoing in the vast spaces of the first cavern. Hoverlamps dolefully lit the scene, throwing huge, distorted shadows on the jagged roof. Gyll forced a smile to his craggy face, knowing what would come.

"It's an easy one tonight, Ulthane. The apprentices have him placed and he's not running too quickly. Isn't that right, McWilms?" D'Mannberg tousled the apprentice's hair with a large, careless hand, his laughter booming from the stones.

McWilms ducked aside from the mistreatment, bowing sketchily to Gyll while casting a dour glance at d'Mannberg. "It's true, sirrah. I gave him the warning and let Ferdin follow. I'll be taking you in the flitter."

"Lose this one, Ulthane, and Mondom'll have you switching places with McWilms here." Serita Iduna, her olive face laughing, touched Gyll's shoulder with an affection that eased the pain of her words. Gyll, knowing, expecting all the gruff humor, stared out to the darkness outside Underasgard. He endured the unpolished wit, the unsubtle humor, though only the full kin dared speak to him in such a manner: the apprentices watched, grinning uneasily, exchanging glances among themselves.

"You've made sure the blade is sharp this time, Ulthane?"

"Look, just follow Aldhelm—he rarely gets lost."

Grin like a fool, old man. You've no one to blame but yourself. Gyll smiled lopsided amusement.

Only Aldhelm remained quiet. He stood in deep shadow near the torn mouth of the cavern, already wearing the wide belt of a bodyshield under his nightcloak. His eyes caught the green-gold light of the lamps; he stared at Gyll. He nodded.

"Ulthane," he said. His voice was dark.

Gyll nodded in return, buckling on the bodyshield that an apprentice handed him. "How do you feel tonight, Aldhelm? We haven't worked together—" He hesitated, damning himself. *We haven't worked together since the failed contract for Gunnar, since I was forced to use my blade on you to stop you from abandoning the code. Fool, learn to think before you wag your tongue so carelessly.*

"It's been a while." A sad smile flickered across Aldhelm's

scarred face—the track of Gyll's vibro. "I remember it very well, though."

His words brought back the memories, and they held all the rancor that existed between them. *Mondom, of all the kin, why did you choose Aldhelm? He'd be the least willing to understand my feelings.* Gyll was suddenly tired, very tired, as if the contract were already over, a long run finished.

Aldhelm moved into the light, checking the Khaelian dagger scabbarded to his belt and letting the nightcloak fall around his tall, muscular figure. "You needn't worry, Ulthane Gyll. I've no intention of letting us fail this contract." A pause. "And we'll do it by the code."

Gyll couldn't read his face, couldn't dredge deeper meanings from the blandly spoken words—it was the problem he always had with Aldhelm: he couldn't pierce the man's emotional armor. Aldhelm turned away, moving with a determined stride to the cavern mouth and beckoning McWilms ahead of him. Gulltopp, the larger of Neweden's two moons, was now rising beyond the trees, silvering the higher branches and silhouetting Aldhelm as he moved into the night, out from the domain of stone.

Gyll, staring, waved the apprentices back to their work and nodded a brief farewell to d'Mannberg and the other Hoorka. He hurried after Aldhelm and McWilms, the well-wishes of his kin following.

Aldhelm had gone to the dawnrock and stopped, McWilms moving on to the flitter that waited near the clearing's edge. The slender tapering pillar of the dawnrock scratched at the sky, the glass receptor at its summit catching the light of Gulltopp. Aldhelm, seeing Gyll approach, touched the dawnrock with his right hand, stroking where the rock was worn to a glossy sheen from the touch of a thousand Hoorka hands: the last ritual upon leaving Underasgard.

Gyll, with a gesture that seemed almost angry, touched the dawnrock in turn—he could feel the warm smoothness of the stone underneath his fingers. The whine of the flitter's engines moved from purr to roar, rebounding from the cliff-face in which the mouth of Underasgard loomed black and empty.

"What did you mean back there, Aldhelm?" Gyll's voice was a harsh whisper, as if the dawnrock were listening.

Aldhelm shrugged. His nightcloak, dark against darkness, swirled about him. "I know what you're feeling, Gyll, whether you want to believe that or not. I know you've grown tired of killing, whatever your reasons, in the past several months. I've watched you, and you wonder too much about the victims. You always did that to an extent, but the tendency is more pronounced now. You think of them far too much for your own good as Hoorka-kin.''

Gyll felt the sting of wounded pride: it flailed his anger, and he felt the blood rush to his face, felt his nails dig into his palms. ''I *made* Hoorka, kin-brother. And I've killed more than you. Over the standards—''

''Over the standards you've done less and less of it. You want to see their faces, you ponder their lives. You empathize. Do they haunt your sleep, too? All those ghosts you've sent to the Hag . . .''

''*Damn* you, man. Hoorka is *my* creation, all the kin follow *my* code, and the code tells us how to feel. You act as if you understand how I feel better than I do.''

''I've always understood you, Ulthane. Ever since you wounded me in the last contract for Gunnar—and I hope the Hag's minions gnaw at Gunnar's soul for eternity. He cost me too much, and I wasn't at all unhappy to see him die. I understood your feelings back then. I understood, and I wasn't angry with you. Did I ever say or do anything to make you think that?''

''It doesn't matter. My feelings aren't within the realm of your concern, Aldhelm.'' The man's patient calm fueled Gyll's anger. He could feel control slipping, knew he had to break off the conversation or risk saying too much. He fiddled with the shoulders of his nightcloak, tightened the strap of the bodyshield with too much concentration.

''I was merely giving you my observations, Gyll.'' Aldhelm's face was still a careful mask.

''Then observe tonight.'' Gyll's head snapped up, his eyes narrowed. ''Watch me, Aldhelm.'' Filled with a fury he longed to vent, Gyll stalked away, slapping the dawnrock once more in passing. His booted feet crackled through dead leaves underfoot with a sound like dry fire. He did not look back to see if Aldhelm followed.

Bondhe Amari, kin of the Guild of Petroleum Refiners, was a man whose mouth was too often ahead of his brain. He was also a poor conspirator.

That much the Hoorka gleaned from their converse with Sirrah Dramian, kin-lord of Amari's guild and the signer of the contract for the man. Dramian, his white hair a proud sign of a long and successful life, had no sympathy for Amari. ''Kill him,'' he'd said to Mondom upon signature. ''I've no cause to begrudge a man scheming to make his way in the guild—the gods know I've done it myself. But this fool is clumsy. The rumors are just too loud for me to ignore. He offends my honor, and I'm too old to challenge him myself. I can afford your damned high price. Kill him." He'd coughed, twisted one of the rings about his finger, gathered his expensive robes about him, and left the caverns, trailing a spoor of perfume.

McWilms brought the flitter down near Undercity. Here, in the oldest sector of Sterka, the buildings massed above on metal stalks that held them above the floods and the mud of the early rains. The air was filled with the foul odor of rotting vegetation. The flitter squelched to a landing in the mud, settling uneasily in the ooze. Gyll and Aldhelm peered out to the clustering of lights, reflecting dully from the wetness below.

"Undercity." Gyll exhaled nasal disgust. "It'll take hours to clean the mud from the boots."

Aldhelm was silent.

McWilms shifted in his seat, glancing over his shoulder to the Hoorka. "Sirrahs, it's not quite that bad, if Amari hasn't shifted positions. Ferdin said to go up the lift there"—he pointed to a diagonal of hoverlamps moving from the river muck to the buildings—"and into Oversector. He's holed up in an abandoned house there. Save your pity for Ferdin. She had to chase Amari through that gunk for a good hour." McWilms grinned at the assassins.

Neither returned his amusement.

The Hoorka flitter had been observed in its landing. Eyes watched from the porches of Oversector as Gyll and Aldhelm stepped out, the mud sucking greedily at their soles. A small crowd had gathered at the terminus to the lift (the mud smeared everywhere, dried into confused footprints). For the most part, they were lassari, though a few wore the insignia of the less-profitable guilds. The spectators eased back from the lift's exit as the grim-faced Hoorka walked out, kicking the clinging filth from their boots. Oddly silent, yet somehow expectant, they backed into shadow, staring.

Gyll leaned toward Aldhelm to whisper as the hungry eyes plucked at them. "This happens more and more. They watch, as if the Hoorka were some damned street entertainers." Aldhelm nodded—sour agreement.

Gyll flicked the cowl of his nightcloak up, shrouding himself. The assassins moved in a pathway ringed with shadows and wraiths. The watchers moved with them, gelid, as the Hoorka moved into the streets of Oversector. Oversector was perhaps the poorest area of Sterka—squalid, far too crowded, and filled with the stench of the river beneath and the poverty above, a subjective fog that was tangible enough to cause Gyll to draw his lips back from teeth in a snarl of disgust. A woman near him, seeing the rictus, drew quickly back in a rustling of cloth.

"To the right, Aldhelm—that's where Ferdin's to be waiting." Gyll swept cold eyes about him. "Carrion birds," he muttered.

The way was ill-lit, for most of the hoverlamps that had been placed here were missing, shattered, or simply not functioning. Gulltopp had not yet risen high enough to light the area. Night was triumphant. A hoverlamp thirty meters away showed the open maw of a cross street and a nightcloaked figure waiting there. The figure held up a hand, the fingers moving in the identification code. Ferdin.

The apprentice was slight, boyish. She shivered as if cold as the two approached. "Sirrahs," she said, bowing. "I see you've brought an audience with you." She scowled at the watchers. "They make you almost afraid to speak. I could always feel them staring, as soon as we moved into Oversector."

"Where's Amari?" Aldhelm's voice brooked no sympathy—a chill reproof, it caused Ferdin to draw herself erect, to stare at the man with eyes gone flat and emotionless. "In a house two doors down on your right, sirrah. I sealed and placed alarms on the other entrances and windows—he has to come out there." A thin index finger impaled darkness, indicating an archway where a hoverlamp bobbed in a portable holding field. It threw knife-edged light at the door. "I set the lamp."

"Did he give you a long chase?". Gyll could see the mud of Undercity caking Ferdin from feet to mid-thigh. The apprentice caught Gyll's glance and smiled tentatively.

"I'm going to spend the rest of the night cleaning myself, as you can see, Ulthane. But no, he hasn't moved in two hours. He has a sting, but other than that he should be easy. McWilms and I could have taken him a hundred times over. If it weren't for the damned watchers . . ."

"Go on then. McWilms is waiting for you in the flitter."

Ferdin nodded her thanks. She let her nightcloak—with the red slash of the apprentice—fall about her and moved into the night.

"You need to talk with the apprentices, Ulthane. They shouldn't be so easily spooked." Aldhelm watched Ferdin's retreating back, glanced with irritation at the watchers along the street.

"You were never bothered?"

"You have to ignore the lassari fools, neh? I concentrate on my task—that's what you taught me as an apprentice, Gyll. I simply follow your teachings." He stared at Gyll.

And I should follow them myself: is that what you tell me, Aldhelm? Once I did, to the exclusion of everything and everyone else. I wish it were that easy now.

"Then let's see if I taught you well," he said.

The doorway to the building was grimed in an irregular semicircle about the handle, the legacy of many unwashed hands. Gyll unsheathed his Khaelian dagger, grimacing at the weight (he preferred his vibro, but the Khaelian weapon had other advantages), and prodded at the entrance plate. The door slid into its niche with a rumble. The Hoorka flattened themselves to either side of the archway.

Aldhelm's fingers moved in the hand code: *I'll go first.*

A quick downward flick of the wrist: *No. Wait.*

The interior darkness remained silent, quiescent. Several curious lassari moved nearer, staring at the Hoorka and peering into the open doorway. Aldhelm feinted toward them with the dagger and they fled.

Now. First Aldhelm then Gyll moved into the room, Aldhelm rolling a flare ahead of them. Night fled to the far corners of the space, startled. Shadows reared and died as the ovoid flare wobbled, bounced from one wall, and came to a shuddering halt.

"Amari?" Gyll called. There was no answer.

The light stabilized. The Hoorka stood in a shabby reception hall that had once been grand. Three archways led out—one directly ahead, one to either side. Two floaters lay keeled over in their holder units, their fabric coverings torn and shredded. A broken holotank sat in a small mound of glassine shards. The floor gritted underfoot. From one corner, a stalkpest went about its foraging, unconcerned.

"Aldhelm, do you see the formal warning? Amari's supposed to have a sting, so there should be—"

"Gyll!"

Gyll turned at Aldhelm's shout, the dagger up and ready. He had only a moment's glimpse of a gaunt apparition in the far archway (frightened dark eyes under a shock of brown hair; a defiant stance) and a fleeting impression of the sting the man held.

The blast struck them.

Gyll's ears ached with the roar, there was a sudden constriction about his body, and he could not move. A dark hail swept around him, and the world slammed him from his feet. His body toppled, stiff.

When the bodyshield released him from its iron grip a second later, the figure was gone. Aldhelm was picking himself up beside him. Slugs from the sting clunked dully to the floor from their nightcloaks; the wall behind them was pitted and torn.

"That cowardly, filthy lassari-sucker," Aldhelm muttered, softly and without inflection. "Without so much as a word to us, without a warning or a thought to his honor and kinship. . . . I can understand the contract for this piece of dung. If it weren't for the shields . . ."

"The bastard," Gyll agreed. He was filled with a sudden rage. All hint of his listlessness was gone, kindled to ash by the rush of adrenaline in the attack's aftermath. He brushed unnecessarily at his nightcloak. He felt as he once had felt—a cool, methodical killer in the service of Dame Fate, a hunter seeking death for the Hag.

"Stay here, Aldhelm—Amari can't escape the house if one of us guards the door. I'll go find him or flush him toward you." Gyll's voice was clipped, high.

"All things considered, Ulthane . . ."

"Neh!" Gyll spat out the word. "His life suddenly offends me, Aldhelm. He's mine. Stay here and be ready."

"He may attempt another lassari stunt, and if we're together . . ."

"We can't talk Amari to the Hag, man." Gyll hefted the dagger in his hand, tapping the floor with an impatient foot. "I insist on this, Aldhelm."

Something in Gyll's demeanor took the fire from Aldhelm's protest. He began to speak but stopped, staring at the older man. He shrugged and moved to the left archway. "I'll wait here for your call, then. If you find him, if you need help . . ."

Gyll shushed Aldhelm with a raised finger. They listened. From the floor above, they heard the sound of furtive movement, a scraping of wood, then silence.

"I won't need your help." Gyll—a dark-clothed wraith—moved into the corridor.

Amari's path was easy to follow: he left behind the detritus of fear and panic. The sting, empty, lay abandoned against the wall a few paces down the corridor, and the dust of the hall was visibly disturbed by his flight. From the end of the corridor, a lift-shaft beckoned. Gyll did not waste time with stealth; he moved quickly to the shaft and peered up.

Nothing.

He tossed the vibro on his belt up the shaft; listened to it clatter on the flooring above. Again, there was no reaction. Gyll let the field take him up.

The second floor was much like the first, a morass of decayed technology and filth. That much he could see in the weary light drifting in from the street's hoverlamp. Amari's retreat had left a scarred track through the dirt. Gyll shook his head. *So easy, so stupid. The bastard acts as no honorable kin, nor does he have the wit to escape the Hag. He panics, and She smiles. Mondom need not have worried. The apprentices could have taken him.* Gyll picked up his vibro from the floor and sheathed it again.

There was a scuffling sound from a room down the hall: Gyll stiffened, ready to move, to dodge or attack. A moment later, the sound was repeated; a scratching of fabric or leather against something hard, or a tentative scrabbling of hands.

"Amari, you bastard, you're Hoorka's now." Gyll clenched the dagger, ready to throw. He squinted into the darkness webbing the hallways, searching for movement. "The Hag waits for you, coward. Come meet Her messenger." His voice was a loud taunt, a deliberate insulting that no kin would tolerate. He called down the shaft to Aldhelm. "I've found him."

Gyll took another flare from his beltpouch and rolled it down the corridor. Shadows chased along the walls—the scrabbling was loud for a second. Gyll smiled: it came from the first door to the right. Hefting his weapon, letting his anger propel him, he moved toward the room.

"Amari, it's hopeless. Come and fight like kin—go to the Hag with that much honor, not like a lassari." He wanted it, wanted the confrontation, the fight; he could feel his heartbeat quicken in anticipation.

He was not answered. He glanced inside the room.

A grimy window smeared light across the floor and halfway up one wall. The interior was dappled, paint hanging in long strips from the walls. Amari crouched in the furthest corner of the room, cocooned in shadow, his back pressed tightly against the wall as if by sheer will he could force his way through. Gyll could see the eyes, frightened, moving nervously. A tongue licked dry, cracked lips.

With two swift steps, Gyll moved to the center of the room. Amari now could not run without going past the assassin. The polished blade of the Khaelian dagger flicked window light across the walls.

"Bondhe Amari, your life is claimed by Hag Death." Gyll

began the ritual for a trapped victim, watching the man. Already, he could feel the anger leeching away, cooled by the man's obvious fear, his helplessness. He tried to kindle it again, keeping in his mind the vision of the ambush, Aldhelm's mocking words, Mondom's galling concern. The effort was only partially successful. Amari sagged against the wall as Gyll spoke; he seemed craven, exhausted, all resistance and pride gone from him. With the Hoorka's words, Amari moaned, shifting his weight, trying to back away from the dark presence.

Gyll couldn't keep the contempt from showing on his face. "Amari, you disgust me. You don't deserve a clean death."

Amari shook his head, a rapid back and forth. Sweat-darkened hair lashed his cheeks. "Hoorka, I'm sorry for the sting. It—" Amari stopped, snagged Gyll's stare with his manic eyes, and then looked away. His right hand brushed hair back from his forehead. "It was desperation. I . . . didn't know what else to do. It shamed me before all kin."

"You can settle your guilt with your gods, then." Gyll forced a harsh edge in his voice, but he could feel that the anger was entirely lost now; it was pretense. Amari disgusted him, repelled him, but there was also an undercurrent of pity. He would kill him, yes, but it was not a deed he would do gladly. "Prepare yourself, Amari kin-less. How do you want to meet the Hag?"

A fractional step forward—Gyll's boots scritched on the grime of the floor. Amari shivered as if cold, pulled upright. "No . . ." The word forced its way past clenched mouth.

"It needn't be this way, Amari. I can use the dagger, yah, but I can also give you a capsule. A lassari's death, but what is that small shame in addition to the rest you bear? It's painless, even enjoyable, I'm told . . ."

A small shaking of his head.

"You can't delay any longer, man. The capsule?" Gyll fumbled in his beltpouch with his free hand, found the capsule and held it out to Amari. *Why do you torture the wretch, old man? Why drag out this farce? It should be over now, the body bundled and given to the contractor. You hesitate, you wait.*

Amari looked sidewise at the capsule, his head half-turned from the Hoorka. His head came around slowly, the gaze always on the palm and the capsule it held. Then something seemed to snap in Amari's eyes. He jerked upright, his hand clapped Gyll's hand away, and he screamed. As the agonized wail jerked Gyll's head back, Amari pushed himself from the wall. Gyll reacted, powered by instinct and training, without thought. He stepped in front of the man, countered with a forearm the wild fist Amari threw. Gyll's dagger slashed forward, sheathing itself deep in Amari's midriff.

Warm, dark, and sluggish blood flooded from the long wound—the low-molecular edge of the Khaelian weapon slicing effortlessly through flesh. Amari gasped, a sound that turned to liquid gurgling. Pink foam flecked his lips. His knees buckled and Gyll stepped back to let the body drop to the floor.

The Hoorka stared down at his hand. Amari's lifeblood stained him to the wrist. Hag Death had come.

"He deserved the slowness, Ulthane."

Gyll turned slowly. Aldhelm stood in the doorway, a silhouette against the guttering brilliance of the flare. The dusty air sparked around him.

"You tell the new kin that they must kill quickly," Aldhelm continued. "You tell them to avoid conversation with the victims. But all rules must be broken, neh?"

Gyll said nothing. He stared at Aldhelm, eyes narrowed.

Aldhelm stepped into the room with unconscious grace. He reached into his pack and handed Gyll the victim's nightcloak. "Let's finish this," he said.

5

The day pretended summer.

Those that could find any excuse to be outdoors took the opportunity. Keep Square was crowded and loud. The Li-Gallant's keep itself was opulent in noon. The sunstar deluged the walls with lemon brilliance and spat aching-bright reflections from the windows.

The main gate of the keep swung back with a resounding clash of metal, the intricate designs wrought there shivering with the violence of the motion. Passersby murmured and paused to watch two people stride from the entrance: the Domoraj, resplendent in his dress uniform, and an older, bearded man who also wore the insignia of Vingi's guard. The latter was speaking loudly to the Domoraj, his arms waving in protest as he half-ran behind him.

"By all the gods, think of your kin, Sucai. You can't abandon them like this, can't leave the guard without its Domoraj. You dishonor yourself, dishonor the Li-Gallant, dishonor your kin. And the Li-Gallant has promised you an erasal tomorrow—'' The man seemed suddenly to realize where they were. He brought himself to a quick halt, eyes narrowing as he glanced around at the frankly curious onlookers. He rubbed gray-white hair, muttered an expletive, then resumed his pursuit of the Domoraj. Sucai was now standing in the center of Keep Square, arms at his sides, staring without seeing the buildings and people around him.

"Domoraj," hissed the man in an agonized whisper. "Come with me, please. I've been your aide for standards, man. You know you can trust Arnor, eh? Let's talk this out. Perhaps too much lujisa . . .'' He grasped at the Domoraj's arm, pulling.

Sucai jerked free of Arnor's grasp, his lips drawn back in a snarl. He spoke for the first time, too loudly for Arnor's taste.

"Leave me alone, you damn fool. I'm no longer your kin."

Arnor stood back, uncertain. His brow furrowed, and he turned about—*too many people. I can't avoid making a scene that'll be the talk of Sterka by nightfall.*

Sucai was plucking at his guild insignia, a small hologram on his right shoulder. He pulled the crest from the fabric savagely, tearing the pin loose. He held it in his hand for a long moment, the sunstar catching the facets of tiny inset jewels. He inhaled —loudly, nasally—filling his chest. His head came up; he stared at the crowd that had gathered around Arnor and himself.

"The person who was once Domoraj of the Li-Gallant Vingi's guild, who is also known as Sucai d'Ancia, declares himself unguilded. He does not deserve kinship." Sucai spoke slowly, using the impersonal mode, insulting himself. He closed his eyes as if in pain. "He is lassari, the former Domoraj. He is Dead . . .'' With the last word, Sucai jammed the pin of the hologram into the palm of his left hand. The first rank of the crowd jumped involuntarily. Arnor started to move forward, then—sensing that the onlookers would brook no interference with a private matter of honor—stood back again, gnawing unconsciously at his forefinger.

Sucai yanked the pin from his flesh. Blood welled out. He smeared the lifeblood across the face of the insignia, then flung it to the tiles of the square. The glassine hologram shattered with a treble finality.

"Domoraj," Arnor said softly.

"There is no Domoraj. He is Dead."

"Sucai, you must know me."

"Sucai is Dead. He sees none of the living." His voice was scratchy, pained, as if shaped from agony.

Sucai began to shed himself of his uniform. The crowd drew closer around him, drawn to the hurt etched on the face. It was a rare sight to come across kin at the moment of their commitment to the Dead. Speculation raced: Why would the Domoraj be so shamed, so full of dishonor that he'd be compelled to seek the solace of the Hag? Yet their mood was also solemn, for there was a redemption of honor in joining the Dead. The Domoraj was now beyond Neweden's laws. He was kin of the Hag.

Arnor began backing away, making his way through the press of people to the gate. He could do nothing. The Domoraj stood naked in the square.

Someone threw him a worn cloak. Sucai accepted it without a word, though his glance conveyed gratefulness. "The Dead?" he asked.

Several voices answered, one louder than the rest. "I saw a procession this morning by Niffengate."

Sucai nodded his thanks and began a slow walk to the west, toward Niffengate. The throngs parted silently before him, watching, whispering.

Sucai looked neither to right nor left. His lips moved in a silent chant. The sunstar pooled blue shadow at his bare feet.

Arnor, shaking his grizzled head, dreading what he would have to tell Vingi, closed the keep gates.

The morning had not gone well. He and Aldhelm had returned to Underasgard early (Gyll plunging his bloodied blade into the earth beside the dawnrock to feed She of the Five Limbs, nodding to the congratulations of his kin), and he had gone back to his rooms. He'd expected to find Mondom there, or at least a note for him to call. He'd had no reason to expect this from her; it had simply been a pleasant hunch that had grown without volition on their trip back, a daydream to take the edge from the unpleasantness of the contract. Expectation had increased, and he'd been surprised to find how tangible his disappointment could be. His room had been empty but for the wort; it had whimpered softly at him. He'd scratched its ear, feeling dull frustration.

Mondom had gone to bed with Serita Iduna.

When he saw her that afternoon, she'd spoken to him, smiling and joking, and asking if he would see Oldin. She touched him with gruff affection. Yet he seemed to sense a forced manner in her friendliness. He wanted to talk to her and lance the boil of his paranoia, but she'd put him off, pleading that Hoorka business called her.

"I know you'll understand, Gyll," she'd said. "You were Thane once."

That had hurt more than his suspicions.

It had driven him into a mild depression that even the unique experience of his flight to the Trader's craft could not dilute. Nor did the pilot of the shuttle help: Gyll had never seen a Motsognir Dwarf before, but if Helgin Hillburrower was representative of his race, they were a gruff and sour lot. He grunted his hello, looked the assassin up and down as if he were a specimen, and grinned savagely. "Like your outfit," he'd said. Gyll could not tell if he was being insulted or not.

Peregrine was huge, massive, looking like a pair of gothic cathedrals glued bottom to bottom and set loose. The Motsognir had whipped the shuttle into a port that was not much smaller than the whole of Underasgard. Around them, the ship was alive with activity: the crew milled in the corridors, nodding to Helgin and staring frankly at the nightcloaked stranger. Gyll could not see enough; he felt the depression leave, shattered by newness. He was inundated with alienness: Down the hall hobbled a bio-pilot, a reengineered human whose nervous system was not set for walking but for guiding ships through the voids between worlds; two people (men? Gyll could not be sure, but both had prominent mammaries) with arms of bare polished metal butted smoothly to flesh; a furred thing like a mating of owl and bear growled at them as they passed. The corridors themselves were set in no sane fashion—seemingly laid out by a deranged architect with a pathological need for misdirection. Gyll was hopelessly lost before they reached Oldin's quarters.

Oldin's rooms were stunning. The place was huge. A thick grass-carpet wandered over hillocks and protrusions—evidently the seating arrangements. Colors, vivid and saturated, swirled restless on the walls, and a large port in the ceiling gave a view of Neweden herself. And set here and there were . . . *things* Gyll could not identify. The arrangement of white globes and blue rods, what was it? Not a sculpture, since it had an obvious control panel affixed. The vial of greasy, rolling smoke; the tank holding what seemed to be only moss-covered rocks; the holos— winged creatures, a neo-dolphin in ceremonial robes, an eerie landscape of storm in which a lightning-creature stalked: all these spoke of the philosophical differences between the Trading

Families and the Alliance, which held all alien things apart from itself.

With a glance of smug contempt, the Motsognir seated himself on a low rise in the carpet as Oldin came into the room. Her face had the delicate hardness of a porcelain doll, the skin silky with an ivory sheen. Her startling eyes were caught in subtle blue, trapped below gilt eyebrows. Here the gravity was heavier than it had been in the rest of *Peregrine*—Gyll decided it was for his benefit—and Oldin moved with a ponderous grace, seemingly uncomfortable in the Neweden-like pull. But it was what she wore that compelled Gyll's attention: it moved, sluggishly. An eye (veined like a bad hangover, a dead black pupil the size of a thumbnail in which Gyll saw himself dimly reflected) gazed back blandly at him from her thick waist. As Gyll stared, it blinked, slowly. A dull black skin covered Oldin's body from ankle to neck, the edges quivering slightly: the amoebic clothing flattered her, thinned the weight that a lower normal gravity and a variant standard of beauty had allowed her to keep. Gyll doubted that she was comfortable. *For effect,* he thought. He stared at the eye.

"Ulthane Gyll, please make yourself comfortable. I've been wanting to meet you for some time now." Her smile dazzled. She noted the direction of his gaze, and the smile widened.

The Motsognir cracked his knuckles, one by one, loudly.

"Helgin," she said, still staring at Gyll, her voice warm, "does not approve of this meeting. You'll quickly learn that Motsognir don't mask their feelings."

"Helgin also does not appreciate being referred to as if he weren't here." The dwarf looked at them, thick eyebrows lowered over deep-set eyes, beard scraggling down his chest. "You'll quickly learn, Ulthane Gyll, that Trader Oldin masks her feelings all too well."

Gyll glanced from one to the other. Oldin didn't appear disturbed by the dwarf's manner, and Gyll, for his part, felt a sudden liking for the Motsognir—something in the gruff manner appealed to him.

A light touch—*by She of the Five, her hands are smooth. Has she ever done manual labor?*—directed him into the room. Gyll pulled away, not wanting to have her clothing contact him.

"You may sit where you like, or have a floater if you prefer." She watched as Gyll chose a spot near but not too near her on the carpeted hills. "I've had refreshments sent up."

As if on cue, the door to her chambers opened and a hover-tray slid in. It came to a halt before Gyll. He looked down at a dish of lustrous, silver ovals, like a nut encased in mother-of-pearl.

"Rhetanseeds," Oldin explained as Gyll reached for one. "They come from well out in the Cygnus sector, well beyond Alliance boundaries. Take one, it will be sufficient."

"Sufficient for what?"

Her smile shone at him. "You don't trust me, Ulthane?"

"M'Dame Oldin, the Hoorka trust only their own kin."

To their right, the dwarf chuckled. "A good trait, Hoorka."

Still smiling, Oldin shook her head. "Nevertheless . . . First, Ulthane, please call me Kaethe. I'm of the Trading Families, and we don't follow Alliance mores, or any other of their rulings. And as for the rhetanseeds—ask the Motsognir. Helgin will tell you that they're harmless."

"I'll tell you, Hoorka, that—so far—no one has ever experienced any ill effects. And I enjoy them myself." Helgin whistled (lips pursed behind the forest of beard), and the tray came toward him, leaving Gyll staring at the seed in his fingers.

Gyll waited, watching as the Motsognir plucked a seed from the tray with a delicate touch made almost humorous by the squat thickness of his fingers, and dropped it into his mouth. Eyes glinting, he stared at Gyll as he chewed. He swallowed, overnoisily, and sighed in satisfaction.

Gyll placed the seed in his mouth, letting it roll on his tongue. It didn't taste—it simply felt smooth. He bit, gingerly.

A welter of taste and smell assaulted him: *cina . . . no, now it's anis . . . too astringent, like lemon, no . . . mint and cloves;* then there was a stimulation behind his eyes—*light!* that burst and faded through the spectrum; finally, a surfeit. It was as if he'd finished a fine, long meal. He was not unpleasantly stuffed, but satiated.

"Shit," he said. Quite eloquently.

Oldin clapped her hands in delight. Her attire, responsive, changed to a webbing of scarlet veins in a field of black. The eye blinked massively. "The aliens—I can't pronounce their name . . ."

"Kaarkg—*whistle*—seer*grumble.*" Helgin. "And I *know* your mouth. It's more than pliant enough to wrap your lips around the name."

"Eater of dung," Oldin said pleasantly.

"Ravisher of month-old corpses," Helgin answered, unperturbed.

Gyll stared. When Oldin turned back to him, the smile was still fixed to her lips. "As I was saying, Ulthane, the creatures used the seeds on extended trips, a form of quick sustenance. We've had great success with them as trade items.''

''She neglects to tell you that the seeds are nonnutritious to the human metabolism. That's what you need to listen for, Ulthane, her unvoiced words.'' Helgin grinned at Gyll from his hillock.

Gyll did not know how to react, whether to be angry or amused. He was caught up in a playlet for which he had no lines, snared in a net of words, all of which seemed important and none of which he understood. He did what he could: he slipped on the mask of his old self—the young Hoorka-thane—and let the cool aloofness of the Hoorka-way guide him.

''I came only to collect payment, m'Dame Oldin.''

''Kaethe.''

''M'Dame Oldin.''

Her mouth turned down, but her eyes danced. Her clothing stared.

''One for the Hoorka,'' said Helgin.

Damn these people, what are they playing at? ''The tales of aliens are quite interesting, but I'm here to collect payment for the contract on Cade Gies. You have the check, I'm sure.'' The last sentence was a cold statement.

''Are the Hoorka always so mercenary and unsociable? You've not smiled since you came, and the lines of your face don't fall naturally into the expression you're wearing.'' She gazed at him, the guileless eyes wide. Her hand brushed clothing-skin; lines of blue radiated out from the touch.

''M'Dame Oldin . . .''

A raised forefinger, languid. ''Kaethe.''

He didn't dispute the correction or acquiesce to it. ''We were hired to perform an assassination. Thanks to Dame Fate, it was done. What else do we need speak of?''

''You'll have your payment. Gratefully.'' As if tired, the eye at her waist closed. ''I was simply interested in *you*, Ulthane. You made the Hoorka from lassari criminals, and I'm aware that you've been attempting to advance the Hoorka beyond the domain of Neweden. The Alliance resists, does it not?''

''We've had a few offworld contracts.''

''But not many. Not to your potential. The Alliance is too cautious of you, too fearful, too parochial in outlook, Ulthane. That's why the Alliance won't let its citizens have much contact with the other races that dwell outside their sphere of influence. They're intolerant of change and new ideas, and social systems

that vary too far from their norm. That's why Neweden has had
so many problems with the Diplos.''

"But the Trading Families..."

Her smile shone, her eyes invited. "The Trading Families are
far more open-minded about such things. We seek out the
unusual and alien, after all. We're more like you, Ulthane. Like
Neweden-kin, we're fiercely loyal to our families; we understand
the concept of kinship, though we don't segregate along occupa-
tional lines. We've no taboos with experimentation and new
ideas—such things tend to be self-controlling. An unviable
concept will extinguish itself or be extinguished. That's not far
from the manner in which Hoorka view their assassinations, is it
not? You say that what's meant to survive *will* survive. You've
reason to be proud of yourself, Ulthane. The code is ingenious in
the way it fits Neweden.''

Her praise warmed him, and he knew he shouldn't let it do so.
It was most likely that the flattery was false. Gyll tore his gaze
away from her and found Helgin. The Motsognir frowned at
him, though the eyes seemed to laugh. Helgin shrugged.

"Don't look at me, Hoorka. *I* haven't dressed like an expensive clown.''

Again, Gyll did not know how to reply. Neither of the two
seemed to take offense at anything said, while to him and all
Neweden, insult was a deadly game to play. "What are you
after?'' he asked finally. He kept the shreds of Hoorka composure around him—distant, always haughty—but he knew Oldin
could read the bewilderment he tried to keep from his voice.

"You want Hoorka offworld.'' Her voice soothed. "You want
a chance to expand the opportunities of your kin.'' The clothing-
eye opened once more; in it, a too-thin Gyll reclined. "Fine. I
believe that the Trading Families can offer Hoorka more than the
Alliance and d'Embry. We have our feuds, also, and we're
concerned with the concept of honor, and we offer a much larger
arena than the Alliance, one virtually without boundaries.''

"D'Embry and the Alliance hold Neweden, and Neweden is
our home.''

"They hold it for the moment, I'll grant.'' A pause. "Solu-
tions can be found for that. You should at least consider us.''

"It's not my choice, even if I were interested. I'm no longer
Thane.''

"Ahh.'' Oldin steepled her hands. She gazed at him over ivory
fingertips. "Does that bother you?''

Damn, is it so obvious to all? Am I so transparent? "No,'' he said, knowing he lied. "It's simply a fact. I still have some small say in the affairs of Hoorka—they *are* my creation. But the old guard must give way sometimes." He tried for half-jovial, felt it come out morose.

"You're not old, Ulthane. The hair is graying, yes, and I'm sure you might find your reflexes a touch slower than they once were, but you're far from old. Experience too, that has its advantages."

His sudden irritation surprised Gyll. It was a complex compound, that ire, full of his own frustration at the night before, the wort, his inability to control the conversation with the Trader, Oldin's teasing. Gyll stood, the veins in his neck standing out, his lined face ruddy. His hand went unbidden to his vibrohilt. "The woman talks incessantly and says nothing." He spoke loudly, using the impersonal mode with bitter relish, knowing that it would spark kin to full anger.

But Oldin was not of Neweden. She didn't move, didn't appear in the least alarmed. "I'm sorry, Ulthane. I simply felt that I'd prefer to make the offer to the creator of Hoorka, no matter who has the titular leadership. It's your training and your guidelines they follow. Therefore it's *you* that interests me. Perhaps I should have approached this another way. Tell the Thane, then; tell her I'd like to speak with her."

Her gaze dropped to his vibro hand. Slowly, he let himself relax, let the arm fall to his side. He came as near to apology as he would allow himself. "All Neweden is quick to anger, m'Dame Oldin."

"Kaethe."—Helgin's basso rumbling. The dwarf looked at Oldin and shrugged. "You would have corrected him, yah?"

"You anticipate me so well."

"You're not given to complexity. It was easy."

A nod to the dwarf and she turned back to Gyll. "Kaethe," she said.

"Kaethe." Gyll gave in. "Irritability is a bad habit of mine."

"No apology is necessary. She of the Five . . . Limbs, is it not? The goddess of ippicators?" She changed the subject without transition. It took Gyll a moment to recover, then he nodded.

"She is the patron of ippicators, and of the Hoorka."

"It's struck me as odd since we've been in Neweden orbit— why hasn't your world made some effort to restore the beast of five legs? Its bones are one of your most valuable resources and surely enough genetic information has been recovered. I've seen the polished bones, and there's nothing more enchanting. With a small stable of the beasts, you could continue to export them without worrying. Cloning..."

"I know of no cloning techniques which don't require live tissue. The ippicator have been extinct for centuries."

"Surely the vast resources of the Alliance..." There was a faint mocking tone in her voice. "Though perhaps they refuse to help you."

"As far as I'm aware, they could do nothing. And besides, a live ippicator would upset Neweden's theology."

"Ahh." Oldin rose to her feet, a quick and graceful motion that startled him. The dark fabric about her moved, the eye blinking in dull surprise. "I'll let you go, Ulthane. I'm sure you've much to do. Helgin will get you the check for the Gies contract. And please talk to the Thane. The Trading Families might have much to offer you, the Oldins in particular."

She came up to him. He could smell a faint musk. It was pleasant, but he didn't know if it was a cologne or the clothing-creature. She smiled, grasping his thick-veined hand in hers. "Come back if you wish, Ulthane. I find the Hoorka fascinating. I'd welcome your company."

He could only nod.

On the way down...

"Well, Hoorka, how do you like the enchanting Oldin?"

"How can you speak of her that way, Helgin? I'm surprised she keeps you in her employ."

"You misunderstand our relationship. The Motsognir have their own means of support. I stay with her simply because I find her interesting, because we like each other."

"You've an odd way of indicating affection."

"She offers me adventure. New sights. A thrill of uncertainty. We never stay in one place too long. The Motsognir lust for that. We've never been a part of man's empires. A Motsognir'd die of boredom in the Alliance. In that, Oldin's right. The Alliance can't like the Hoorka, Ulthane. Give them time, and they'll start looking for ways to keep your people contained, safe and ineffective. The Alliance is just a gigantic inertia-machine seeking to preserve itself. Its vision is inward; it's satisfied with the status quo. And the more it tries to preserve itself, the larger the cracks that are going to appear."

"You talk like a philosopher, Helgin."

The dwarf turned a yellow-laced eye toward Gyll. "You just have no ear for sophistry, Ulthane. You're too used to people telling you the truth."

They entered Neweden's atmosphere. The planet welcomed them back with a roaring of mock thunder.

Outside the caverns, the sunstar had settled below the horizon. The night denizens prowled the hills. Deep in Underasgard, Gyll had gone to a spot far from the usual Hoorka lairs. He'd not expected to be disturbed there. He was mistaken in that assumption.

Gyll watched as Cranmer placed a bottle and two glasses on the rock beside him. The clink of glass against stone was loud in the stillness. To one side, a dimmed hoverlamp oscillated golden-green inside the barred cage of a headless ippicator skeleton. Light alternated with shadow on the walls of the cavern. On the rock, the bottle tilted dangerously. "What's that?" Gyll asked.

"Lubricant."

Gyll's eyebrows rose quizzically. He cocked his head.

"You're too literal sometimes, Gyll." The smile did not leave that mouth. It seemed permanently affixed. "It's wine. I thought it'd be a nice gesture. I haven't seen much of you recently."

"A lot going on."

"And you haven't talked to me about any of it. I thought I'd track you down and just talk—the wine'll ease a dry throat."

Cranmer sat. Gyll could see a slight wince as the coldness of the stones made itself felt through the fabric of Cranmer's pants. "You people have to move this planet closer to the sunstar," Cranmer said, noticing Gyll's attention. "I'm always freezing." Despite the heavy jacket he wore, Cranmer hugged himself.

"It keeps the wines chilled."

"Was that a joke?" Cranmer asked with too much surprise in his voice. "Ulthane, you're a constant revelation."

"Cranmer, you're a constant nuisance. If you're going to stay, at least pour the wine." Gyll's voice was dull, as if with fatigue or disgust. He had turned away from Cranmer, staring at the ippicator's skeleton, mesmerized. Cranmer pursed his lips appraisingly. He tugged the sleeves of his jacket down over his wrists, then began talking as if he'd noticed nothing.

"I was in Sterka earlier today," he said, reaching for the bottle and pouring a goodly amount into each glass. "I've a few things you might be interested in hearing."

He placed a glass beside Gyll. The Hoorka glanced at it, then returned to his preoccupied stance. Cranmer sipped his wine, watching, waiting, then shrugged. He settled himself on the rock. "D'Embry's got Diplo security checking out Cade Gies. Seems she doesn't like the thought that Oldin could have an

Alliance citizen killed and not inform her as to the reasons. I don't think it's because of any affection for Gies or revulsion because of his death. D'Embry just doesn't care to be left in the dark.''

Gyll grunted a reply. Cranmer glanced up to where the shadows of the ippicator's ribs flickered on the jagged roof. He set his glass down. "I also heard that Potok is supposedly considering a truth duel. The gossip all over Sterka is that the Li-Gallant is responsible for Gunnar's murder. The Domoraj joined the Dead yesterday, and that's supposedly an indication of his shame with the Li-Gallant. Everyone expects the challenge to be given within a few days of the funeral.''

Gyll had slowly turned to face Cranmer. His face was in light, but a rib-shadow striped him from shoulder to chest. His head seemed to float in air. "Vingi and Potok would be the combatants?''

"Isn't that the basis of truth-duel—the opponents have to be highly placed in the guilds, and the stakes enormous?''

"Yah.'' A smile came and went. "That'd be a travesty.''

"Would it serve justice?''

Gyll shrugged. "Dame Fate is supposed to guide the hands and rule the outcome—that way the assertion is proved true or false. If you believe that the Dame does so, then yah, justice is served.''

"What about you, Ulthane? Do *you* believe?''

Gyll turned away again. "I believe it's probably a well-calculated political move on Potok's part. If he thinks he can best Vingi at truth-duel—and Vingi *can't* refuse—he stands to gain quite a bit. I imagine a large monetary fine would be levied, maybe seats in the Assembly given up. It could ruin either guild. A risk, but a calculated one. And the people will be entertained, whether they believe or not.'' He stared into shadow, into the arch of bone.

"Cynical, Gyll.''

"I feel that way.'' Once more he turned. Light raked across his lined face. "I saw Oldin this morning—she made me think about other possibilities. And afterward, I went into Sterka.'' Gyll paused. His eyes narrowed. "If you're recording this, Cranmer, turn it off. What I have to say isn't for anyone else's ears.''

Cranmer spread his hands in innocence. "You don't trust my discretion?''

"No.''

A small grin. "Ah, well. I've not been recording, Ulthane.''

"Good. Cranmer, do you remember the night of Gunnar's death? We were in the outer caves. I'd just killed a stalkpest."

"Aldhelm came out—he was leaving the caverns."

Gyll nodded. "He told us he was going to see an Irastian smith who was visiting Sterka. I checked all the local smiths, on a whim. I don't know why I was so suspicious. None of the smiths had seen Aldhelm that night. None had kin visiting from Irast."

"Aldhelm gave you no names. Maybe it was someone you missed. Maybe the smith was visiting true-family. That's uncommon, but it happens."

"Maybe Aldhelm lied. In which case, what was it he wanted to do in Sterka that he didn't want to discuss with kin?"

Cranmer had no answer. He drank from his glass. "Have you talked with Mondom about this?"

Gyll's laugh was a short exhalation. "It's always the same thing: 'Have you talked with Mondom?' I sometimes even ask that myself. Once, once, Cranmer, that wouldn't have been needed to be asked." Gyll shook his head slowly. "I haven't seen her since I returned. I was supposed to meet with her after seeing Oldin, but she wasn't in Underasgard—some business with a kin-lord in Illicatta. I won't see her until Gunnar's funeral tomorrow."

"Then confront Aldhelm. Talk to him."

"No. It's not my place." There was an edge of bitterness in Gyll's voice. "I'm not Thane, after all. And I'm not sure it's something I really want to do. Aldhelm is kin; he knows what honor is, and we have to trust our kin to uphold that honor, neh?" Gyll—habitual—moved fingers through graying hair. "I don't know, Sond. I don't know. I'm not sure what I feel this moment. I'm of two minds. One part of me wants to leap in, take over the active role again, even if it means a confrontation with Mondom. Egotistically, I think I'm the only one who truly understands Hoorka, what I meant it to be, what it should do. And the rest . . . Maybe I'm just being bitter. I keep thinking it's all Mondom's problem now. Let her work it out. I can't even say too much to her for fear that she'll think I'm interfering, usurping her authority. We've already fought over that. And she *is* my friend, my lover. I don't want to ruin that. She's the closest to me of the kin. So what would *you* do, scholar?"

Cranmer waited a long moment before replying. "I think I might drink my wine."

Slowly, Gyll smiled. He glanced down as if seeing the glass for the first time. "You know," he said, "that may just be the right solution."

6

An excerpt from the acousidots of Sondall-Cadhurst Cranmer. The following excerpt is from a conversation between Ulthane Gyll and Cranmer. The lack of background noise and the echoing resonance indicate that the conversation took place in a secluded area of the caverns. The dating of the segment is only approximate. It is included among several other undated recordings, all evidently clandestine.

EXCERPT FROM THE DOT OF 5.15.217:

"I think I might drink my wine." (Cranmer)

"You know, that may just be the right solution. You'll have to excuse my mood, Sond. It's everything taken all together, not just one thing. I let myself get into these depressions, and then I have to come here and think myself out of it. It goes away in time." (Here there is the sound of drinking, a clatter of glass on stone.) "But then you know all that already."

"Still, I'm glad that you don't mind talking about it."

"I don't mind because I trust you to go no further with it. And I have to admit that it's sometimes nice to have someone listen, to talk out loud and hear myself try to explain—you can see the flaws in your logic. It wouldn't work with everyone, though; you won't let this get beyond the two of us."

(Cranmer laughs with an edge of nervousness. After a moment, Ulthane Gyll joins in.)

"Gyll, your trouble is that you're an idealist. Everyone else around you is a pragmatist."

"Is that so bad?"

"It is when you constantly assume that they all think the same way you do."

The two Hoorka were seated in the stands of the guilded kin, a part of the crowd filling Tri-Guild Church square. The lassari, gawking at the expensive display of mourning, huddled at the southern edge while the guilded kin were comfortable beneath a

large weathershield near the church. It was not a pleasant day for
Gunnar's funeral. The sunstar shrouded itself in clouds and the
sky wept, a constant drizzle. The lassari shifted restlessly under
improvised shelters.

The censers, borne by a troop of young boys representing all
the guilds sworn to Gunnar-Potok's rule-guild, had just passed in
golden splendor. The acrid fumes still hung in the air, a pall the
rain was dissipating rapidly. The youths had looked frankly
miserable. Their gilt finery had been soaked and clung to their
skin, their breaths steaming in the chill air. The procession was
moving slowly down the lane between the lassari crowds and the
bleachers of the kin: a trio of pipes, followed by a phalanx of
musicians with krumhorns and tabors; then the beast-dancers
from Irast acting out for the fifth time that day—they were
becoming rather bored—the death of the Great Ippicator, twirling
with awkward arabesques in their five-legged costumes.

Gyll shifted in his seat, restless. "We need to talk, Mondom.
Oldin had an offer—I think we should hear it."

"Yah?" Her gaze was on the beast-dancers. "It will wait until
we get back to Underasgard. This isn't the place for business.
Besides, my butt's gone to sleep."

Following the beast-dancers, a large floater passed bearing the
dignitaries of local guilds, a score of kin-lords. Those absent
were most conspicuous. The Li-Gallant's guards, as the policing
force for Neweden, were present, but Vingi himself was not.
Instead, the Li-Gallant had sent his recording secretary, pleading
government business as an excuse. The Hoorka had also been
asked to join the group on the floater, but Mondom had cited
their code's insistence on strict neutrality and had instead sat
with the mass of guilded kin in the stands.

A smaller floater followed, preceding the bier. In it, the
Regent d'Embry stared dourly at the crowds. Her face, under the
weathershield, reflected bland sympathy, a public mask. Rigid,
she neither moved nor glanced about.

"Do you think we can really trust her, Mondom?" Gyll
nodded toward d'Embry. "Look at her, so stiff—and yet we let
her hold the future of Hoorka."

"We haven't a choice in that, Gyll. That's what you always
told me."

"Yah, but I don't like it. If there were an alternative . . . I'll
bet she has to peel off that face every night."

And last, the bier. It was flanked by all Gunnar's kin, their faces
chalky with white funeral paint. The rain, in their long march, had

streaked and splattered the paint. They looked sufficiently mournful, the turquoise guild-robes tattered and rent, the shoulders dotted with random blotches and smears from the thick paste on their faces. The bier moved slowly, majestically. It was a floating cloudlet, pulsing a deep sapphire from somewhere in the fog that surrounded it. On the mist lay Gunnar, atop a pyre of scented wood. Grotesques, small imps, raced about the edges of the cloud, their miniature faces wracked with pain and grief. As the bier approached Tri-Guild Church, a hidden choir began the descant to the dead; the sapphire glow went amber, the Hag's color. The choir reached a crescendo as Potok came forward toward the cloud-wrapped floater, bearing a torch. It hissed in the drizzle.

Suddenly, a flare arced out from the midst of the lassari. Screeching and wailing as it climbed, the projectile exploded high above the square, a false sun. Heads turned in shock, Potok stood in uncertain surprise, the choir faltered to a ragged halt.

The flare's appearance was answered by a shout from the lassari. "Renard!" was the cry. The ranks of lassari seemed to boil, some trying to back away from the square, others surging forward. With the rest of the guilded kin, Gyll and Mondom came to their feet in the stands as several lassari rushed the bier. They bore crude weapons. Rough hands shoved aside the startled Potok. A group of the lassari grasped through the clouds of the bier, pulling and tearing. The mist faded, revealing a bare skeletal framework of steel and wiring. The grotesques became mournfully immobile. The lassari pushed, the bier tilted.

A cry of anguish came from the guilded kin, now beginning to recover their senses. But they had no leader and hampered each other more than helped: the rush from the stands was slow, tangled. The lassari pushed again as Potok's kin tried to stop them. The bier toppled in its field, canting over. The pyre broke loose, spilling wood and Gunnar's body to the wet pavement. A roar of triumph came from the insurgents—"Renard!"—a howl of outrage from the kin.

Gyll watched the confusion in the stands, the chaos in the square. "Let's go, Mondom—we can't do anything here."

"But the damned lassari . . ."

"Vingi's guards are coming. There's enough confusion already. We'd only add to it."

The guards moved, belatedly, attacking with crowd-prods and tanglefeet webs. But they were too far from the bier to get to the focus of turmoil; the lassari made use of the confusion to dart back into the mob. The crowd screamed as one—guilded kin and

lassari—as the guards forced their way in pursuit, using their
weapons indiscriminately.

The lassari (and some of the kin), angered now, began to
resist, fighting back as well as they could. Someone—a plant-pet
wrapped about his shoulders—shouted and lassari moved away
to harry the guards. People milled in the square, seeking escape, seeking an outlet for anger, seeking someone to strike.

Chaos held sway. The drizzle became a downpour.

M'Dame Tha. d'Embry was furious. A thundercloud of emotion preceded her into Diplo Center. The staff glanced up from
terminals and desks as she rumbled through: they quickly decided that to pretend ignorance was the best course. The sight was
tragicomic, though a glance at the enraged face forbade laughter. D'Embry's dress tunic was disheveled, soiled, and wet. Her
weathershield belt was broken, the casing cracked. Her white
hair hung in limp strands, the mouth was cemented with deep
wrinkles. Her eyes arced fire.

Heads stayed down, attentive to their tasks.

She stormed into her office, leaving behind a wet legacy of her
passage, and barked at the com-unit on the desk. "Karl, get in
here. Bring a warm towel. Several of them. Now."

D'Embry turned and glared out her window. A shiny-wet
Sterka Port stared back, blanketed in thick clouds. The skull of a
large ippicator gazed blindly through the rain, a gift from the
Hoorka. A symbol of this world, it seemed to laugh at her. "A
damned barbarian place," she muttered. "Gods, I'm sick of it."

Karl entered, towels in hand. He gave one to d'Embry with a
carefully expressionless face.

"Don't stare, Karl. It's not polite. And I know you saw the
procession on the holotank." She fixed him with a sour gaze.

"Yah, m'Dame."

D'Embry scowled. Karl made no elaboration. She glanced
down; Karl held a flimsy in one hand. "What's that?"

"A contract proposal for the Hoorka," he answered, holding it
out to her. "It came over the relay from Niffleheim while . . ."
He hesitated. "While you were out."

D'Embry glared. She toweled her hair, ignoring the flimsy,
then saw that the towel was stained with her pinkish bodytint.
"Damn." She threw the towel to a corner and snatched the
flimsy with a wiry hand.

"It could be important, m'Dame. A Moache Mining official is
the signator."

"Screw Moache Mining—and don't look at me that way. I know the meaning of the word." She tossed the paper to her desk, shaking her head. "The frigging Hoorka keep nagging me, and the whole structure of Neweden seems to be cracking around me. You saw that lassari outburst, Karl. Someone—some *one*—orchestrated that. It wasn't just a spontaneous upwelling. That was a person's name the lassari were yelling. It was *planned,* by this Renard, to hit right where Neweden would feel it the most. The incident will enrage the guilded kin and harden their attitude toward the lassari, and it'll inflame the kinless. It couldn't have been better designed to cause this world grief."

She suddenly slumped into her floater with a sigh, as if all energy had deserted her. Seated, she cupped her chin in her hands, shaking her damp head. "The damned contract can wait a few hours—I'm not so sure that I want the Hoorka to work this. I don't want to see or hear anything having to do with Neweden or any of its idiotic people for the next two hours. See to it, Karl."

"M'Dame . . ."

"*Do* it." She didn't look at him. She stared at the replica of d'Vellia's *Gehenna* standing in one corner of the room. The door hushed shut behind Karl.

"You could've retired to that estate on Arlin. Remember that, you fool old lady. You *asked* for this assignment. You couldn't trust it to anyone else, could you? You had to go and *ask* for it."

It was normal and customary for Hoorka to engage in practice bouts. There was, in fact, an unofficial ranking among the kin as to who was the most proficient with vibrofoils. Gyll and, later, Mondom, had done nothing to stop this covert hierarchy despite the fact that it was not covered in the Hoorka code. Their silence on the matter promulgated its continuation.

Normally, a match drew little attention. Even Cranmer, after recording diligently the first several that followed his arrival, had stopped dropping by the practice room. The kin who happened to be in the area might stop to throw in a comment and the results certainly traveled quickly in the gossip of the kin, but few set aside other activities to become a spectator.

The bout between Aldhelm and d'Mannberg was the exception. Aldhelm was generally acknowledged to be one of the best Hoorka with vibrofoil and he was the unofficial leader of the duelists. The kin would seek out his matches to stare and search for weaknesses to exploit. D'Mannberg's presence amplified the interest: Aldhelm and d'Mannberg had for some time been at odds. The last time they had fought, it had gone strangely. Aldhelm, to the surprise and shame of his kin, had put a display of his prowess ahead of adherence to the etiquette of kin-dueling. Before Thane Gyll, Aldhelm had hurt and angered d'Mannberg unjustifiably. Since that time, the rancor had lain between him and d'Mannberg.

The sympathy was with d'Mannberg. The betting favored Aldhelm.

Cranmer was fiddling with his equipment, watched by a skeptical McWilms. The apprentice grimaced at the tangle of holocameras and controls. "Have you placed the cameras correctly?"

Cranmer glanced back over his shoulder. "I've been doing this for a decade. Since before you joined the Hoorka."

"You told me that last time, but the 'cube was all jumbled. Poor placement."

"For an apprentice, you're damned impertinent. Are you gonna help or just offer your expert advice?"

"I'll help. You're going to need it to get set up in time. Aldhelm's just come in."

D'Mannberg was already present, stripped to the waist. He was simply huge—a tall and massive man, his hair and beard shining red in the glow of the light-fungi that lined the room. To the casual eye, he appeared obese—his kin knew better. D'Mannberg was surprisingly fast for his weight, and the flesh masked muscle rather than fat. Aldhelm, readying himself to one side, was more traditionally muscular with a wedged torso. He slid his vibrofoil from its sheath; it whined through the air. The light-fungi tinged his skin, perspiration sheened his back.

D'Mannberg readied his own weapon, clicking it on. The orange-tipped marker shot from the hilt to its full extension, defining the length of the nearly invisible wire. The blade thrummed its power. He deactivated the blade, watching Aldhelm loosen up. "You still want the match, Aldhelm?"

Aldhelm glanced at d'Mannberg, the scar standing out on his face. He gave a noncommittal smile. "Who have you gotten to judge it, kin-brother?"

D'Mannberg turned, surveying the kin who were beginning to crowd the perimeter of the strip. "I'd have asked Ulthane Gyll or Thane Mondom, but neither is here. Sartas?"

Sartas nodded his willingness, stepping forward. Both Hoorka handed their weapons to Sartas. He examined each blade, locking

hem on the practice setting—the vibro would sting enormously,
but would not cut flesh. The desire to avoid a touch was
quite real; painful welts would still form. Sartas touched the foils
together: sparks hissed and flared, dying on the earth of the
cavern floor. He handed the weapons back and strode over to a
rack of vibrofoils, taking one out and activating it.

"Take your places, kin-brothers," he said, standing in mid-
strip. His olive face moved from Aldhelm to d'Mannberg. "The
match is five touches. All code strictures apply—a lost weapon
may be recovered without penalty and the entire body is a valid
target. The two of you will disengage when I call halt, or you'll
face my blade. Remember that it's not on the lower setting." He
paused. "Ready?"

They nodded, assuming the *en garde* position.

Sartas lowered his vibro and stepped from the strip. "Begin."

Beat, beat: a wailing shook the cavern, sparks rained to the
ground. D'Mannberg, seeing Aldhelm's foil in the fourth guard,
attacked in the high outside line to be met by a beat parry.
Riposte, parry, and counter-riposte: there was a whining slap,
loud in the room, as Ric's blade found Aldhelm's bicep.

"Halt!" Sartas stepped forward, knocking away the foils.
"Touch for d'Mannberg."

Aldhelm stood back, his face sullen, a hand kneading his arm.
Ric grinned. "That's payment for the last time we met, neh? I'm
not as slow as you might think, and you've given me a fair
amount of incentive. She of the Five doesn't care for those who
ignore the etiquette."

Aldhelm's face was emotionless. "One touch doesn't make a
match, either. And you're a large target." Then, too slowly,
"Kin-brother."

A mumbling from the spectators: those Hoorka as yet unsure
of the depth of ill-feeling between the two were quickly con-
vinced. Cranmer, behind the shelter of his equipment, pursed
thin lips. "What'd you think, McWilms?"

The youth's eyes were alight. "Aldhelm looked lethargic, sleepy.
That was very sloppy work on his part. But keep recording, Sond,
keep recording. This looks like it might be good."

"You're a bloodthirsty bastard."

"Yah, ain't I." He grinned.

Sartas scowled at the verbal exchange between Aldhelm and
d'Mannberg. He slapped his vibro at the floor, kicking up dirt.
"Sirrahs, please return to your positions. And watch your
tongues. We're kin here, and while I'm judge, you'll act it." His

dark eyes moved from man to man. Slowly, they both bowed to him.

"Take your positions again, then." He waited, then stepped back once more. "Begin."

This time Aldhelm was more cautious and less sleepily over-confident. He seemed to be awakening to full arousal, more aware of the match. His vibrotip danced now, flickering as he probed d'Mannberg's defense, backing the larger man slowly down the strip with short, frantic attacks that never let d'Mannberg regain the initiative. Still, all the attacks were successfully met. Aldhelm moved forward, then lunged into the open line, his body extended. D'Mannberg, swiftness belying his bulk, leapt backward and the vibrotip missed. He grinned at Aldhelm.

Now Ric counter-parried and riposted, taking the right of way. Bare feet hushed against the earth, sweat varnished their skin and made dark strands of their hair. Foils slapped and wailed.

"D'Mannberg's improved. A lot."

"Ulthane Gyll's been working with him. That, and he has a revenge to seek here. And Aldhelm still doesn't seem to be fully alert."

D'Mannberg let the tip of his vibro dip slightly away from the high line, as if his arm were becoming tired. Aldhelm took the proffered opening without hesitation, responding with a thrust. D'Mannberg was waiting; his foil screeched along the length of Aldhelm's, bringing them briefly closer, and he kicked out underneath Aldhelm's vibro hand. Aldhelm's hand opened with the impact and his vibrofoil slithered to the ground. D'Mannberg stepped away immediately, before Sartas could move to intervene.

D'Mannberg spread his arms wide. "Pick up your vibro, Aldhelm. We both know the etiquette, neh?" The sarcasm in his voice was obvious.

"D'Mannberg—" Sartas began, threateningly, but Aldhelm waved him silent. Scowling, he bent at the waist and recovered his weapon, checking the setting on the ring control once more. He did not look at d'Mannberg. He was too calm, too reserved. The smile left d'Mannberg's face; he crouched and rose quickly, exercising his legs.

"Gods, McWilms, look at Aldhelm's face." In the monitor holocube, Aldhelm's visage came into focus. "He looks like a killer I once interviewed. He has the same tautness to him....Hell, I can't explain it, but I see it."

"Don't have to explain, Sond. D'Mannberg had better see to his defense. Aldhelm's awake now."

They began: a quick flickering of vibros as Aldhelm went into a furious compound attack, feinting low and coming high, getting the strong of his blade to the weak of d'Mannberg's. D'Mannberg kicked again, but found Aldhelm's thigh rather than his knee. Thrust, beat parry, and a riposte to the inside low line—Aldhelm's vibro slipped over the guard of d'Mannberg's foil but stopped a millimeter short of a touch. D'Mannberg hesitated, open, but Aldhelm didn't take the advantage; d'Mannberg knocked away Aldhelm's blade with a beat. D'Mannberg's sweat-beaded face registered puzzlement. He disengaged, and Aldhelm did not follow.

"You had me." D'Mannberg's vibro was still up, waiting, in the fourth guard. Sweat dripped from his beard.

Aldhelm shrugged.

"My leg isn't a good enough touch? Is that it, Aldhelm? You want something more painful?" His face was flushed with anger. Above the heart, on the face, near the genitals—there the lash of vibrofoil was excruciating.

Aldhelm's face was set in stone. Cold, the eyes; white on red, the scar twitched. "I missed you, that's all."

"What would my pain prove to you? I'm your kin, not some lassari you can toy with."

"Kin believe kin, don't they? Then believe me. I missed you."

"By the Hag, Aldhelm, all the rest saw it too . . ."

"Sirrahs!" Sartas's foil whipped down between them. "If you wish to duel, I'll referee. If you want to argue rather than meet blades, go to the common room. It's all one to me, but you're wasting my time. Assume a ready position or deactivate your foils."

Aldhelm turned to Sartas. "D'Mannberg's eyes are as blind as an ippicator's."

D'Mannberg reacted as most guilded kin would to an insult in the impersonal mode. His ruddy face flared with rage. He spat out a response in the same mode. "Aldhelm has the voice of a lassari. He can speak no truth."

The words cracked Aldhelm's icy calm. With a guttural shout, he flung his foil aside and lunged for d'Mannberg. But Sartas moved too quickly. His strong hands grasped Aldhelm's arm, slipping on sweat, then clamping down. D'Mannberg had begun to move in defense, but other kin restrained him, arms around neck and waist. Both men strained to be released.

D'Mannberg spat on the ground. In his fury, he spoke the

question that many kin had thought but none had voiced. "At least I know where I was the night Gunnar was killed. Aldhelm, alone of the kin, wasn't in Underasgard. Did Aldhelm kill him, sneaking like a cowardly lassari?" D'Mannberg stared directly at Aldhelm, waiting.

"Let me go, Sartas. Please." Aldhelm slumped in Sartas's grasp. His voice was dull. "Let me go. I won't dishonor myself." Sartas, slowly, loosed his hold. Aldhelm shrugged once, shaking his head, while the kin watched him warily. Aldhelm nodded to d'Mannberg.

"You can think what you want, kin-brother," Aldhelm said. "It doesn't matter when Hag Death breathes in your direction. And you were right. I wanted the most painful touch—I was angry, angry with myself *and* you. Still, I shouldn't treat kin so badly. And I did *not* kill Gunnar." He stood, hands on hips. "Believe it if you will."

Then he turned and walked from the room. His kin, surprised and (perhaps) disappointed that a bloodfeud had not been declared, watched him go.

"Damn." Cranmer exhaled shakily.

"Yah," McWilms agreed. "An interesting recording you have there, scholar."

D'Mannberg, released from the restraining hands of his kin, clicked off his vibrofoil, sheathing it forcefully.

"Bastard," he muttered.

Mondom cuddled the wort in her arms, stroking the serrated ear flaps gently. Orangish fur floated about her, clinging to the fabric of her nightcloak; she shook her head, sending hair flying. She could see scaly skin showing through bare patches on the wort's shell. "When did it get this way?" she asked. "Have you named it yet?"

Gyll smiled at the multiple questions. "It's been getting worse in the last few days, and Renier's given me a salve that might help. The poor thing doesn't seem to be in pain otherwise, though it's still too weak to stand for long, and it doesn't eat much. I don't know . . . And I'm not going to name it yet—I don't want to get attached to it just to have the Hag take it for Her own pet."

Gyll sat on the edge of his bedfield, uniform shirt off, boots on the floor beside him, nightcloak thrown in one corner. He shrugged.

"You don't like making commitments unless you're certain of

the outcome? Is that what you're saying, Gyll? That doesn't sound like the philosophy of the person that would have created Hoorka, not an idealist. After all, the Hag might have taken all Hoorka for pets, too." A smile; she patted the wort.

"Yah." He nodded in submission. "Let's just say I haven't found a name I like yet—it's got nothing to do with being attached to the damn thing. Will you spend the night with me?"

"Make a commitment without being sure of the outcome? Never." She stroked the wort a final time, sneezing as she did so, wrinkling her nose at Gyll's sudden laughter. She placed the creature back in its cage. The wort growled once in protest, then lay on its side, panting. "So . . . We never had a chance to talk this morning, not with all the commotion. You wanted to tell me about Oldin?"

"Yah. I found her interesting. Very much so."

A raising of eyebrows.

"Oh, yes," Gyll continued. "She finds men with graying hair very sensual. She seduced me almost before I could walk in the door . . ." He stopped, grinning. "I was never very good at that type of fantasy, huh? She *is* striking in her own way, though that's not what I wanted to talk to you about. And you needn't look so innocent—you've gone to bed with people on a whim."

"Hah. You've been spying."

Gyll didn't respond to her teasing. "It was all business. And she said a few things that we need to explore."

"We?"

"Hoorka." He leaned back on the bedfield. "You and I."

"Mmm." Mondom crossed the room and sat next to Gyll, one leg up, facing him. She reached down to touch his thigh. "Then talk. You got payment?"

"Yah." He shook his head. "That's unimportant. What Oldin *did* hint at was an offer for a more challenging and open field for the Hoorka. She didn't give any specifics, but the suggestion was there, if we wish to check it further." He shifted position and Mondom's hand slipped from his leg. She made no move to put it back. "I think we should find out more, Mondom."

"Work with the Trading Families? The Alliance wouldn't allow it, Gyll. D'Embry'd ban us from offworld work again."

"I know she'd try."

"Then why do you even think of considering it? Neweden's ruled by the Alliance—if d'Embry wants Oldin gone, she just has to order it. If the Alliance bitch doesn't want us to work

Trader contracts—and she won't—she'd have no difficulty stopping us."

"You didn't see what I saw on the ship, Mondom. It was like . . . like having my eyes opened after being blind. Gods, that's a common metaphor. Still . . . Listen, a long time ago I saw what I could do with a gang of common lassari, and I was satisfied with what I'd made for a while. Then I managed to get the Alliance interested in the Hoorka, thinking about the new vistas that would open before us if we could move beyond this one world—I thought *that* was my life-goal. You know I've been moody for some time: I think I was simply dissatisfied. That ship—the Trading Families dwell in a larger world than the Alliance, Mondom. I saw a Motsognir—you know how rare they are. I encountered new spices, new smells, new sounds—*alien* things, from cultures totally unlike any the Alliance knows. And Oldin, in her own way, seems as if she might actually *care* about the Hoorka, to understand what I've set up. The way she describes the Families . . ."

"The way she describes the Families is probably the way she thinks you'll like best. And the Alliance holds Neweden, not the Families."

"For now."

Mondom laughed, but her laughter had little amusement in it. "Gyll, the Trading Families aren't going to come and take Neweden from the Alliance. They have agreements, and the Alliance is too strong." She rose, shaking her head. Gyll watched her, watched her turn and face him again. "I just received a contract from d'Embry this evening. Offworld—a place called Heritage. You see, Gyll, we *are* beginning to make real progress, to see the completion of what you set out to make. Vingi can't really oppose us any longer—he has no leverage anymore. Gods, it's all you worked for, and you're still willing to consider this intangible offer of Oldin's?"

"You didn't see the ship."

"I don't need to."

"Mondom, Hoorka must—"

She severed his words with a violent movement of her hand. "*I'm* Thane, Gyll. Don't tell me that Hoorka 'must' do anything." As Gyll stared, startled by her sudden vehemence, she softened her tone, the lines of her face gentling. "You gave me the responsibility of leadership, neh? Because you didn't want it. Has that changed?"

"I'm simply trying to give you some information."

"But you insist that I act upon it, the way you want me to. No," she said as Gyll began a protest, "you expect Hoorka to follow your lead, as it once did."

"Were I still Thane," he answered, choosing his words carefully, "I'd still listen."

"Gyll"—wearily—"you gave up the title."

"I was..." His voice trailed off.

"You're feeling sorry for yourself."

"*Don't tell me what I'm feeling, Mondom!*" Gyll's anger flared as quickly as had Mondom's. He sat, abruptly, a forefinger pointing in warning.

"Then don't tell me what I have to do as Thane." She wasn't infected by Gyll's quick rage. Her lips twitched with the beginning of a word, then pursed in concentration. "It has nothing to do with Oldin, does it, Gyll? You know it. It's because I'm Thane. I *can* guess at how you feel. If you made a mistake in giving up the leadership, I'm sorry that you feel that way. But it's not a mistake that can be rectified now. It all adds up to that, Gyll—your boredom with Hoorka matters, your moodiness, your lackluster performance on your contracts..."

"Aldhelm?"

"I don't understand."

"Has Aldhelm been talking to you, giving you tales about the Amari contract? Remember, Mondom, Aldhelm was the one that counseled me to abandon the code in the Gunnar contracts; it was Aldhelm who was in Sterka the night Gunnar was murdered."

"Gyll, that's an outrageous accusation." Her face echoed inner distaste. "I'm ashamed that you'd say that. Don't you trust kin? How does the code-line go? 'All Hoorka are kin. You must trust kin implicitly, above all else. Kin do not lie to kin, kin do not conceal their inner feelings from kin.'"

"I know the code." Gyll swept an arm through the air as if waving away her words. "I wrote it, neh? I don't need a recital." Gyll struggled with his temper, wrestled it into grudging quiet. "Mondom," he continued, more reasonably, "I apologize for that. Let's get back to the question of Oldin. I do find her offer tantalizing. The possibilities might be good for us."

Mondom's stance was rigid, legs well apart, hands at her waist. "No, Gyll, I don't think so. Neweden belongs to the Alliance. We have to work with them or they'll confine us here, take away all we've worked for. Don't you remember your own arguments with Aldhelm a half-standard ago? He wanted Hoorka to shift away from the Alliance too, even if his view was inward rather than outward. You refused to consider it—because of what the Alliance might do. We don't know that the Trading Families can truly offer us anything. Oldin doesn't run them, isn't necessarily speaking for her grandsire, as far as we know. D'Embry has *real* power here, not just in words.''

''But if the offer is tangible, if it could give more power to Hoorka . . .''

''I don't see how that could be, Gyll. Stay away from her. The Traders are devious. They're also centered a long way from Neweden.''

''Is that an order?''

''Does it need to be?''

Stalemate. Gyll stared at Mondom, willing her to yield as she once would have, to defer to his wishes and sit beside him again. He knew himself too well; the words of apology he should utter were chained. They couldn't break loose of his pride. One of them had to give, Mondom or Gyll—she to yield or he to nod his head in acceptance.

She didn't. He wouldn't.

Gyll glanced away, looking down at the thick-knuckled hands, at the too-paunchy waist beginning to creep over his belt. *Have I just lost her as friend and lover? Is this what I bequeathed her? —by She of the Five, she's much as I was, as I still am. I am right, I am right this time, and I can't get her to listen*. He glanced up; Mondom had not moved. ''If we can't talk about it, we won't, then. I'd still like you to stay with me tonight.'' He already knew the answer.

Her eyes were suddenly very bright, very moist. She shook her head, the barest of motions, her lower lip caught between small teeth. ''I don't think so, Gyll. Part of me would like to, very much, but—'' A pause. She hugged herself, staring at the ceiling, the wort, and finally back to Gyll.

''I don't think so,'' she said. ''No.''

7

''Who have you been contracted to kill?''

''The rumors are that you've been retained by Moache Mining.''

''Can you tell us who contacted your organization on Neweden?''

"Why do you feel that the Alliance is willing to let the Hoorka work in social structures other than your own?"

The questions echoed in the steel vastness of Home Port. The three Hoorka, two full kin and an apprentice, did not answer. They watched a nervous Alliance official check their baggage and examine the traveling visas issued by Regent d'Embry, ignoring the cluster of reporters that had accosted them on their arrival on Heritage.

"Please, sirrahs—this isn't a vacation world. We know it's not that."

"If it's Moache Mining, then you have to be working for Guillene, and your victim has to be de Sezimbra. Why deny it?"

"Do you enjoy the killing, sirrahs?"

Sartas glanced up quickly. He swept his nightcloak over his shoulder, baring the much-used vibro that hung on his belt. Behind him, Renier and McWilms stood away from the Alliance official, their stance suddenly wary and erect. Sartas glowered at the gaggle of reporters. "I only enjoy," he said, enunciating very slowly and clearly, "killing those who insult me and my kin." His flat stare held the eyes of the man who had made the last remark. His right hand touched the hilt of his weapon.

The reporters were suddenly mute but for a nervous coughing and the shuffling of feet.

"Have you finished with us, sirrah?" Sartas turned back to the official. His manner was curt but polite: the Hoorka aloofness.

"You're free to go. I hope you enjoy your stay." The man's last words trailed off into silence. He half-smiled, half-shrugged. "Habit," he said.

Picking up their duffels, the Hoorka began moving toward the arched entrance of the port terminal. The reporters stood aside to let them pass. Except for one, they didn't follow.

He was a short and stout man wearing a luminescent jacket and knee-length pants—Niffleheim fashion. He pursued the Hoorka, matching strides with Sartas. The assassin glanced at the man once but kept walking.

"Wieglin, with the *Longago Journal*," the man said in identification. "Listen, there aren't many secrets on Heritage. It's a poor, lousy world. There aren't but a handful here that could even think of affording your services. It has to be someone with Moache, eh? Why deny it?" He panted in the effort to keep abreast of the longer-legged Hoorka.

"We haven't denied *or* acknowledged it. The contract's signer will be revealed if the attempt is successful." Sartas spoke without looking at Wieglin. Renier, to his right, broached the entrance, the doorshields dilating.

"Ahh, the *attempt*..." The hot and dry air of Heritage assaulted them, billowing out the nightcloaks and sucking hungrily at the sweat that appeared on their brows. Harsh sunlight cast sharp-edged shadows at their feet. Sartas motioned and McWilms went to procure a flitter from a stand. Wieglin persisted, wheezing.

"You only attempt to kill the victim, like it's a mystical game. Well, it won't work here. Moache—Guillene—demands results, not sophistry. If they thought they could kill de Sezimbra and get away with it legally, they'd do it. Even Moache Mining has to play within some of the laws, and de Sezimbra's too smart to have an accident. It's only because the Alliance let you people out of your cloister. Death is too easy an answer to problems."

"Leave us be." Sartas tried to ignore the man, hooding his face with the nightcloak and staring out at the sun-baked landscape. Already, he missed the coolness of Neweden's day.

"I'll leave in a minute, after I say my piece. I've been on this world for the last three months because I know there's a story here in what de Sezimbra's been doing, because I know that Guillene's hand is bearing down too much on these people. He bleeds them as dry as the sands. Yah, it's all legal since they're indentured laborers, and all of 'em signed the documents. That doesn't—or shouldn't—make them chattel. De Sezimbra's working to change all that. The money you get from this job is going to be tainted with the blood of every man and woman on Heritage. Guillene is a foul bastard."

"If the victim—*whoever* he or she is—is meant to live, Dame Fate will see to the preservation of life."

"I'm sure that's comforting to all involved. Those who de Sezimbra was helping will hug their children and tell them 'Don't worry, he was destined to die.' That's a real balm."

The flow of words came to a halt as Sartas and Renier, without a word, strode toward their flitter, now stopped a few meters away. The Hoorka threw their luggage in the compartment and swung into the blessed air conditioning of the car. The flitter, in a swirling of dust, left Wieglin behind, hands on hips.

"Welcome to Heritage, eh?" Among themselves, they could finally relax. Renier grinned at Sartas.

"I always thought other worlds'd be exotic, beautiful places. So much for that fantasy. I'm already looking forward to the return. The heat's going to kill me."

They rode through the streets of Home, Heritage's only city. The rest of that world's settlements were the metal expanses of the mining platforms, rumbling colossi moving inexorably across the landscape and leaving behind a trail of pits and broken rock. Home was a collection of small, squat buildings, sitting in the eternal dust, squalid and hot and noisy. Children playing in the bare yards turned to watch the flitter pass; curious eyes stared at them from shuttered windows. Once, a rock flung by an unseen hand cracked off the windshield; a few blocks further on, garbage rained down on them from a second story window. The people they saw were mostly sullen, unsmiling, as drab as the buildings around them. Their unspoken dislike was palpable. Only the rich rode flitters, and the rich had to be somehow connected with Moache Mining. The tension burned at the Hoorka like the noon sun.

But when the flitter passed the columns of a high, black shield-wall surrounding Park Hill, the vista changed: desert to tropical oasis. Here, hedged by lush greenery and verdant lawns, lived the upper echelon of Heritage. The severity of the sun was masked by foliage as the dreariness of the indentured workers was hidden from the officials of Moache and the offworld visitors. The Hoorka drove past a grove of bubble trees and onto the grounds of the hostel. Sartas, already disturbed by the world, concluded their business with the clerk brusquely, grabbing the keys to their rooms.

"Let's get this over with." He scowled. "Quickly."

De Sezimbra's house stood in the lee of small brown hills a few kilometers from the outskirts of Home. The building was a low, small affair, a few outbuildings as attendants. Shabbily constructed, as well, McWilms noted as he approached. McWilms was both hot and tired after the walk from Park Hill. Sartas had not allowed him use of a flitter, an annoyance he'd nursed from irritation to exasperation on the walk. His nightcloak stifled him, his undertunic was wetly irritating with circles of perspiration, and his patience was at a low ebb. He wanted nothing more than to complete his task and get back to the comfortable and dark rooms at the hostel. He kicked at road dust.

He was certain that he was being watched as he turned from the road onto the path leading to the house. He could feel the pressure of a stare from the outbuildings, from the polarized windows of the house. He forced himself into the role of the aloof, disdainful Hoorka. *Like Aldhelm or the old man himself.*

Don't let them know how you feel; become an instrument in the hands of She of the Five Limbs. He tried on Sartas's scowl, found that it fit, and went to the door.

A flat viewscreen was set in the metal of the door. It had already been activated by the time he stood before it: swirling tongues of abstract color were tangled there. A voice came from the screen. "Your business?" it asked curtly, a basso query.

McWilms stared at the screen with narrowed eyes, the scowl a mask. "My business is only with Sirrah Marco de Sezimbra. I would speak with him, and in the flesh." He found himself lowering his voice to compete with the dark tones of the doorwarden; he cracked only slightly.

"And if he doesn't wish to see you?"

"It would be to his advantage not to refuse."

Silence. The screen went to a bland gray-blue. A few seconds later, the door irised open, jerking into its slots. McWilms recognized the man who stood behind it, but checked the bio-monitor on his belt as a matter of course. The light on the monitor glowed emerald—the man was de Sezimbra. McWilms made a deep obeisance. "Sirrah de Sezimbra."

"You have the advantage of me, I'm afraid." Marco de Sezimbra was tall, dark-skinned, and handsome. He half-smiled at McWilms, his eyes gentle and puzzled. "I apologize for my ward. He tends to be rather surly with strangers—Heritage being what it is."

"I'm Apprentice McWilms of the Hoorka, and the apology isn't necessary, sirrah," McWilms said without the smile that would have made his words friendly. He found himself liking the man, a quick affection. Not, he told himself, that it would affect his performance. And if de Sezimbra appeared overtly amiable, those around him were more cautious. A man and a woman stood behind and to either side of de Sezimbra, holding stings with the muzzles pointed unwaveringly at McWilms. The apprentice nodded inwardly. "My own task is small and I stress" —with a glance at the man's armed companions—"that I intend no harm. Marco de Sezimbra, your life has been placed in the hands of the Hoorka and our patron, She of the Five Limbs."

A quizzical stare, a furtive glance at his companions—de Sezimbra clenched and unclenched his hands. "I don't understand."

"A contract has been signed for an attempt on your life." McWilms was patient but dourly serious. *It's easier on Neweden. What I've already said would have been more than enough. The man doesn't yet realize . . .* "The contract will begin at 14:17

local time and end at 23:10; that's the local equivalent of twelve
Neweden hours. Your life lies with the whims of Dame Fate.
Should you still be alive at 23:10, Hoorka will pursue you no
longer."

"Your organization means to kill me?" He seemed on the
verge of astonished amusement, as if he still weren't certain that
this wasn't a cruel jest.

"The Hoorka have no personal interest in your death. We
work for others. We're simply instruments in the hands of
another person."

From behind de Sezimbra, the woman spoke. "And if we kill
you now, you with the small task?"

"Rowenna—" de Sezimbra began, but McWilms interrupted.

"I'm but an apprentice, m'Dame, a messenger. My fate is
always in the hands of the Dame. But my death won't affect the
contract. I've nothing to do with it—that's the task of full kin.
And there are other options. You may still buy out the contract."

"How much is it?"

"Ten thousand—that's what the signer paid."

De Sezimbra smiled sadly. "He's obviously richer than me."

"Then you must trust Dame Fate."

"What of my friends, the others living here?" De Sezimbra
indicated the area with a nod. He didn't seem overly upset or
surprised. It was as if he'd been expecting something of the sort;
now that it had happened, he could remain calm.

McWilms knew now that he truly liked the man. Most of the
victims were quivering and fearful when told of the contract. He
found himself hoping that the Dame would be kind. "The
contract is only for *your* life, sirrah. If you're protected, we'll
attempt to kill only you, but no promises can be made. Other
people have been killed before, when they interfere with the
Dame. Even Hoorka have died—and we expect you to defend
yourself. It's your choice. We adjust our strategy to the situation,
for the victim must always retain his chance."

"If I run? By myself?"

"Then none of those here will be harmed, and my kin will
carry less."

A nod. De Sezimbra's gaze had an inward look. Rowenna, the
sting still directed at McWilms, shook her head vehemently.
"You can't do it, Marco. I won't let you." Her voice was quiet,
the face haggard. "It's Guillene," she said, looking at McWilms
as if she expected confirmation. "It's that frigging Moache
bastard. The coward can't even do his own dirty work...."

His lover, then. Or she wants to be. The way she stands near him, the possessiveness in her gaze... "If the contract is successful, the signer will be made known." *Calm, always calm.* "If Sirrah de Sezimbra lives, then, by the code, we'll reveal nothing and simply leave Heritage. It's not a person's destiny to know beforehand by whose hand he'll die." The last sentence was stiff, a quotation.

De Sezimbra was caught in an icy peace. He nodded to McWilms as pleasantly as he might to a dinner companion. "I should be grateful, I suppose," he said, speaking to all of them. "We knew the danger of coming here and trying to stop the injustice. I thought we'd simply be deported on some trumped-up charge. This..." A mournful shaking of his head. "It could've been a simple, brutal murder, as well. At least this way I seem to retain some chance. I don't understand why Guillene would do it this way, but I'm glad."

He seemed to come back to himself then. The eyes flicked back into focus, the melancholy half-smile returned to his mahogany face. He nodded to McWilms. "Is that all you have to tell me?"

"Just one thing more." McWilms reached under his nightcloak, watching the two with the stings. Then his hand came out, proffered toward de Sezimbra as if for a handshake. De Sezimbra took the hand, then suddenly drew back—his palm was wet. The muzzles of the stings came up. Rowenna seemed on the verge of firing, but de Sezimbra shook his head. "No, I'm not harmed." He glanced at the hand; the moisture was rapidly drying. "At least I don't think so. A tracer?" he asked.

McWilms nodded.

"I could wash the hand."

"It's not that easily removed." McWilms glanced at Rowenna, her face a rictus of anger and concern. "We don't wish accidental deaths. In our own way, we Hoorka are very reverent of life." He moved back a step, squinting against the sun. "My task is done. I wish you luck, Sirrah de Sezimbra."

"And I wish your people none, Apprentice McWilms." De Sezimbra almost smiled. "I'd like to talk with you again, though. At 23:11, perhaps?"

McWilms made another, deeper obeisance. "May She of the Five Limbs watch you." With that, he turned and walked down the dusty path, retracing his steps. He heard the door creak shut behind him, heard the beginning of Rowenna's protest.

He didn't go far. He'd scouted the terrain earlier, finding a hidden niche between two boulders on a hill that gave him a view of the house. Cursing the sun and the heat, he settled down to wait.

He did not wait too long. Almost an hour later, the door to the house opened and de Sezimbra stepped out, a pack on his back. McWilms smiled. *I knew he'd be alone. He's too proud and sensitive to let the others aid him—and he's an effective enough leader to make his word stand against all the arguments. Good. Sartas and Renier can have the hunt of knives, since he isn't carrying a bodyshield. They'll be pleased.*

Unaware of McWilms's surveillance, de Sezimbra settled the pack on his shoulders and walked west, toward the wind-swept foothills and the falling sun.

It was 14:33.

16:51. Sartas and Renier readied themselves in their rooms. McWilms had been reporting back to them at fifteen-minute intervals. The preparations had been minimal, since McWilms had informed them that de Sezimbra was both alone and carrying no bodyshield: an extra nightcloak for the possible body, the tracker for the dye on the victim's body, a tachyon relay (the purchase of which had depleted the Hoorka treasury, but which Mondom insisted was necessary by the code)—it transmitted the arrival of dawn at Underasgard. No stings, no bodyshields, nothing but the vibros. Both of the Hoorka were satisfied with that. It was one of Ulthane Gyll's tenets that killing should be a personal matter, an intimate deed. It's only then that one understands the responsibility involved. A sting, an aast, even to some extent the Khaelian daggers, all allowed the wielder to stand back from the moment of death, to cloak the Hag with distance.

Not tonight. They would face Her at handsbreadth.

They were waiting for the flitter. Heritage seemed to sense the beginning of the contract, the nearness of the Hag. When Sartas and Renier had come into the lobby, everyone had turned to look—a group of people staring over a game of vari-resolve, a couple playing a hologame, those simply reading on the floaters.

"The rumors must have spread. Now we're the vicious, nasty Hoorka," whispered Renier.

"Yah. And we'll eat the flesh of the victim afterward. . . ." A scowl. "Just simple, bloodthirsty monsters."

They moved from shade into the bright heat. A man stood near the entrance to the hostel, one hand shielding his eyes. In the lushness of Park Hill, he was an anomaly, dressed in clean but plain and cheap clothing, his feet bare rather than sandalled, his hair cropped close in the fashion of the miners. He saw the Hoorka, blinking against the furnace of the sky.

"Sirrahs," he called out.

Sartas paused, Renier behind. "We've no time for chatter, sirrah." Sartas began to turn away to wave to the approaching flitter, but the man moved a step toward the Hoorka, still speaking.

"You can't do this." The tenor voice quavered, and the man took another tentative step, within an arm's reach of their nightcloaks. "De Sezimbra is a good man."

"Good men die as easily as bad ones. That's not our concern, and we haven't time to argue philosophy." Renier was gentler with the intruder than Sartas would have been. He and Sartas turned to move toward the flitter, but the man stepped in front of them; nervously, but deliberately. "In the name of humanity, you can't do this." His voice was quiet; it was more effective because of that. "They won't say it, most of 'em, 'cause they're afraid of Moache and Guillene. But de Sezimbra is someone who helped us. We don't want to see this happen."

The Hoorka had halted, each gauging the man. "Out of the way, sirrah." Sartas made as if to push his way forward, but the man stepped back and held up his hand. It held a sting.

"I'm sorry, but I can't let it happen." The voice trembled, the apology was ludicrous, but the finger was steady on the trigger. Sartas watched the hand, breathing shallowly. "Better that I be killed than Marco. He's worth more to us—let Guillene do what he wants with me."

The finger went white with sudden pressure . . .

. . . but the Hoorka were already moving, Sartas to the right, Renier dropping left and rolling. The sting cracked and bucked; pellets chipped paint from the hostel's wall. The man did not have time for a second shot. Sartas lunged, grasping the man's forearm and twisting violently. Bone cracked, loud in the sudden stillness, and the sting fell to the grass. Sartas pushed and the man stumbled, moaning in pain. Renier had already recovered the sting. He pointed it at the fallen man.

"Death," Renier said, his voice gentle, "isn't an easy gift. Dame Fate must want the victim, and you must remember that the victim will always be willing to trade your life for his. In that, you're lucky that we're Hoorka. We don't kill when it's not needed."

With a practiced motion, Renier detached the clip from the

sting and slipped it into a pouch of his nightcloak. He tossed the weapon into a clump of shrubbery. "Get the arm seen to soon," he said. "It shouldn't be a bad break."

The Hoorka left him, kneeling in shock, as the hostel denizens emerged, blinking, to view the excitement.

Sartas said nothing until they were in the flitter. Then he touched Renier on the shoulder, a squeeze of affection. "This looks like one of the contracts we're going to hate, one that gets in your dreams. I'll be glad when we get back to Neweden, kin-brother."

Renier nodded in agreement.

18:41. They'd left McWilms behind nearly an hour ago, panting-tired and liberally coated with the dust of Heritage. They'd had to leave the flitter at the outskirts of Home, where the broadcast power faded. From there, they'd rented a local groundcar, a decrepit device burning a noisome and smoky liquid fuel. Sartas had been dubious, but the machine had proved durable enough to climb the rough terrain.

McWilms had had little to report: de Sezimbra was moving slowly but steadily to the west, into higher and more broken country. They told the apprentice to stay with the vehicle until he heard from them. Then they began the real pursuit—on foot, facing the same difficulties as their quarry.

The dye-detector placed de Sezimbra a kilometer and a half from them. They could follow that trace until they came too close: the detector would cease functioning when the victim was within two hundred meters, another example of the code's insistence that the victim be given a chance of escape. And the detector gave them only a modicum of aid. It indicated only direction and distance. In the twisted, rock-strewn landscape of steep hills, they could not travel for long in a straight path. They had to turn and backtrack more than once, their way blocked, moving back and forth among the brown-red stones and gritty earth. The land was torn, dry, and nearly barren, though not lifeless. Now and then they'd glimpse a shadowed form staring at them; the assassins would grasp their vibrohilts, not knowing which creatures were dangerous or what form an attack might take.

In his familiarity with Heritage, de Sezimbra had a decided edge.

They found the first sign of him as the sun eased itself down on the spikes of nearby mountains. A scrabbling of pebbles lay at the bottom of an incline, and there was a mark higher up where weathered rock had broken loose to leave lighter stone exposed. Looking further, they found a scrap of bloodstained cloth. The blood was still wet.

"He fell, then. Scraped himself fairly well too—the cloth's saturated. Think it'll slow him down?"

Renier shrugged, pulling his nightcloak tighter about him. Already the oppressive heat of the day was waning; the chill of night hung in the shadows. "Maybe, if he cut his leg or side. In any case, he'll probably be more careful now—that in itself'll hold him back."

They scrambled up the slope, sure now of their path and alert for small signs of the man's passage. Twilight shaded the sky. A few minutes later, the orb of the sun entirely gone, Renier pulled from his pouch a pair of light-enhancers. A sallow moon hoisted itself in the east. The rocks hid deep shadows, but the landscape was bright enough for them to continue at the same pace. They were gaining quickly on de Sezimbra.

"Renier . . ."

The assassin turned, his eyes goggled with the enhancers. "Yah?"

"The detector went off a few minutes ago. I thought he was just on the edge of the range and it'd come back on, but it hasn't. We're near him."

Their vibros hissed from sheaths, thrumming as if glad to be released from confinement.

The Hoorka followed the man's trail: a scuffling of dirt, displaced rocks, the marks of boot heels. The going was rough, always west and upward. A cliff scarred with vertical slashes like the wounds of a giant claw walled them to the right. On their left, the path fell off steeply into a deep ravine—they could hear the sound of running water in the darkness. The ledge narrowed as they went higher and they were forced to move single file for a time, until the gouged cliff shattered itself into a small plateau littered with large boulders. Hiding places abounded. Sartas muttered a curse.

"We'll have to search here, damn him. Looks as if the cliff begins again just ahead. You start there—see if you can tell whether he's gone on. If not, start working back toward me. If we've got him trapped here, we can go home."

Renier nodded, already moving. Sartas began a slow examination of the area, vibro always at ready, feeling a tension in the muscles of his back. He'd felt the thrill of that tension before—it had always betokened the presence of the victim.

Sartas heard the commotion first: a muffled cry of "Hoorka!" followed by a fleshy thud and the dopplering whine of a vibro moving through air. Sartas ran toward the sounds, dodging between boulders, and suddenly getting a clear view.

Near the edge of the ravine, Renier was grappling with de Sezimbra. Somehow, the assassin had been stripped of his vibro; it flailed the ground nearby. De Sezimbra seemed to know the art of hand-to-hand combat. As Sartas watched (still running, wondering whether a thrown vibro would be accurate enough and rejecting the idea) de Sezimbra twisted out of Renier's grasp, kicking with a surprisingly agile movement. With a wailing cry of frustration, Renier stumbled and fell, slipping over the ravine's edge. His fingers scrabbled for a hold as de Sezimbra turned to see Sartas, still meters away, striding toward him. Sartas cursed inwardly: by the time Renier could scramble up again, de Sezimbra would be gone. Again he fought the impulse to throw his weapon—too far, and a twirling vibro was as likely to hit with hilt as well as edge. De Sezimbra scooped up Renier's weapon and ran.

The victim was gone; Renier had yet to reappear. The code was explicit on the point: if kin might be in danger, the victim was to be ignored until the kin's status was determined. Sartas peered over the edge of the depression, thumbing the enhancers to full power. He thought he could make out the figure of a man, but it could well be a trick of shadows. "Renier," he called softly, then more loudly.

The only reply was a faint echo. "By the frigging Hag—" Sartas glanced about—no, de Sezimbra was too far away by now. He could always find the trail again. He decided Renier must be unconscious, must have struck his head on a rock. The code and his own emotions tallied; he made his way carefully down the steep incline, grasping at rocks, slipping, sliding. He cursed de Sezimbra, cursed the Dame, cursed Renier.

It had to have been a freak, a whim of the Dame. When Sartas saw Renier, he halted his descent suddenly, grabbing for a handhold as rocks slid from under his feet. There was no mistaking the angle at which Renier's head rested against his shoulder or the stiff arms that seemed to hug the earth. Sartas had seen death enough, had heard the Hag's cackling at close quarters. He knew, knew from the stillness, from the feel of it.

Renier was dead.

He came down more slowly now. No reason to hurry. Renier might have been asleep from the appearance of the body. Sartas, his hands gentle, turned Renier on his side, rocks cascading below them. The left temple was a jellied depression, the skull crushed with blood trickling sluggishly over the open wound. With no hope, Sartas felt for a pulse and found none. He hunkered down beside the body, bracing himself. Sighing, he invoked She of the Five, performing a quick rite for the dead kin. His words were quick, his gaze restless and always avoiding the body.

He fumbled in the pocket of his uniform, pulling out a small beacon. He touched one face of the device and set it beside Renier. Then he thumbed on his relay.

"McWilms?" He waited a moment, then spoke more harshly. "Damn you, boy, you'd better answer."

"Here, sirrah." The words were tinny and distant, surprised and questioning. "You got de Sezimbra?"

"No," Sartas spat. "Renier is dead. I've set the beacon for you to follow. Trace it and take care of the body—I did the short rites, but I want you to give him the longer code-rite. Get the car as near as you can—we'll need it." He spoke flatly, almost tonelessly; it was not a voice to interrupt. "Do you understand all that?"

"Yah, sirrah." A pause and a crackling of electronic thunder. "What of de Sezimbra?"

"If he was important to you, I'd have said so, ass." Sartas let go the transmission button and breathed deeply, in and out. Then: "I'm after the man now. Hurry yourself. I don't know what carrion eaters live here, but if that body is touched, I'll take it out of your hide. Understood?"

"I've already left."

Sartas crouched, feeling the loose stones moving underfoot. His legs ached with the night's run. "Hag-kin," he muttered to himself, glancing down at the corpse. "He was luckier than we thought, neh? A worthy opponent. He'll be a fit companion for you, Renier, one to be proud of. I admire him. He's got fire and determination." The assassin reached down to touch the broken face. "You were a fine kin. All Hoorka will miss you."

He straightened, leaning against the slope. He glanced up at the jagged, moon-glazed summit of the ravine.

He began climbing.

21:45. It had been easy to find de Sezimbra's trail. The detector had shown him an image for only a quarter of an hour

and had then gone quiet. The fight with Renier—the brush with
the Hag's talons—had evidently frightened the man. He left the
spoor of panic and fear, no attempt at stealth. Upward, west-
ward, climbing toward the cold, hard sky, pushed by the adrenaline of death-fright . . .

But Sartas knew that his energy would only be a temporary
ally. He'd seen it in other contracts. De Sezimbra had had the
longer run, and the Hoorka were conditioned for the punishment.
Time was still on Sartas's side, if he could get closer.

He found himself filled with a grudging admiration for de
Sezimbra. He'd expected the man to be easy prey, but he'd
seriously underestimated his resources. That might have cost
Renier his life. Hoorka had died on contracts before—not many,
but it was something that was expected at times. The Hoorka
knew victims would strike back, would struggle against death;
for some kin, Sartas was aware, that implicit danger was excit-
ing, titillating. Renier had not been one of those, however. Sartas
wished him peace in the afterlife. His kin's death drove him,
made him ache for revenge, but the anger was tempered with
respect for de Sezimbra. He felt curiously remote from the
sadness, holding it back from his consciousness for the time
being. Later, he'd mourn and weep with the rest of his kin,
would feel emptied as Renier's body went back to ash in the
soot-smeared Cavern of the Dead.

In de Sezimbra's place, Sartas would have done the same. He
approved of de Sezimbra for that, but he could kill that which he
admired. He forced himself to concentrate on his task; all the rest
could wait.

He'd seen that de Sezimbra was tiring: the marks were now
fresh on the dirt and stone, and the sparse vegetation that the
man trampled had yet to spring back up. Close. Sartas pressed
himself, moved a bit faster. Soon.

It was not a prepossessing scene: Sartas slipped into a narrow
cleft in the cliff wall, following the tracks. The crevice opened
out suddenly into a natural amphitheater, a hollow perhaps thirty
meters across surrounded by dour gray walls of stone. There was
little cover but the moon-shadow. The light-enhancer pierced the
murk easily enough. Sartas could see de Sezimbra crouched
opposite the entrance, his clothing torn, his side bloody with
scratches, his dark skin shiny with perspiration. Panting, he still
held Renier's vibro in his hand, but it was not activated. He'd
trapped himself.

Sartas, his nightcloak swirling about him as he halted, stared at de Sezimbra. The man was still, not certain that he'd been seen. "Marco de Sezimbra, your life has been claimed by Hag Death."

The assassin's voice, stentorian in the night stillness, startled de Sezimbra. He shook himself, disbelieving, then stood, his breath ragged. "I'm not yet dead, sirrah. And for whom other than this Hag Death do you want me?"

"That information's not for you." Curtly, but not unwillingly, Sartas answered. The man could go nowhere, there was still enough time. If he wanted to talk, let him.

"Ahh." De Sezimbra nodded. "It doesn't matter, really. I know it's Guillene and Moache. He's the only one that would think that he has enough reason. You'll really let me go at 23:10?"

"I *would* have." The emphasis was pronounced.

The ghost of a smile played at the corners of de Sezimbra's mouth. "You still might need to. You won't throw your vibro— that's a low probability attack. You have to come and get me, and I could conceivably get past you."

"Or you could use the vibro."

This time he did smile. "I'm afraid it's not my forte. I'd rather be sneaky."

"You won't get past. Try and you'll feel my blade. I've more pleasant means of death, if you're willing to concede the inevitable. You won't get past." Sartas spoke with confidence, but he remembered Renier; he could not afford to underestimate the man again.

De Sezimbra was almost amiable. He stepped forward into the wash of moonlight, letting his pack drop from his shoulders. He limped slightly, favoring his left leg. "I've been on other worlds that didn't want me, sirrah. I've learned how to defend myself to an extent. Had to. I might not be the easy target you suppose. And I never concede inevitabilities. That's too complacent an attitude. It allows you to let injustices continue. I fight back, instead. Ask your friend—he's waiting on the other side of the cleft, isn't he?"

A spasm of pain twisted Sartas's face, a shadow. "You don't know? You killed him, de Sezimbra." A pause. "He waits for you, but it's not here."

"No." Shock and surprise were loud in the denial. "I wasn't intending that . . . I didn't hold back, that's true, but he was going to kill *me* if I didn't get away. I thought the fall would give me time . . . I checked with Niffleheim. They said the Hoorka were scrupulous, would follow their code. All I wanted was the time." His eyes pleaded. *A man who's never killed*, Sartas thought, *and who hadn't really contemplated the possibility of having to do so.* "I'm sorry," de Sezimbra said. "I didn't want that to happen. Believe me." He seemed genuinely perturbed, concerned.

"A victim that doesn't resist the Hag deserves his fate. And our apprentice must have told you—we don't take a person's fate out of the hands of their gods. I congratulate you on your skill," he remarked stonily. "Dame Fate was with you. It wasn't your time yet. It is now."

"Dame Fate may still be with me."

"If She is, you'll know soon enough."

Sartas said no more. He moved slowly into the open, watching de Sezimbra, waiting for the man to move, to commit himself. Back, to the left: de Sezimbra retreated, eyes glancing from side to side wildly, looking for an avenue of escape. The Hoorka moved inexorably toward him.

De Sezimbra flicked on his vibro.

It happened quickly. De Sezimbra suddenly leapt straight forward, far more agilely than Sartas expected—the limp was gone, a deception. The man's vibro thrust at Sartas, but the Hoorka, despite his surprise, was already countering. He turned, evading the blade, and slashed with his own weapon, hearing the whine of the vibro and the tearing of cloth. De Sezimbra groaned with pain as the vibro raked his side, and he kicked at Sartas's groin. Sartas deflected the blow harmlessly, lunging. This time he found his target. De Sezimbra staggered back wordlessly, dropping his weapon, hands clenched to his stomach. Blood, bright arterial blood, was slick around his fingers. He moaned, looking up at Sartas. He seemed about to speak; his mouth worked, but no words came. He nodded, almost a salutation, and slipped to his knees. Grunting, de Sezimbra tried to rise again and found he could not. He looked up at the sky, at the watching moon.

He fell to his side on the rocks.

"If I could've denied the Dame's whim, I would have, de Sezimbra," Sartas whispered. "If a man deserved to live . . . I wish you'd been luckier."

The Hag came to Heritage for a second time that night.

Sheathing his vibro (he would not clean it again until he returned to Neweden and could feed She of the Five), Sartas called McWilms, giving the apprentice his position. While he

waited, he gave de Sezimbra the rite of the dead and wrapped the
body in the spare nightcloak.

In time, McWilms arrived, and they took the body back to the
car. On their way to Home, the tachyon relay on Sartas's belt
suddenly shrilled, startling them both.

At Underasgard, morning light had touched the dawnrock.

They could not help but attract attention as they entered the
boundaries of Home. The throaty rumble of the groundcar shook
the sleepy ones from their beds and turned the heads of those on
the streets. All stared at the death-apparitions: the dust-lathered
Hoorka in the open car, dark in the fluttering nightcloaks; the
silent bundles in the back, wrapped in black and gray cloth.

They knew, the inhabitants of Home. The Hoorka could sense
the news spreading through the city, welling outward.

Guillene's home was set well back from the street that wandered
through Park Hill. It was further held aloof by a high wall and a
wrought-steel gate flanked by two guards. The Hoorka rode
toward it through a scurrying of people. Already a crowd had
formed before the gates, standing silent across the lane, moving
with a quiet restlessness. The guards, dour-faced, perhaps a little
frightened, uneasily watched the mob grow, crowd-prods in
hand. One whispered into a relay button on his lapel as the
Hoorka rode up, shattering the night stillness.

The groundcar shuddered to a halt, the roar of the engine died.
Sartas and McWilms, the cowls up on their nightcloaks, dismounted
and picked up the bundle behind Sartas, handling it with a
curious gentleness. They laid it before the gate as Guillene's men
watched, as the mute faces across the street stared. The crowd
swayed, murmured. "Is Sirrah Guillene here?" Sartas asked.

The guard to whom he spoke didn't have a chance to reply.
From the darkness beyond the gate, a figure moved into sight.
The muttering of the crowd increased. "I'm Phillipe Guillene,
Hoorka." He was tall and slight, his hair a crescent of silver
around the dome of his head, and the robe he wore spoke of
silken wealth. The voice was smooth, aristocratic. Gray eyes
glanced down at the wrapped body outside the gate. "Is that de
Sezimbra?"

"It is. Your contract has been fulfilled. Do you need to see the
face?"

He glanced up. Sartas could see quick horror in the man's
eyes. *So that's why he would pay Hoorka, then. He doesn't want*

to be near death. "No," Guillene said, his voice rushed. "I believe you."

There was a concerted whispering in the ranks of people across the way. Guillene looked, seemed to see the spectators for the first time. He looked at them rather than Sartas. "De Sezimbra was to be an example to them," he said. "The man was a troublemaker and a fool."

"I found him to be a brave and honorable opponent." Beneath the shadowed hood, Sartas's eyes glittered. He defied Guillene to gainsay him.

Guillene's face flushed with irritation, visible even in the dim light of the gate-lamps and the moon. He tugged at the belt of his robe, drawing it tighter around his waist. "You needn't speak your opinions here, Hoorka. I paid you—and well—for your work. It's now done. You may return to Neweden. I want nothing more to do with you."

"And the body?"

"My people will throw it on the slagheaps with the rest of the filth."

Sartas said nothing, but his stance altered subtly. Behind him, McWilms sensed the shift in attitude; he moved back and to one side, in a better position to support Sartas if trouble developed. The crowd-murmurs grew louder, though none of them made a move to cross the street, and none spoke loudly enough for Guillene to understand words. If they were angry with Guillene's treatment of de Sezimbra, they were also cowed.

"De Sezimbra deserves better rites." Sartas spoke slowly, loudly. "As I said, I found him to be courageous and honorable."

Like steel striking steel, his words drew sparks from Guillene. The man reared back as if struck. His eyebrows lowered, his lips parted, and the noble face was suddenly ugly. "*I* decide what is to happen on Heritage, Hoorka. If I say that the body is to be given to the slagheap, then that will be done." He gestured curtly to his guards. "Take it," he said.

Sartas stepped forward, an arm sweeping aside his nightcloak, his hand pulling the brown-stained vibro from its sheath. It whined eagerly; behind him, Sartas could hear the harmony of McWilms's own weapon. The guards, suddenly uncertain, stopped, caught between obedience and fear. They looked back at Guillene.

"Marco de Sezimbra faced Hag Death with honor," Sartas hissed, poised over the body. "I won't have him dishonored now. You'll lose your lives if you try. Sirrah Guillene, unless you want bloodfeud declared against you, tell them to stay away."

Guillene's face was taut, his neck corded with unvented anger. "This isn't your little backward world, Hoorka. There's no bloodfeud here, no kin. The man died because I willed it so. He's to be an example to my employees—I *warned* him to leave Heritage, to go before I was forced to take stronger measures. He stayed. He chose his fate. You stop me now, and you give an unwanted meaning to his death. That's not what I paid for. I won't have it."

"You paid for death. Nothing else." Sartas spoke to Guillene, but he watched the guards, who backed away one step. "The meaning and results of a person's death aren't in your hands but the gods'. You aren't able to pay for that. De Sezimbra will be given the proper rites or more than one person will join him in the Hag's dance. You can summon enough people to overcome us, true, but that'll only give more emphasis to de Sezimbra's death, neh?" Adamantine, that voice, with no hue of weakness. His vibro hummed threateningly, the luminous tip unwavering.

"We'll take the body back to his people." The voice came from the front ranks of the watching crowd; as Sartas glanced that way, a woman stepped out into the light of the gate-lamps. She was plain, heavy, clothed like a miner or lassari laborer. Behind her two men as nondescript as she stepped forward, heads down. "De Sezimbra helped my family once. We'll take the body and do what's proper, sirrah." Her voice was an odd mixture of servility and determination.

Sartas glared, uncertain. He didn't trust these people, so much like lassari, so used to doing Guillene's bidding. Lassari could not be trusted. It was a bitter lesson all guilded kin learned. Turn your back on them, and you'd better be prepared for the thrust of the knife.

Guillene raged behind his ornate barrier. "I'll have your shift masters cut your wages—your family will never leave Heritage. That's the cost of touching that body."

"Sirrah Guillene, I'm sorry, but the assassin is right. De Sezimbra deserves to be treated better than a common thief." She could not defy Guillene for long; her gaze dropped at his scowl. Behind her, the men shuffled their feet.

"You'll do this properly, woman?" Sartas asked.

She glanced at the angry Guillene. A nod, tentative at first, stronger . . . "Might never leave Heritage anyway. I'll take the body back to his cabin and his people. If we may?"

Sartas, slowly, stood aside, still unsure but swayed by the look on Guillene's face. "You *will* do it," he said again.

"By my word," she replied. Sartas nodded and watched the two men lift the body and turn back into the crowd. The mass of people parted wordlessly, flowing back around them. Guillene, with a broken cry of frustration and rage, turned and strode back toward his house. "I won't forget this, Hoorka." The words came from the night.

Sartas and McWilms, a wary eye on the silent guards, sheathed their weapons. The groundcar roared as they made their way back to the hostel.

The following day was as pastoral as Heritage seemed capable of being. The sky was sooty blue, tinged with orange on the horizon where the metallic cross-hatching of a mining platform gnawed the distant hills. The sun was unrelenting: too hot, too bright, too oppressive.

Sartas and McWilms were pleased. They would be gone soon.

The flitter held the day's warmth in abeyance, circulating cool air through the glassed compartment in which they sat. The windows were polarized to cut the glare, and the scenery passed—ten meters below them—at a tolerable speed. The flitter purred along its predetermined course. The Hoorka relaxed, heads back on the cushioned seats, eyes half-closed.

"Gorgeous view, neh?" McWilms was half-turned, looking down at the orangish landscape.

"I'll be damned glad to leave it. Underasgard'll be very pleasant, even with having to tell Thane Mondom that we need to prepare a wake for Renier." He glanced back. A heavy, oblong case was secured to the back of the flitter.

"When do we reach the Port?"

"An hour. Just lie back. Relax."

McWilms sighed and closed his eyes. Thus it was that he didn't see the grove of trees to their right nor the gout of fire that blackened the leaves there with sudden fury. Both Hoorka were only momentarily conscious of the wrenching lurch as something tore into the shell of the flitter, shredding the plasti-steel, ripping off the guiding power vanes. The canopy sheltering them flew apart in crystalline shards; the next lurch of the flitter threw them both from the craft, blessedly oblivious.

Orange and black: flame and smoke tore at the craft and flung it to the ground.

The wreckage plowed into earth a hundred meters from the still bodies, carving a blackened gouge in the gritty dust, burning. Neither Hoorka saw the figures that came from the grove and stood over them, silent and grim-faced.

"They're dead?"

"This one is. The other'll be soon enough. No, don't bother to kill him—let 'im suffer."

It was nearly thirty minutes before the nonarrival of the flitter caused a puzzled Diplo at the Port terminal to send an investigating team out after the tardy vehicle. Neither Sartas nor McWilms heard the exclamations of surprise and concern as the Diplo crew arrived at the still-smouldering mass of twisted metal.

Hag Death, grinning eternally, returned again to Heritage.

8

An excerpt from the acousidots of Sondall-Cadhurst Cranmer. This transcript is one of the rarities. In the Family Cranmer Archives there is a dot with what seems to be a live recording of the following scene, but the fidelity is terrible and much of the dot is indecipherable. Evidently Cranmer felt the conversation to be of some import, for he immediately did a dictation of the conversation as he remembered it. It was a method to which he had to resort on other occasions. The concealed microphones sometimes failed. It was, in his own words, "a penance one pays for being dishonest."

EXCERPT FROM THE DOT OF 5.28.217:

"Gyll was not much in a mood to see me. 'Don't even bother, Cranmer,' was all he said when I knocked at his door. I persisted noisily, though, and eventually he had to answer. He looked angry and tired. His eyes were red-veined and he moved with a jerky sullenness.

" 'Don't you ever listen?' he growled. 'I'm not interested in talking to anyone.'

"I put on the jolly-old-Cranmer face that Gyll seems to consider the real me. 'Talking can be a catharsis of sorts, you know. You'll feel better afterward; it's guaranteed. I always find that . . .' I went on like that for a time, until through weariness or self-defense, Gyll stepped back to let me in. He'd evidently been cleaning his weapon—the tools were spread out on his bed and the vibrowire was extended. The wort sat quietly in its cage, its head turning to watch us. Gyll sat on the bed, pretending to be absorbed in his task. I took the one floater in the room, asking if he'd heard anything new about the Heritage foul-up.

"Gyll has an interesting face. For all his talk of the code and Hoorka aloofness, anyone that knows his habitual ticks and grimaces can read him. He's virtually without guile. I love playing cards against him: he can't bluff. When he's mad, he looks at you from slightly under his eyebrows, his lower lip sticks out a little, and the mouth turns down. All the wrinkles on his face get a little deeper. All those things happened then. 'I don't know anything,' he said. 'Mondom insisted on going to see d'Embry alone. She should have let me go in her place, Cranmer. I know that cold bitch of a regent, Mondom doesn't. She's likely to get some placating story . . .' He stopped and began to polish the vibrowire vigorously.

"I grunted and *hmmm*ed a few times in sympathy. 'What interests me is the contract itself,' I told him. I let him know that I'd checked with the Center files and from what I could glean, de Sezimbra was exactly what the miners thought him to be—a good man, a gadfly (and a needed one) to the Alliance. And Moache Mining'd been involved in questionable practices before. 'Does it bother you that the Hoorka have killed an honorable man in the service of a dishonorable bastard, a man who has no sense of moral right or wrong, at least in the way Neweden views such things?'

"That brought his head up. He set the vibro aside too gently. The way he looked at me, I could see that the question was one that was already nagging at him. 'What the Dame wills to happen, happens. And if Hoorka hadn't killed the man, someone else would have, without giving de Sezimbra his proper chance.' But he said it without fire, without conviction.

"I replied that no doubt the fact that it was all the Dame's will was very comforting. 'And no doubt she meant for the flitter to be ambushed, too.'

"Gyll gave me the aggravated look—the one that comes right before anger. 'Because something is fated doesn't mean that it's also right. You know that. What happened with Renier; that was understandable, even expected in its own way. But what Guillene did to the other two . . . If that man were on Neweden, bloodfeud would be declared without a thought, and it'd be a slow death if I found him.'

"I figured I had one more push before Gyll got angry and I had to shut up for a while. That's Gyll's way: you have to dig at the man to get him to talk, and all the prodding makes him irritable. 'Guillene's offworld,' I reminded him. 'You can't do a damned thing to him. And in any case, Mondom's handling it, not you.'

"He didn't say anything at all, which was unlike him. He picked up the vibro again, reeled the wire back into the hilt and attached the holding plate. Then he jammed the weapon back into the sheath and stood up. He stared down at me. 'Cranmer, one day the looseness of your tongue is going to cause it to be cut out,' he said, and then he walked out of the room.

"The wort whimpered at his retreating back. And I sat there wishing that there was another way to get Gyll to react—jabbing holes in a person's dreams is depressing.

"And in any case, I *like* my tongue."

Thane Mondom was possessed by rage. It sat, an indigestable and bitter lump in her gut. Frustration gnawed at her stomach; sorrow battered at her, demanding release.

Two Hoorka dead, Renier by a contracted victim, but Sartas slain by a cowardly ambush. And McWilms—she'd just left his rooms in the Center Hospital. The surgeon had said that the boy would recover, but Mondom had seen the misshapen face under the med-pad and the empty socket of his shoulder where they were preparing the arm bud. He might attend his initiation as full kin, but it would be many months before he could take his place in the rotation. The condition of McWilms, his mute helplessness and pain, made her the most angry. Death, *that* she could understand, could cope with, but the boy's mutilation...

She strode into the brilliant lobby of Diplo Center, the sunstar a mockery at her back, and demanded to see Regent d'Embry. The startled Diplo she accosted mumbled nervously and whispered into her com-unit. The Diplo's eyes spoke of contempt, but her voice was blandly polite. "The Regent is able to see you now."

"She didn't have a choice." Mondom strode away.

D'Embry's office was awash with lemon sunlight. It glared from the holocube of d'Vellia's *Gehennah* in the corner; a wedge of light shimmered across the carpet and over her desk, slashing across the Regent's thin body but leaving the face in shadow. D'Embry herself was a mobile sunbeam, her hands, shoulders, and earlobes dashed with yellow skintint. Only her much-lined face was at odds with the day. Her mouth was down-turned, the icy-blue eyes serious.

"Come in, Thane Mondom. I have to admit that I was

expecting to see someone from the Hoorka today. I was sorry to hear about the problems with the Heritage contract.''

"*Problems?...*" Mondom glared at the woman. *So frigging secure behind that desk. She doesn't care about Renier, Sartas, or McWilms. If she feels any sorrow, it's only because of the trouble she'll have over Heritage.* "You have an interesting way of phrasing things, m'Dame.''

D'Embry toyed with an ippicator bone on her desk. The polished surface caught the light, held it and amplified it, lustrous. Thin fingers, yellow against the bone's subtle ivory, turned the piece and set it down again. "You think I haven't any feelings for your kin in your loss. Believe me, Thane Mondom, I do." She looked up, and Mondom was caught in her young-old eyes. "When you've lived as long as I have, you've had to lose those that were close to you. I *do* understand how you have to feel, the anger. The Alliance will pay the cost of McWilms's hospitalization. Consider it a gesture of our concern for your feelings—I shouldn't have let you work that contract. The situation was far too volatile.''

"Have you seen him?''

"Apprentice McWilms? No.''

"I have." Mondom tore herself away from d'Embry's steady regard, going to the window. The lawn of the Center stretched out to the flat expanse of Sterka Port. In sunlight, the head of the large ippicator before the Center stared sightlessly at distant port workers. "They told me that half his face had been torn away, like someone had scrubbed at it with a file," she said, staring outward. "He was just a mass of bleeding, shredded tissue. The right arm had been crushed, flattened, the bones shattered. He'd nearly bled to death. Both legs broken, severe internal injuries. Maybe here on Neweden he'd've died, unconscious. Now he gets to live with the agony—and I'll have to tell him that it's the better option. Sartas's injuries had been worse. I think in some ways he's luckier.''

She turned back into the room. D'Embry was watching her, silent, hands folded on her desktop. "And *you*, damn you, sit back there and talk about *problems* on Heritage," Mondom shouted. "Well, they were people, and my kin, and I feel their hurt." She paused, breathing heavily once, and when she continued, the voice was more controlled. "My people are going to want to declare bloodfeud. I can't say that I disagree with that.''

"Bloodfeud's not possible.''

"Your own report says that Sartas argued with Guillene, went against his orders. Guillene threatened Sartas, publicly."

"There's no proof that Guillene was responsible for the attack."

"Who the hell else?" Mondom laughed in exasperation and disgust.

D'Embry shrugged, but her gaze was sympathetic. "De Sezimbra was popular among the miners—it could have been a group of them, or perhaps even de Sezimbra's associates. It didn't have to be Guillene."

"None of the others have any reason to harm Hoorka. We're simply the weapon, not the hand that wields it. Would you destroy a vibro and let the man go that used it?"

"I'd be tempted to destroy both." Then d'Embry sighed, leaning back in her floater. "Heritage isn't Neweden, Thane. They've a different governing structure, a different set of laws. Believe me, I understand your anger and frustration, but there's very little I can do about it."

"Because Moache Mining is involved? Is that it? I'll wager that the word reached you from Niffleheim before the bodies were even loaded on the ship, neh? Leave Heritage alone, ignore the murder of Hoorka." Mondom's fury boiled; she fought to hold it back, knowing it would either make her cry or rage and knowing that d'Embry would just sit there and watch, unmoved. She stood opposite the Regent, leaning down, her hands on the polished surface of the desk.

D'Embry hesitated before answering, and Mondom wondered what emotion clouded those clear eyes for a breath. "Moache Mining *is* powerful," d'Embry admitted. "I can't answer for Diplo Center on Heritage. But *I've* had no instruction from Niffleheim or Moache. And even if I had, my actions would be my own."

There was a fierce pride on the Regent's face.

Mondom glanced at the ippicator bone on the desk, with an inward prayer to She of the Five. "But you still won't let Hoorka act as we wish."

"Only because I don't want Hoorka getting involved in something too big for them. I'll do everything I can. It's an offworld matter, Thane." Reaching out, d'Embry touched Mondom's callused hand with her softer, vein-webbed one, yellow against tanned flesh. Mondom began to pull away from the contact, but d'Embry held her with gentle pressure. "No matter what you want done," the Regent continued, "it'll have to be handled through Diplo channels and in accordance with Heritage's own laws, which are the laws of the Alliance. We'll try to find the people responsible, I promise you that. I'll push them if I have to, and I'm a very good, experienced pusher. It was just this kind of situation that worried me when I allowed the Hoorka to work offworld, Thane. Don't make my fears become reality, or I'll have little choice." A quick squeeze of fingers, and a surprising warmth in d'Embry's eyes: Mondom found herself listening, the anger momentarily background.

The Regent moved her hand back. Mondom pulled herself erect. "I understand you, Regent. I do. But you'd better get results and a punishment thât's satisfactory to Hoorka. I've only so much power to sway my kin, and they're enraged and bitter."

"You're the Thane. They *have* to understand, or at least obey."

Mondom smiled, lopsided. "I'm Thane, yah. But obedience is another matter, sometimes... Ulthane Gyll could do it, but Ulthane Gyll also doesn't *take* orders well, nor do some of the others." She glanced away, slowly looking about the uncluttered room. When she looked back, she had again become the arrogant Hoorka-thane.

"You'd better see that something is done quickly, m'Dame," Mondom said. "You might find that it benefits both you and Neweden."

The Li-Gallant Vingi found his new Domoraj to be rather less intelligent and less given to moody introspection than the former holder of that title. The combination was more to his liking.

The Domoraj faced Vingi from the corner of his room, which held the rods of the Battier Radiance. Vingi was naked in the glare of the Battier, rolls of fat girdling his body. Seeing the Domoraj enter the room, he reached out and turned off the device, putting on a worn blue robe that hung from one of the posts. This Domoraj is a buffoon, he decided as the light began to fade. He'd keep him for a while, but already the thought of a successor concerned him. Someone younger, more pliable to Vingi's whims. The Li-Gallant moved to his desk, folding thick hands over the scattered flimsies there, his rings flicking parti-colored light about the room.

"You may sit, Domoraj." Vingi watched the man. The new leader of his guard force was older, paunchier, and Vingi found that the man's smile seemed cruelly superficial—it touched only his mouth. The eyes sat too close to the prominent nose; the

uniform he wore was too tight, meant for a younger version of
the man. "I hope my lack of proper attire didn't upset you too
much."

"Not at all, Li-Gallant."

Vingi had seen the Domoraj's face when he entered the office.
"You don't lie well, Domoraj."

The man's smile wavered, like a flame guttering in wind.
"Li-Gallant..."

"It's not that awful, man, but you should learn to be more
careful. I don't like pretension with my staff, Domoraj. You
needn't feel threatened." Vingi waited, but the Domoraj said
nothing more. He patted his ample stomach. "I've had a most
interesting communication from Sirrah Potok," Vingi continued.
"It seems that he was most perturbed by the slowness of your
security forces during the lassari attack on Gunnar's bier."

A slow nod. "Li-Gallant, the attack was so sudden, so
unexpected, and with the discomfort of the rain—"

Vingi halted the litany of excuses with an abrupt hand movement. He'd discovered enough—the Domoraj had fear of him.
"I can understand your problems, Domoraj. Your much-lamented
predecessor could have done no better."

The Domoraj relaxed perceptibly. He tugged at his uniform,
settling it more comfortably around his shoulders. "I'm impressed
by your assessment of the situation, Li-Gallant." He smiled.

"I'm sure you are." Vingi returned the smile. "However, I
think you misunderstand me. I see your difficulties, yah, but I do
not excuse you for them. That was a very sloppy example of
your ability to control my forces, a ground for severe reprimand
if not an outright dismissal. Do you understand me now, Domoraj?"

Vingi watched the smugness evaporate from the Domoraj, saw
the beads of nervous sweat pearl on the forehead. "Li-Gallant—"
the Domoraj began.

Vingi ignored the burgeoning plea, knowing what the man
would say. "It *would* be sufficient for punishment if it didn't fit
well with my own plans. Potok's guild has been shown, publicly,
to be weak, lassari-prey. Your incompetence worked well,
unintentionally, for you did manage to quell the attack when you
finally moved. What worries me is whether Dame Fate will
allow such a coincidence twice. If I need a disciplined force and
can't have one..."

"Li-Gallant, I assure you that it can't happen again. I was just
beginning my command then. My methods are just now having

effect. In a few months, you'll have an exceptionally well-trained and eager force."

Vingi's lips curled in a half-smile, half-sneer. "Yet I have to have a scapegoat for the Assembly, Domoraj. I can't entirely let the incident go by. Your people were slow. I want you to choose one of your lieutenants—he will be made responsible for the tardiness, and publicly reprimanded."

"Li-Gallant . . ."

"You will do it, Domoraj." Vingi nodded. "And you'll continue to work on the discipline, won't you?"

The Domoraj bowed his head in acceptance.

"Good. You see, Domoraj, I might have some small use for your vaunted training. Potok has challenged me to truth-duel. The Magistrate's Guild has accepted the proposal, and I need to reply by this evening. Potok accuses me of the death of Gunnar."

"You'll not accept it?"

"Oh, but I will. Gods, man, all guilded kin think me guilty already. If I decline, it will be certain to them. Dame Fate will guide my hand, and I believe that Potok will find me in better condition than he suspects. You *do* think me innocent, don't you, Domoraj?" Vingi cocked his head, his several chins jiggling.

"Yes, sirrah. Of course." The Domoraj did his best to appear shocked by the implication that he would not believe his kin-lord. Vingi was not particularly impressed by the acting. *Look at him—those eyes can hide nothing; all his acting is in the mouth. He knows that I tried to slay Gunnar with the Hoorka, knows that I once had Domoraj Sucai send someone after him, and he knows that the Domoraj was recently plagued by guilt. The whispers have been heard—he thinks that the Domoraj joined the Dead because I forced him to dishonor once too often, that I killed Gunnar through him.*

Vingi looked down at immaculately groomed fingernails. "I'm pleased that you're so sure of my innocence."

"Sirrah, what penalties have been demanded?"

"For Potok's guild: loss of five seats in the Assembly; Potok will step down as kin-lord, exiling himself in Irast. Also, we'll receive a large tithe for reparation of the harm that the false accusation has done us. Should we lose (and I know you'll not let that occur, Domoraj), the Assembly will be dissolved and a new election held at once. Our guild must pay the election expenses. I will also retire as kin-lord to an exile of my own choosing so long as it is not within fifteen hundred kilometers of Sterka. We'd be ruined, financially and politically."

"Yet you'll risk that?" Fear showed in the Domoraj; in his stiffness, in the restlessly clenching hands. If the guild were gone, so was his own stature. Vingi gambled with all of them.

"I prefer a quick death to a slow one, Domoraj. My kin-father would have felt the same. If I were to refuse, within five standards all the penalties set out against us would have occurred anyway. The rumors would have done Potok's work for him—I know he hopes for refusal. And I don't intend to lose. Potok isn't young, and if he's not as . . . ahh, large as myself, I doubt that he's any more used to labor. You'll train me, Domoraj; Potok has no one in his guild as well versed in fighting skills."

"Li-Gallant, I can only do so much in a short time—when is the duel?"

"In three days."

"Potok will also be preparing."

"Then you'd best do the better job, neh?"

To that, the Domoraj had no answer.

"But what does it *do*?" the dwarf kept insisting.

"You can see it and hear it as well as anyone," Oldin replied, sounding exasperated. "*That's* what it does."

"Things have to do something. You can't sell them if they don't."

"Now that's your typical bullshit, Helgin."

The instrument sat in the middle of Oldin's rooms, an ovoid a half-meter across impaled on the tip of a four-sided pyramid. The facets of the pyramid gleamed like cut crystal; from the milky depths a light pulsed, always an aching purple-black that seemed to be just on the edge of the visible spectrum. The device emitted discordant squeals and grunts like a mortally sounded trombone. It was not pleasant to see or hear. Helgin was damned if he could find a pattern in the timing or melody in the pitch. He said as much to Oldin.

"So it wasn't meant for Motsognir sensibilities, Helgin. I won't try selling them to the dwarves, then. Or maybe you're just tone-deaf."

Helgin scowled behind his ruddy beard. He walked up to the object with his rolling gait and reached out to touch. Slick, smooth, cold—far colder than the room. He looked at his fingertip. "Who got you this damned piece of junk?"

"Siljun—he bought three hundred of them on speculation. Said the race that manufactures them puts them around all their buildings. He also said that the noise kept him up all night."

"I can imagine. By Huard's cock, I don't know what you're going to do with them."

"I've got fifty of them. Siljun kept the rest. I thought I might try selling them as some kind of rejuvenation device. Just make 'em expensive enough, give a little tale about how they're important in the natives' ritual orgies . . . They'll sell. And they'll work because people want them to work—the placebo effect."

"Yah." Helgin stared at the woman. Oldin was swathed in layers of cloth, an iridescent wrap that wandered about her body in complicated windings. It complimented Oldin's stocky physique—enticing, but promised endless troubles with removal. Helgin decided that it fit her well. "You're a dishonest bitch, Kaethe."

"Only when I need to be. At other times I can be quite nice, as you know." She smiled sweetly down at the Motsognir. "I'm going to try selling a few of these with the next load down to Neweden. And speaking of that world—how is Renard? Have you talked with him since the funeral?"

The alien artifact burbled and wheezed through the last part of her question. Helgin was close enough—he kicked out with a sandalled foot. The device rocked heavily and subsided into penitent hisses. Helgin grinned. "I talked to him. He said things are proceeding fairly well. Said to mention to Grandsire FitzEvard that he was right—all Neweden needed was a few pushes in the right places. If the Li-Gallant can retain his power and his viciousness, you'll get what you're after, eventually." Hands on squat, wide hips, he regarded her from under the shadowed ledge of eyebrows. "You should at least express a modicum of remorse, Kaethe-dear. We're discussing the sabotage of an entire society for your grandsire's whims."

She nodded distractedly. "Remorse isn't something taught to the Oldins."

"Too bad. Otherwise, you're almost human. I could almost come to like you." He spoke gruffly, but Oldin smiled at him. From the ovoid came a whimpering in melancholy violet.

"I'm just doing what Grandsire's asked—he doesn't tell me why. I hope the altered Neweden is what Grandsire wants. I wonder if there'll be anything left of the caste system?"

"Like the lassari? He might want them—a built-in servile class. Or are you thinking of other things?" He scowled, twisting his beard. "Anytime you induce change, you destroy something good. The Motsognir found that out when we took Naglfar as home—we gave up much of our culture that was sound and viable when we became wanderers. But we'd lose just as much by settling again. Neweden was changing anyway. I think that's what your grandsire knew. He decided to hasten the change—that's something more easily done than destroying an ongoing and vital society. But I'll be damned if I know what he wants from Neweden.''

Helgin shrugged and sat on the grass-carpet, leaning back against the now-quiet artifact. Where his back touched the device, a purplish nimbus welled outward.

"Did Renard say he needed anything?"

"Neh. He's been here long enough to feel comfortable. He said he'd wait for the next ship before he left. Wants to make sure that everything goes well, that he doesn't need to make adjustments.''

A nod. "Have you seen Gyll—the Hoorka?"

Helgin—mouth pursed, eyes wincing—pulled a hair from his beard. He regarded the red-flecked, coarse strand. "Why? Is he something your grandsire wants you to save?"

"He said nothing about them.''

"That's why I wondered at your talk about an 'offer' to them. Are you playing at a whim yourself, Kaethe?''

Again, a shrug. Her gilded eyebrows rose, fell. She looked up at the viewport in the ceiling. "Grandsire rewards all those who follow his orders. But he rewards best the ones that show initiative. The Hoorka are . . . interesting. And Gyll's ideals are close enough to that of the Families to be potentially useful. The Hoorka could conceivably work with us. I wasn't entirely false about the possibility of transplanting the Hoorka. The Oldins could use Gyll's skills, his dedication, and I think he'd be more happy with us than the Alliance.'' She looked down at him, a speculative gleam in her eyes. "And you seemed to take a liking to him, dwarf.''

"I did.'' He stared flatly back. "He resembles the Motsognir in temperament—he could be as stubbornly disagreeable as me. And I don't like to see people I like get hurt. So if you're just lying to yourself again, why don't you forget the Hoorka?''

"He could be useful.'' She was looking at the viewport again. Neweden was a bright curve at the lower edge. Sleipnir was a pockmarked face set in black.

For no apparent reason, the ovoid suddenly gurgled and screamed—a high-pitched discord at loud volume. Helgin, leaning back against it, catapulted himself across the room, rolling up against the far wall. Kaethe, hands over ears, laughed at him.

Helgin shot a venomous glance at her amusement, picked

himself off the floor, and strode back across the room to the
wailing machine. Grunting, he pushed at the ovoid. It moved,
then settled heavily back into place. Helgin pushed again, and
this time it toppled, striking the floor with a sharp crack. The
banshee howl died—leaving only Kaethe's giggling—and the
lights on the base flickered once before fading.

"Damn you, you might have warned me about that." Helgin
spat on the broken machine. "Now you only have to sell
forty-nine."

9

Dinner in Underasgard. The long cavern (calcite deposits
stained a pale tan—though where Felling's apprentices had been
set to scrubbing, they were milky white) was filled with rude
tables and the loud talk of kin. The full Hoorka had gathered to
one end of the cavern, which was fragrant with Felling's stew;
from the kitchen entrance, the pale faces of the youngest apprentices looked out, sweat-slick, at the doings of their elders.

"The Thane won't do as Sartas's honor deserves. She's just
sitting back and letting d'Embry make excuses." Aldhelm slapped
the table in front of him for emphasis. "The Hag gnaws at his
soul, and we've done nothing to stop Her."

"If that's your feeling, why don't you complain to the Thane
when she's here to defend herself?" retorted d'Mannberg from
down the length of the table. A susurration of agreement came
from those around him. "She's doing what she feels is best for
Hoorka, and you've sworn allegiance to her. Unless your word's
no better than a lassari's, save your complaints for Council.
She'll listen to you, and answer."

"Would that do any good, kin-brother?" Aldhelm stood, one
foot up on his stool, arms crossed over his knees. The scar on his
cheek was glazed with lamplight. Before any of the kin could
reply, he continued. "It's not just Sartas. McWilms is in the
Center Hospital. And remember that Eorl was killed by lassari,
and we've never found his murderer. We're losing our honor—
and we'll lose more if Sartas and McWilms aren't avenged. The
tale's already common gossip, and the guilded kin are still
muttering about us. Ask Ulthane Gyll—he hasn't said anything

about Thane Mondom's decision, and I'd wager that he's not in agreement with her on this.''

"You didn't follow the Ulthane's lead when he was Thane. Why are you suddenly claiming him as an ally?'' Serita Iduna, sitting beside Ric, cocked her head at Aldhelm. She leaned forward, her elbows smearing moisture across the wood. "We've suffered no worse than the other guilded kin, at least those around Sterka. We're all involved with the lassari problems— look at Gunnar's funeral.''

"Sartas and McWilms weren't attacked by lassari.'' Bachier spoke in defense of Aldhelm.

"That's true, but the guilded kin talk about Hoorka because it's known that Gunnar escaped us twice. They think a Hoorka might have been involved in his death. I almost don't blame them.'' D'Mannberg had been looking at Serita; now his gaze moved to Aldhelm. The significance of his glance wasn't lost on the other kin, but Aldhelm did not seem to notice. "If you hadn't asked for permission to visit Sterka that night, Aldhelm, Hoorka couldn't be suspect.''

"I'm sorry, but I wasn't aware at that time that Gunnar was going to be killed.''

The air between the two of them was charged. Bachier hurried to fill the silence. "We have problems—no one disputes that,'' he said, glancing from one to the other. "But internal bickering isn't going to solve anything. Yah, I don't like the fact that the Thane is willing to wait for d'Embry to act, but she also said that she wouldn't wait forever. We followed Ulthane Gyll's rulings—''

"Thane Mondom isn't Ulthane Gyll,'' said Aldhelm.

"She *is* Thane,'' Bachier insisted. "And she was the Ulthane's choice.''

"Choices aren't always good,'' Aldhelm retorted. "Mark my words. Mondom won't do anything for Sartas because *d'Embry* won't do anything. I'm sick of the Alliance and their games.''

"So we should limit ourselves to Neweden?'' D'Mannberg shifted his massive bulk on the stool. Wood creaked under him. "Maybe we should even make a bid for power and kill a few of the kin-lords, neh?''

Aldhelm glared. "And why *not* just Neweden? It's our culture and our society. That's what killed Sartas. And why don't you just say all that's on your mind, d'Mannberg? You think I killed Gunnar without giving him proper warning and a chance to defend himself? I live by the code, even when I feel it's wrong.''

"Is that why you felt Ulthane Gyll's vibro, because you

followed the code? We all know better, Aldhelm. You almost ignored it once, and that was with Gunnar, too.''

"I'd still never slay a person from shameful ambush, without letting Dame Fate have Her chance.''

"You can say that,'' d'Mannberg said with some heat. "You talk a good defense, but words are just words.'' Deliberately, he turned away from Aldhelm, looking at the other kin around him. "You see, Aldhelm is always right. The rest of us are just too stupid to see it.''

"Talk *to* me if you've something to say, man.'' Aldhelm trembled with interior rage.

D'Mannberg ignored him, continuing to speak to the others. "He'd ignore the code on the practice strip, but expects us to believe him in all other things. If Aldhelm thinks I'm that stupid, he's an ass.''

Aldhelm's face went scarlet, his hand moving to his vibrohilt. His stool clattered backward, his boots stamped packed earth. Aldhelm pulled the hilt from the sheath and flung it down in front of d'Mannberg. It skidded across the table's surface, stopping hilt foremost half off the wooden planks. D'Mannberg looked up at Aldhelm, a long slow smile forming behind the russet beard. "First blood, kin-brother?''

Aldhelm, tight-lipped, nodded.

Serita, behind d'Mannberg, gestured to the wide-eyed apprentices staring from the door to the kitchens. "Get Thane Mondom and Ulthane Gyll,'' she said, gesturing harshly. "Move, you fools!''

They stood before the Thane, Aldhelm and d'Mannberg. Aldhelm seemed tense, on edge, his arms akimbo. His weight shifted from foot to foot, impatient, and he watched Mondom with a grimace of pride. D'Mannberg seemed eagerly confident, legs wide like a surly dwarf given stature. He seemed almost happy—his blue eyes danced from the Thane to Ulthane Gyll.

Mondom liked neither one's attitude. She also did not like the way Gyll sat behind her, silent, one hip up on the edge of her desk like some critical overseer. Mondom paced, back and forth between the desk and the two antagonistic Hoorka, trying to find some way to discharge the tension in the room, trying to ignore her own feeling of pessimistic inevitability. She seemed tiny against d'Mannberg's height and girth, sour when placed next to Aldhelm's masked stoicism. *Much the way d'Embry seems to me. Too damn much like d'Embry.*

"The two of you do nothing but argue. I'm sick of hearing about it—you can't settle it talking, can't fight it out on the practice strips. Now you demand first blood—what was it this time?" She could hear the irritation in her voice, melded with fear of her inadequacy—sharp, petty, nasal.

D'Mannberg glanced at Aldhelm and shrugged. "Does it matter, Thane?" he asked. "We seem to be able to reach no better solution. My honor would like the blood he demands."

"Your honor also demands that you do what's best for Hoorka-kin. Fighting among ourselves only weakens Hoorka. We've enough problems at the moment without risking injury to appease somebody's wounded pride." All the time walking—to the desk, back again.

"You fought Bachier, Thane." Despite his restlessness, Aldhelm's voice was calm. His eyes seemed to mock her. "That was no doubt a great help to our kin."

In the midst of a step, Mondom whirled about, her nightcloak billowing out like a dark wing. "I *had* to fight Bachier—he insulted me during Council. Every decision I make seems to be grounds for open discussion among the elder kin; I had to prove myself worthy to be Thane, and I had no wish to hurt Bachier. I've seen the two of you, watched you both. You circle each other like tiger cubs, constantly seeing how far you can go before the other lashes out with claws. You want to hurt each other too much."

"We only want first blood, Thane. Nothing more. It's our right, under the code, to be allowed to have it," Aldhelm said.

Mondom nodded. She inhaled, held it, then let the breath go with a sigh. "Can't you wait a few nights, see if it's still this important to you then? If your blood cools, maybe you'll be able to talk out your misunderstanding. I'd be happy to arbitrate, to help the two of you sift out the problems."

"You can't stop them, Thane." Gyll spoke from behind her, his voice natural, unstressed: a simple, factual statement. She turned to him, accusing.

"How can you be so certain of that?"

"Look at them." He nodded to the two assassins. "Neither of them wants to give in. Give it up, Thane. Let them have first blood."

Mondom blinked in surprised anger at Gyll's indiscreet candor. Feeling the boil of temper rising, she turned back to d'Mannberg and Aldhelm. "You won't wait? You insist on immediate satisfaction?"

D'Mannberg nodded, echoed by Aldhelm.

"Then you can have it." Her voice was clipped, curt, official. She cloaked her feelings in the mask of distant authority. "Ulthane Gyll will judge the match. Call my apprentice as you leave, Aldhelm. Have her inform the kin of the match. Then prepare yourselves. You may go."

She watched them leave, stonily, wrapping her nightcloak around her as if cold. As the door crashed shut behind them, she looked back to Gyll.

"*Don't*"—heavily—"*ever* advise me in that manner again, Gyll."

"You've told me you want my advice."

"As a friend advises a friend. Not like a god advises his worshippers."

"Mondom—"

"You can leave too, Gyll."

He was suddenly contrite. "Mondom, I'm sorry . . . I was way too brusque and you deserve to be angry. It just seemed so obvious that they wouldn't have it any other way. I know what d'Mannberg thinks about Aldhelm—you must have heard what he said during their last practice."

Mondom suddenly lost her anger. Her shoulders slumped beneath the dark cloth of the nightcloak. "I've heard you voice the same suspicion—that Aldhelm might have murdered Gunnar. I still don't believe that, Gyll. And it's not worth shedding blood over."

"If it's true?"

"I believe my kin."

Gyll hesitated. The rest of the tale was on his tongue—his suspicion that Aldhelm had lied that night, his subsequent failure at finding the supposed Irastian smith. It was, after all, the Thane's business—if kin had done the dishonorable deed, then it was the Thane's right to be aware of that and to mete out the punishment. Yet he couldn't say it. He told himself that it was because it was still uncertain—Gyll might have missed the smith, or perhaps Aldhelm had some other task in Sterka that night, and Gyll had also not had the opportunity to confront Aldhelm directly. Whatever the reason, he said nothing; just nodded at Mondom's statement, wondering at his own arrogance in keeping this from her.

Mondom smiled, touching his hand. "Hey, you have to judge this, neh? Go on, Gyll. I'll be there in a few minutes." A pause. She almost smiled. "Yah?"

Gyll squeezed her hand. He left.

Mondom slumped back against her desk. "Damn," she muttered to the walls.

The practice room, noisy with conversation, was crowded. The Hoorka-kin found what room they could, jostling good-naturedly. All other activity in Underasgard had stopped. A few Hoorka, vibrofoils in hand, stood about with sweat-slicked skin, breaths quick and loud, their own practice abandoned. Even Felling, with his stained apron over the swell of his paunch, was present. The blood-duel was not to be missed.

It would be quick. All of them knew that. First blood only (though it was whispered by some who had seen the two before that Aldhelm would not be contented with a simple scratch), and Ulthane Gyll was notorious for being a quick hand with his own foil in judging such matches. A nick would end it, if Gyll had his way. Cranmer, an apprentice towing his hoverholos, was hastily setting up his recording equipment, casting appealing glances at Gyll. The Ulthane strode back and forth along the chosen strip as Aldhelm and d'Mannberg feinted with shadows at either end.

Gyll glanced at Mondom as she entered the cavern. She moved forward as the ranks gave way before her, leaving her standing in a small, clear circle of ground. Gyll didn't know if that was deference or an indication of some uneasiness in her presence. He did know that the kin had never treated him so, and he could see from her stance that she was uncomfortable with the distancing. Mondom nodded/shrugged to him.

Gyll stepped to center strip. "Kin-brothers, are you both ready?"

His clear baritone sent the muttering of the kin into silence. Aldhelm and d'Mannberg came to the middle of the strip.

"Your weapons, please." Gyll quickly examined the vibrofoils (pull the control ring down, twist it sideways three clicks, let it snap back into position, locked), then he plunged the foils into dirt alongside the strip. Both went in easily, earth kicking up around the tips and the shivering vibrowire. He handed back the weapons and pulled his own foil from the rack. As the growl of vibros grew loud, he checked his own blade. "You will remember that this is first blood only," Gyll said. "If either of you try to go beyond that, you'll also be fighting my blade. Neither the Thane nor I wish kin to fight in this way—when it's necessary, you'll do it by the code." He glanced from one to the other.

Ric d'Mannberg was tense—his nervousness showed in the

banded swirl of muscles in the back of his hands, thick fingers
flexing over the foil's grip. The polished guard threw back the
underwater light of the nearest light-fungi; a slash of emerald
crawled his arm. He rubbed his beard with a forefinger, scuffled
the packed, resilient earth with bare feet.

Aldhelm was an enigma. The vibrofoil was held casually, the
luminous tip down and swaying a few centimeters above the
lined dirt. He glanced at d'Mannberg with a curious lethargy, as
if the anger had cooled to a dispassionate dislike, as if he no
longer viewed d'Mannberg as a person, but as a problem to be
studied for the best method of execution. He simply nodded at
Gyll's admonition.

"This is the last chance," Gyll continued. "I'd prefer that
you reconsider. A disagreement, as Thane Mondom told you"—
he glanced at her; yes, she'd noticed the contrition in his
voice—"needn't be settled by blood."

"On Neweden, that seems to be the way of things, Ulthane.
Everyone supposes that you must seek blood to redeem yourself." Aldhelm didn't look at Gyll, but at d'Mannberg. The tip
of his foil swayed. A muscle in his jaw twitched the scarred
cheek. "I assume d'Mannberg still stands by his words to me?"

"Did I say any untruths, Aldhelm?" asked d'Mannberg.

The scar flicked again, fungi-light staining the flesh. "It
doesn't really matter, does it?"

"We'll let the Dame decide." D'Mannberg let the tip of his
vibrofoil graze Aldhelm's weapon. Metal whined and clashed;
the foils bucked in their hands.

Gyll whipped his foil up, knocking the weapons aside. "You'll
begin when I start you, not before." His eyes warned. *Watch this
one carefully,* he told himself. *There's been too much hurting of
kin.* "Salute each other and begin," he said. He stepped back
from the strip.

Vibrofoils came up, met high with a clashing that sent quick
sparks cascading to the earth. Their vibrations thrilled the air.
Then the foils moved in a sudden dance, d'Mannberg stepping
forward with an audible grunt, taking the high inside line. Parry
and riposte—Aldhelm's weapon moved with a lithe grace, and
the meeting of foils gave birth to a bright, dying rain as
vibrowire hissed in anger. Aldhelm moved his blade in a quick
circle, a counter-parry of quarte, then lunged to the high inside
line. D'Mannberg knocked the foil away with a beat, stepping
back, but Aldhelm's foil pursued. D'Mannberg kicked at Aldhelm's
foil hand, suddenly, but his foot found only air and as he

wavered off-balance, Aldhelm thrust. Vibros screamed, whining as the foils scraped along each other's length. The kin could see d'Mannberg's foil held too low, the guard allowing access to shoulder and bicep. The larger man desperately lifted the weapon as Aldhelm's foil slithered toward him. An intake of breath— those beside the strip were certain of a touch. Gyll moved forward, ready to halt them; Mondom, in her inviolate circle, frowned.

But Aldhelm moved back, two quick steps, disengaging. D'Mannberg didn't pursue. The cavern was suddenly quiet without the clashing of vibrofoils. The two Hoorka stared at one another. A droplet of sweat ran from d'Mannberg's temple into his matted beard. Some inner communication seemed to leap from man to man. Then d'Mannberg took a step, sweeping his foil in a wide, looping arc like a saber. Aldhelm batted it aside easily. The foils barked metallically.

A breath.

Then Aldhelm took the initiative once more, quickly backing d'Mannberg down the strip. His foil beat d'Mannberg's aside; he kicked out, his foot nearly finding d'Mannberg's knee, slamming into the thick muscle of the thigh. The huge assassin stumbled backward and Aldhelm lunged.

But d'Mannberg was powered by instinct, going with the motion and half-falling to one side. His own counter-thrust was made in desperation, blind, trying to find Aldhelm before he himself was touched. His foil came under Aldhelm's foil, past the flailing arm (even as he felt the agony of Aldhelm's blade in his shoulder), and into Aldhelm's unprotected stomach. The weight of Aldhelm's lunge added force to d'Mannberg's foil. The weapon, slicing upward, parted diaphragm from stomach, slid into lung tissue, the vibro tearing at flesh. Aldhelm, a look of astonishment on his scarred face, fell even as Gyll cried "Halt!" and strode forward. D'Mannberg—eyes wide, his breath halting—had already snapped off his vibro. Blood-slick wire hissed into the hilt. Aldhelm was prone, hands clutched over his belly, his foil kicking dust beside him. Thick blood flowed around his fingers, ran down his hands and arms. Gyll tossed his weapon aside and crouched beside the man. D'Mannberg knelt, bewildered, as the stasis holding the Hoorka broke.

"Aldhelm . . ." Gyll could feel dread twisting his bowels. He could almost smell the Hag's breath in the odor of stale sweat and bitter steel, the faint tang of lifeblood. Aldhelm grimaced in agony.

"By the Hag—" he muttered through clenched teeth. He looked up at Gyll, pain clouding his eyes. "Ulthane . . ."

"Don't talk, man. Rest. We'll get you to the Center Hospital." Gyll glanced up as Mondom thrust her way through the kin around the fallen assassin. She took a quick look at Aldhelm—her mouth a line of concern—and snapped orders to the kin. "Iduna, get the flitter ready. Cranmer, get on your Center link and tell them we're coming. You three—get a floater for Aldhelm. Move!" She knelt beside Gyll, touching Aldhelm's hands lightly and moving them aside. She winced as she saw the wound.

"Ulthane, Thane . . ." Aldhelm's voice was weak; it brought their heads down. "I didn't kill Gunnar. I've no reason to lie, now. Believe me, I didn't kill him."

"Nobody thinks you did," Mondom said. She looked at Gyll, her glance angry. "Now be still. Let Bachier take care of the bleeding."

Gyll and Mondom moved aside as Bachier—now in charge of the healing for the guild since Renier's death—began to minister to Aldhelm. They went to d'Mannberg.

His wound was surface. It bled profusely, but the damage was slight. "Is he—" d'Mannberg began.

Gyll shook his head. "It's an ugly wound, Ric."

D'Mannberg threw the hilt of his foil to the ground. It bounced among the kin's feet. "Thane, Ulthane, I didn't mean for that to happen. It was just a blind thrust, and if he hadn't been moving . . ." A look of pain thinned his mouth, furrowed his brow. He blinked away sweat. "We've lost too many kin. I didn't care for Aldhelm, I admit; we fought all the time of late. But I wouldn't have deliberately . . ."

"We know." Mondom laid a hand on his shoulder—the flesh was cool, wet. "Get the rest of them out of here, Ric, and get your shoulder looked at," she said. "And make sure Cranmer's stopped filming."

"It's not enough to lose Eorl and Sartas," she said as d'Mannberg began moving the Hoorka from the cavern, as Aldhelm, moaning, was placed on a floater and rushed away. "We have to find ways of killing ourselves. He's not going to make it, is he?"

"I don't think so." He couldn't think of a gentler way of saying it, and he didn't feel like lying.

Mondom swore. "Damn it, Gyll," she said at last. "Why did you give me all this?"

"Would you want me to take it back?"

Her chin trembled for a moment, flesh puckering. He thought she might cry, but she shook her head again. "I don't think so, Gyll. But do you want it?"

When he didn't answer, she moved away from him, watching as the last of the kin left the cavern. Then, the room silent and empty, she did cry. Gyll, stricken, didn't know how to comfort her. He could only hold her, hand snared in her hair, pulling her to him.

Tri-Guild Church was a blaze of pageantry. The immense space held within its fluted walls was a welter of light from drifting hoverlamps in field-holders high above the crowds. A phalanx of stained-glass windows (ippicators rampant, Dame Fate with Her enigmatic smile, the Hag leering down) threw wide shafts of colored brilliance down on the massed kin; a scurrying montage of brightly dyed cloth and stain-altered sunlight. Peddlers of refreshments called their wares as they shoved passage through the throngs on the floor and in the temporary stands along the walls. The cries were loud above the murmur of conversation.

Only guilded kin were present. For the rest, the spectacle was being broadcast to a huge holotank set in Tri-Guild Square. Lassari or kin unfortunate enough to be unable to afford seats inside—they milled in the square.

Truth-duel: when between the Li-Gallant and his largest rival, it was an event to fascinate Neweden. It would be seen in Illi, in the Northern Waste, along the Sundered Sea, in Remeale on Kotta Plain. Even the Diplos were present, high on the tiered decks, conspicuous in the bright clothing of the Alliance and gathered around the aged, slight figure of Regent d'Embry.

Truth-duel: on Neweden, it was a venerable but rare institution, invoked only in cases of extreme suspicion where normal judicial procedure could not be followed or guilt proven by evidence. It was avoided because the Guild of Magistrates put the heaviest of penalties upon it. The loss of truth-duel was considered irrevocable admission of guilt. There was no appeal from the judgment of the five deities of truth.

Already the Revelate of Tri-Guild Church had invoked the Five, whose images stood at the points of a star-shaped stage. His orange robes ablaze—tongues of unsearing flame licking up and down the seams; as the hoverlamps faded into dimness and opaque covers slid over the stained-glass panels, he was quite impressive—he named them. One by one, the deities burned with a gout of crimson flame, then threw a tight yellow beam across to its neighbors. The perimeter of the stage was then laced with intersecting lines that would repel unprotected flesh. Only the two combatants would be allowed egress to the interior. The Revelate, invocation complete, led the assembly in a brief prayer as his flaming robes flickered. He raised his hands in a gesture of religious ecstasy—the church, plunged into sudden darkness, was then assaulted by aching white brilliance slicing from above and below the star-stage. An involuntary gasp came from the onlookers. Now, somber in their green vestments (the color of justice), each with a priceless chain of ippicator bone-beads, the elder magistrates moved slowly into the sun-blaze, their slaveboys (naked except for jeweled collars) supporting them. They moved to the corners of the stage, each to a deity's right hand.

And finally, greeted by a sea-roar of anticipation, Vingi and Potok walked onto the dais. Each wore only a simple white cloth around his loins and a wrist bracelet of some dull metal. They were flooded in the fury of a nova. Vingi was a hillock of flesh, his gross folds puckered with cellulite, his breasts almost like a woman's but for the hairiness of his chest. Yet he moved with a strange grace despite his grotesque appearance. He did not provoke laughter, but a strange silence. Potok seemed only out of shape, his bald head shining, the body of an overweight man given to little or no exercise. He was small beside Vingi, but appeared to be far more mobile. Neither looked the part of fighter.

The beams from the truth-deities parted as they approached, falling back into place behind them. The magistrate at the head of the star-stage tottered a step forward, leaning heavily on the shoulder of his slaveboy.

"Your bracelets, please," he said. Hidden amplifiers gave his voice deific proportions. "Place them at the edge of the arena."

Vingi and Potok did as requested, removing the iron circlets from their wrists. A nod from the magistrate, and his attendant darted forward (beams breaking around him), grasped the bracelets, and came back to his station. The magistrate touched the panting head with affection, a small smile on his lips. "Your weapons, sirrahs," he said, looking up again.

Rising slowly from the center of the star-stage, a platform held two crowd-prods. A simple rubber grip, a stubby metal cylinder, a thumb contact: they were simple weapons, but capable of delivering a jarring shock to the nervous system. Applied in the right area or to the body in general a number of times, they could

reduce a person to gibbering, slack-jawed shock or unconsciousness.
Vingi and Potok picked up their prods, holding them in uncertain
hands. The platform sank and became flush with the floor again.

"The truth-duel is now initiated," the magistrate said as his
fellows nodded. "If one of you asks to yield or is unable to
continue the duel, the other will be adjudged the victor and the
penalties previously decided upon will be given. There will be
no rest periods, no pauses, no particular rules. You cannot leave
the star-stage until the gods have ruled—the gods will guide your
hands and destinies, for one of you lies."

The magistrate stepped back, leaning on his slaveboy. He
nodded in the shadow of his truth-deity. "Begin."

Prod-metal flicked light over the expectant faces in the crowd:
Vingi swung his weapon up and back. Potok hefted his prod,
feeling its weight. The guild-kin of each rule-guild shouted their
support.

The Li-Gallant took a ponderous step forward. His flesh
jiggled about his waist, on his thighs. Potok was obviously much
quicker; he moved forward and to the side, swinging his prod. A
clatter of steel: Vingi, arms moving, blocked Potok's intended
blow with his prod. Potok, moving as Vingi turned slowly to
attack, swung again and touched the Li-Gallant. A shrill buzzing
came from the prod, a choked-off moan escaped Vingi's lips.
The touch was above the kidneys, just under the ribcage. Vingi's
face went red, his eyes watered.

But he still followed Potok, if slowly, who had stopped to see
what effect the prod had on his opponent. The Li-Gallant's arm
swept out (light-glare shimmering the prod's length); Potok,
startled, beat at the weapon. Vingi, for all his girth, masked
muscle beneath the continents of flesh. His prod bullied past
Potok's flailing defense to touch the man on the right side of the
chest. Potok groaned as the prod crackled like a lightning stroke.
He stumbled backward as Vingi thrust at him again. Once more,
Potok's greater agility saved him.

Both were now more cautious, having been hit once. As the
crowd settled back into noisy restlessness, as the partisan kin
cheered, the two played a game of patience. Potok would lunge
and dart back, Vingi would attempt to maneuver Potok into a
corner where the Li-Gallant's greater reach and strength gave
him the advantage. To the connoisseur of finesse and grace, the
match was a dismal farce. It was far too slow. The cheering
waned. A few more touches were scored, but the duel dragged
on: fifteen minutes, half an hour. Both men were now obviously

tired; sweat dappled the star-stage, darkening the cloth about their waists and shining on their backs. Slowly, the eventual outcome was becoming apparent to the spectators. Vingi's kin began to become noisy; Potok's guild was watchful, quiet, afraid.

Vingi was stronger, in better shape, and more able to bear the stinging bruises of the crowd-prod. Potok, fish-mouthed and gasping, struggled to stay one step beyond Vingi's reach. His attacks had become little but desultory feints that did nothing to drive the Li-Gallant back. Vingi stalked his prey, moving slowly, but always moving.

Vingi stepped, and his bearlike arms pummeled air; his prod clacked as he struck Potok's weapon. The prod shivered in Potok's grasp, and Vingi struck at it again. The prod slithered away from Potok, clattering across the floor. Potok, his eyes frightened, moved to recover his weapon (his kin moaning as one), and Vingi lunged.

The Li-Gallant's prod found its mark.

Potok screamed, a wailing cry that echoed in the hall, now lost in the joyous whistling from Vingi's kin. Potok rolled, reaching out for his prod with desperate, wide-spread fingers. Vingi's huge foot came down on the hand, hard. The cracking of bones could be heard in the nearest rows, and Vingi's prod ran the length of Potok's spine. The squeal of agony choked off suddenly. Potok's head lolled against the floor.

It was over.

The yellow beams from the deities faded, the aching glare of the star-stage altered to sapphire as Vingi stepped away from Potok. He smiled. The magistrate moved forward to declare him victor.

To declare him truthful and innocent.

It was much later when Gyll finally returned to his rooms. The wort mewled at him—he'd missed its feeding. He stared at the animal, wondering. *How can you be alive, so improbably, when Hag Death snatches at everything else around me? You damn thing, you weren't built for survival, yet you continue to fight...* He reached down over the cage to stroke the furred hardness of the shell.

It had all gone wrong so quickly—so needlessly. Aldhelm had not survived the trip to the hospital. Yet the death was still an unreality, a dream—*he wasn't meant to go that way, not by the hands of his own kin, accidentally. That was how it was in the early days of Hoorka, before I disciplined them, before the code was set.* He sat on the edge of the bedfield, staring at his hands knotted on his lap. The hands were a network of tiny cracks, whitely dry, the light reflecting satin on the surface, golden-shadowed in the wrinkles.

Why did you give me all this, Gyll? Mondom's words kept coming back, insistent. *But do you want it?*

He could feel a sense of change, like a faint spice-smell in the chill dark air of Underasgard. And for the first time, he welcomed change. He thought he knew the answer to Mondom's questions. He didn't care for that answer, knowing what it might mean. But more and more he was certain.

10

An excerpt from the acousidots of Sondall-Cadhurst Cranmer. The following is part of several interviews Cranmer recorded outside the context of the Hoorka. It is perhaps more interesting in how it reflects Cranmer's own shift in attitude over the standards he spent on Neweden. As Cranmer remarks in his Wanderer's Musings *(Niffleheim University Press, 252), it took him quite some time to readjust to our society after living in that society. Certainly the Cranmer I knew before the Hoorka study would never have been so patronizing. He began, afterward, to wonder if the attitude of the elite toward those below them wasn't something lying dormant in all people, and to question whether his humanistic views weren't merely a civilized veneer far too easily scratched away. Cranmer, ever afterward, was active in social reform, perhaps to the detriment of his status in his field; it is not good for one engaged in the study of societies to be active in endeavoring to change the one in which he lives.*

The lassari of this interview has never been identified—another indication of the odd and uncharacteristic contempt that exudes from Cranmer in this dot.

EXCERPT FROM THE DOT OF 9.26.215:

"You're a lassari?"

(A moment's silence.)

"Speak up, woman, and show some wit. This is an audio

recording. Your nods don't register. And please don't look so frightened of me. Now, you're a lassari?''

"Yes, sirrah." (The voice trembles a bit; contralto, a bit rough.)

"And you live . . . ?"

"In Brentwood. My true-father has a place there, sirrah. He doesn't mind my staying."

"Do you work?"

"How'ya mean, sirrah? I do what I have to do, certainly."

"You needn't take offense. I'm interested purely as a scholar. What do you charge for your, ahh, services?"

"Are'ya interested, sirrah? For you, I could—"

"Have you looked at yourself? No, this is simply for my notes. If I need comfort, I can find the Courtesan's Guild.''

(She laughs, then stops quickly as if afraid of offending Cranmer.) "The guild-women are far too expensive for the likes of what I get, sirrah. I'm not skilled or pretty enough to join 'em. And I'm cheap."

"But that allows you to survive."

"Like the rest of lassari. You do what you can, as long as you want. After, there's always the Dead. You can find 'em if you need."

"You don't sound as if you enjoy your life."

"Neweden's fine for the guilded kin, sirrah. If you ain't kin, then maybe next time Dame Fate'll be kinder—I went to a seeress once, and she told me that I'd been kin in earlier lives, that I'd be kin again. It feels right. So you accept it—if you kick back now, then maybe the Dame'll kick *you* when She steals you from the Hag again, send you back lassari again. Or maybe She'll just leave you there as one of the Hag's handservants."

"Don't you ever get angry? You people act like complacent cows."

"When you're jussar, you're angry. You forget to get angry when you become lassari, when no guild wants you. You live better and longer that way."

"A complacent attitude."

"Hmm?"

"Damn . . . ahh, never mind."

"I'd like to see someone pull the lassari together, demand something better for us and make it stick. If that person ever comes along, maybe I'll join 'im. Until that happens, I'll stay quiet."

*   *   *

Gyll tried to strike a balance between unabashed staring and nonchalance. He didn't succeed.

Kaethe Oldin reclined on a grassy hillock in her chambers between four metal pillars that radiated a golden light. It made every centimeter of exposed flesh glisten; being nude, she glistened quite a bit. Ulthane Gyll, on whose cool and strict world casual nudity was uncommon, felt rather provincial and uncomfortable. He didn't know where to put his gaze. Beside and below him, Helgin—who had ushered him into Kaethe's rooms—chuckled.

Kaethe sat up on one elbow. A gilt eyebrow winked light at him; she smiled. "Ulthane Gyll. I'm glad to see you again. A moment—let me get rid of the Battier." She reached out, languid, to touch one of the posts. The glow dimmed, the Battier receded into the floor. All the light in the room now came from the panels on the walls and Neweden, floating beyond the viewport.

"Kaethe thinks that an angelic glow can be achieved from the outside, rather than requiring a saintly interior," Helgin commented. Grunting, he seated himself on the carpet, crossing his stubby legs underneath himself.

Gyll nodded, not knowing how else to reply. Helgin disconcerted him. Gyll knew that he wouldn't tolerate such casual insult from guilded kin. On Neweden, the Motsognir would either prove himself to be an excellent foilsman or die. But, as she had the last time, Oldin reacted as if she'd expected his sourness. She nodded sweetly to the dwarf.

"If saintliness were required, you wouldn't light the darkness either." She stopped, laughing suddenly. Her laugh was crystalline; Gyll found himself smiling in response. "I've embarrassed you, haven't I?" she said, looking at Gyll. "I'm sorry, I just forgot where"—she tapped at a wall. It opened, revealing a closet, and she plucked a robe from its fasteners, slipping it about her shoulders—"I was for a moment. I hope I haven't..."

"You haven't." Gyll paused, searching for something else to say. "The view was...interesting."

A smile rewarded his effort.

"And if you think the exposure wasn't deliberate—despite the fact that Kaethe could use some exercise—you're a fool, Ulthane." Helgin; gruff, scowling. He plucked at the grass-carpet.

Gyll started involuntarily, smile evaporating into frown. His eyes narrowed, folding the crow's-feet at their corners deeper. "I think what I please, Motsognir, and I'm *not* a fool."

The dwarf snorted laughter and slapped the carpet with his hand. "You Newedeners antagonize too easily. It's no fun baiting you. I tell you, Hoorka—I'm good with any weapon you can name, even better with my hands, and I'm a damned small target to hit."

The wizened, beard-hidden face was comically furious.

Despite himself, Gyll found his irritation gone. He shook his head into the dwarf's red-veined stare. Helgin's lips drew back from teeth: he leered. "Try me sometime, Ulthane."

"Keep talking like you do, and I probably will."

Oldin had lain back down on the hillock again, upper body supported on elbows behind her, legs crossed at ankles. "The two of you complement each other. The Family Oldin could use both Motsognir and Hoorka." She glanced questioningly at Gyll. "The reason I asked to see you again, Ulthane, was to find out whether you had talked with Thane Mondom."

A shrug. The port view shifted as *Peregrine* made an orbital adjustment. Ocean-blue light swept across the floor toward Gyll, moving with his shrug. "I've talked with Thane Mondom, and I'm sorry I haven't responded before now—much has been happening." He thought of Mondom; when he'd left Underasgard, she'd been making arrangements for the construction of Aldhelm's pyre. "She doesn't appear interested."

"But *you* are?"

Gyll wondered if he were that easy to read, but decided not to deny his interest—if it was a game she played, he'd go along for now. "To an extent, I am."

"Good. The Family Oldin can offer Hoorka far more than the Alliance. The Oldins are quite strong among the Trading Families, and we could use your skills to enhance that—the exact manner in which the Hoorka might operate would of course be up to you." She sat up, smiling. "My offer, then, is this. Come with me when I return to OldinHome—as soon as my business is done here. Spend time among the Family societies, see what you need to see, and determine how you can devise a code to allow you to work with and for us. I think you could fashion the code to work within our context."

"Trader Oldin—"

She shook her head. "I won't try to correct you this time, Ulthane. But 'Kaethe' would be preferable to 'Trader Oldin.' This is hardly a formal meeting, neh?"

Gyll hesitated, began a "Kaethe" and ended elsewhere. "I once used a vibro on a kin-brother who insisted that I change the code to fit a situation. I feel that strongly about it—if you think that the Hoorka-code must be changed to work within your society, then perhaps I should leave now and waste no more of our time." The remembrance of Aldhelm conjured by his words brought back the dull ache of his death. Gyll choked down the ghost, forcing his mind to stay on the subject.

"I didn't mean to suggest anything distasteful to you," Kaethe said. "I know you created the code, managed to bring order out of chaos, and the code fits Neweden's society ingeniously. I expect that you could devise a Hoorka-guild under another similar culture. I compliment you by saying that you could change the code, believe me. In any case, your coming with me to OldinHome binds you to nothing. I'd pay you as an adviser—ten thousand, in Alliance currency if that's what you want, for a third-standard of your time. No restrictions beyond that. Just come and see the Families' society, perhaps give a suggestion or two to our fighting masters to enhance their training, and make your decision later."

"Your words still say the same, even under the sugarcoating. The code works, m'Dame," he said, stubbornly.

"On *Neweden* it works, Ulthane," she answered, lifting her hands as if in supplication. "You've never been offworld, never seen the varieties of structures I have. No one code can work for them all. I know about Heritage, about the killing of your kin—it's part of the same problem, Ulthane. You're a Neweden native, born here. What works for Neweden *might not*"—he could see her watching his face carefully for reaction—"work elsewhere. I can understand your reluctance to abandon what's taken you so far, but I'd be silly not to warn you about inflexibility. It's not a survival trait, Ulthane. Not even in a society as static as that here. And I think you're a survivor."

"You talk a lot like Aldhelm."

"Aldhelm?"

"He is . . ." Gyll's lips tightened, his brow furrowed. The pain and anger and sorrow nagged at him again. *Down. Stay down.* "He was one of my advisers. A good friend at one time. He told me much the same thing once—we never could agree on it, and it drove us apart."

"Did you reconcile yourselves?"

Down. "No. I followed the code and insisted that he do the same." For a moment he thought of telling her everything, of the struggle that ended with Aldhelm feeling the bite of Gyll's vibro as Gunnar fled before them. But something held him back, as if by saying nothing he apologized to Aldhelm. "He did as I said, and it worked."

Kaethe sat forward, hugging legs to breasts, looking at him with her chin set on knees. "Nothing in this universe is a stasis."

"Perhaps not, but Neweden hasn't changed significantly in two centuries."

She stared at him, unblinking; the intensity of her gaze made Gyll uncomfortable. The gilt eyebrows shivered with reflected planet-light. "It will. Believe me, Ulthane, Neweden will change. When it does, and it might be sooner than you believe, nothing will be the same here. The Hoorka will have to change with Neweden or your guild will die."

Her certainty worried Gyll. He wondered at her fervor. "I was Thane for a few decades. The code has always managed to bring us through crises. It's the only thing that allows us to work on Neweden—if the Li-Gallant thought we'd ever break our ways, he'd have us hunted down. The code is the one thing that sets us apart from lassari and jussar..."

"You're not Thane anymore. And if the society on which the code is based changes, then you needn't worry about the Li-Gallant. He'll be facing his own problems. The code would be outmoded, a confining set of useless rules which'll bring you death."

Gyll scowled. "Everything brings death. Just living brings the Hag closer every day. Perhaps we needn't talk further, m'Dame."

Kaethe suddenly uncurled herself, standing. She tugged at her robe's belt, stretched. "I want to show you something, Ulthane." She turned to Helgin. He was picking at his toenails, seemingly oblivious to the conversation. "Helgin, you know what I want. Would you get it?"

The Motsognir rose to his feet slowly, joints cracking. "At your service, oh master..." he said with too much joviality. He glanced at Gyll. "Ulthane, in this she might be right. The Motsognir have seen many ways of life in our exile on Naglfar. Some things change very slowly. It may take centuries to see the flow, but all things do change." He left the room.

Helgin returned a few minutes later, a large hover-tray bobbing behind him on a tether-line. On the tray, inside a nutrient tank scaled with bubbles, floated a creature the size of a wort. Eyes closed, the embryonic head large and the limbs but half-formed, it was still recognizable. Gyll had seen it in a hundred renderings.

Ippicator.

Helgin grinned enigmatically, Kaethe sank down on the carpet again as if weary of standing in the Neweden-like gravity. They both watched as Gyll went up to the hover-tray and stared. He thought for a moment that it might be a replica, but it moved, a faint quivering that had nothing of the mechanical in it. The head turned slightly, the limbs twitched. Gyll marveled at it, at the smoothness of the orangish skin (in the replicas he'd seen, they had always been slate-gray). He touched the tank—it was warm. "It's real," he said, and immediately felt foolish. Emotions twisted at him—ones he'd thought safely removed. *It goes deep; Neweden training, Neweden religions. Even for one who doesn't entirely believe, it's hard to shake off the ties. An ippicator, the gods' pets . . .* "I thought . . ."

"That I said it was impossible. I know." She looked at him over steepled hands. "It *is* impossible, if live tissue isn't present. The Trading Families are *old,* Ulthane, older than the Alliance or even Huard. Our roots lie back with the First Empire. We've been to many places, sometimes before anyone else. I checked with Oldin Archives. They had a specimen of tissue, a frozen sample—evidently the Oldin captain who came here first found the five-legged beasts fascinating too, enough to have taken the sample against future cloning. I had it sent here."

"It sounds like a damned expensive way to impress Hoorka." Gyll watched the embryo turning slowly in the tides of the tank, still trying to decide what he felt.

"She's spent more on other failures—it's a family trait, I think," Helgin rumbled. "Throw enough money at something, and it solves everything."

"I bought your services, didn't I, Motsognir?" Kaethe smiled at the dwarf, then turned back to Gyll. "The fifth leg, incidentally, is a sensing device—the beast fed on the tender roots of certain grasses that were also the favorite of a local burrowing insect. The 'leg' extends a small horny spike into the soil, and the ippicator can hear the grubs moving. Where there are grubs, there are roots—the poor creatures are virtually blind. You know, the Archives didn't even know they possessed the sample. We could've been breeding them for the bones. It'd have to be in small quantities, of course, or we'd drive down the prices, but . . ." Again, that slow smile. "You see, it wasn't necessarily just to impress Hoorka."

"Yah, don't expect altruism of Traders, Ulthane. They threw the word out of their dictionaries." Helgin scratched at his dense growth of beard.

Gyll frowned. He forced his gaze away from the ippicator. "She of the Five Limbs . . . All of Neweden would curse you for a heretic for this, m'Dame Oldin. The ippicator is sacred in some way to nearly all guilded kin. This fetus is an abomination."

"To you, also?"

"I was brought up to believe in Neweden's gods. My true-mother was devout. She worshipped every day, praying that her jussar son would become guilded kin. My true-father—he·didn't believe; he was an offworlder. He'd scoff, and then they'd fight. . . . Me, I sometimes believe, and I always must seem to do so. I believe mostly in myself and the code. But I look at this thing, and I feel disgust. Ippicators belong to the gods and the dead."

His hands plunged into the pockets of his nightcloak. He shifted from foot to foot. "I guess it's not easy to escape your conditioning."

"I'll have it destroyed, Ulthane. Helgin—"

"No!" His own vehemence startled Gyll. He shook his head. *Calm, always calm. That's the way of the code.* "Yes, destroy it, but wait until I've left. I want to look at it some more, fix it in my mind. Then send it to the Hag."

"As you wish."

"Trader Oldin, I had thought only to tell you that Thane Mondom had no interest in your offer. She speaks for Hoorka."

Kaethe leaned back. Neweden light bathed her. "And you?"

"I've made my life Hoorka's." He stared at her, suddenly the aloof Hoorka again.

"I'm much less interested in Hoorka as a whole than in the person who created them." A muscle tugged at the edges of her mouth. "I'll ask one thing of you, Ulthane. Repeat what I've said to Thane Mondom. Ten thousand—simply for you to look at the Trading Families. We can see a time coming when we might need Hoorka. There are movements in human space, Ulthane, tides that are swelling. When these movements end, the Alliance will no longer be the way of the future."

Helgin laughed into the silence that followed her statement. Both Kaethe and Gyll looked at the dwarf. "Nor might be the way of the Families, Kaethe. The safest way is to be a Motsognir and hide on Naglfar. But, Ulthane, you'll find more Motsognir on Trader ships than on Alliance planets. That may tell you something."

"Are the Traders threatening the Alliance?" Gyll asked.

"We always have, implicitly." Oldin shrugged. "And that's

all I can say. But I'll make you another offer, to make the original one more tangible. I'd hoped that the gift of an ippicator would please you, but I've misjudged Neweden on that. No matter, it will die.'' Kaethe waved a hand in dismissal. ''Ulthane, the tale I've heard is that the Hoorka lost two men on Heritage, and that another lies in Center hospital. I've also heard that the Regent d'Embry has refused to allow you to pursue bloodfeud.''

''That's true enough.''

Kaethe nodded. ''I will provide—as a gesture of goodwill— one Hoorka free passage to and from Heritage. What you do there is entirely up to you. The Alliance won't know unless Hoorka tells them, or you're not as adept as I've been led to believe. If you're not, then perhaps I should reconsider the offer anyway.''

''Hoorka don't kill without warning.''

''I know that transmissions have gone back and forth from Diplo Center here to Heritage. Guillene knows that Hoorka wanted the declaration, believe me. Bloodfeud is a Neweden custom, Ulthane. If Moache Mining thought Guillene in any real trouble, they'd pull him offworld, give him a new name and face. The man has no respect for you, or your kin wouldn't have been slain. Moache Mining has no respect for you, or Guillene would be gone. You know what to do on Neweden—you can't say the same anywhere else.''

Quiet. The ippicator's tank burbled. Helgin dug at his bearded chin. Neweden performed a slow somersault in the port.

''Guillene knows what you'd like to do,'' Kaethe continued. ''He just doesn't believe you capable of it.''

''I'll tell Thane Mondom,'' Gyll replied. But he knew what he wanted. He knew that if the decision were his, he'd make the pact now. He'd never liked or trusted d'Embry and the Alliance, but they'd offered the only path for Hoorka's growth. If he were Thane again . . .

Gyll said no more to Kaethe.

When he'd gone, Helgin came back to Kaethe's rooms, shading his eyes against the reborn radiance of the Battier, relishing the lowered gravity. The ippicator's tray was gone.

''He was quiet on the way down,'' Helgin grumbled. ''Pensive and withdrawn. You've confused him, Kaethe.''

''Only for a bit. He'll do it, Helgin. If he has the will I think he has, he'll find a way.''

''No matter what it costs him? Kaethe-dear, you sound as if you're gaining respect for the man—that's unlike you. I don't think you enjoy the idea of what Renard is doing to Neweden, either. Gods, woman, are you growing a conscience?''

Kaethe smiled benignly. ''If I am, Grandsire'll rip it out by the roots when we get back.''

Gyll could see the tension in Mondom from the moment he entered her room. She stood before her desk, a pile of flimsies behind her, an apprentice in front. She dismissed the boy with uncharacteristic gruffness as Gyll came in; when she looked at him, he saw that her face was drawn and haggard, the skin pale.

''You haven't slept,'' he said.

''It shows, neh?'' Mondom managed a wan smile and collapsed onto her bedfield with a sigh. Sitting, legs dangling, she rubbed at her eyes with the heels of her hands. ''I couldn't seem to rest much last night. I kept seeing Aldhelm, that terrible wound; Sartas, too. I didn't want to take a pill, so I just kept tossing until I got up and went to the Cavern of the Dead—made sure the apprentices were doing everything right. Looked at the body for a while. Then I came back here and went over the records—we're not broke yet. You?''

''I managed to sleep. Not too well, though, and not long.''

''You don't look so bad. Did you talk with Oldin?''

''Kaethe? Yah.''

''Kaethe?'' Mondom repeated. ''So you're on a first name basis with her. Is she attractive, Gyll?''

''The Traders like their women chunkier than Neweden.''

''You've never had an offworlder, have you? Have you asked her yet?'' Mondom seemed to find his discomfiture amusing. Her eyes—drawn in lines of blood—laughed at him. Gyll leaned against the wall, watching. ''I'm sorry, Gyll,'' she said at last. ''I couldn't resist teasing you a bit. What did Oldin have to say?''

''I told her that you weren't interested in her offer. She asked us to reconsider. She wants one of us to go with her for a third-standard, and she said she'd pay ten thousand for that, with no other obligations.'' Gyll was careful, slow. Cloth whispered against stone as he shifted.

''Ten thousand just to see the Trader society?''

''To see them, decide whether Hoorka could work with them, and to give them advice on their training.''

Mondom lay back slowly, sighing. She closed her eyes. ''Ten thousand is a lot. But there's nothing to reconsider, Gyll. Not in my opinion. Neweden belongs to the Alliance, and Hoorka to

Neweden. It's *your* dream we're chasing, after all. You should be more vehement about it than me." The eyes opened, found him. "You should know better than any of us that we can't go with the Traders, no matter what they offer."

"She'll ferry a Hoorka to Heritage. With no restrictions, without the Alliance knowing."

"Gyll"—wearily.

"No, Mondom." He levered himself away from the wall, striding over to the bedfield and sitting beside her. He took her hand in his, forcing enthusiasm into his voice. He was surprised at how easily it came. "The Alliance won't know. The Hoorka can go to Heritage, do what's necessary to avenge Sartas and McWilms, and return. The Alliance won't be able to prove that it was us, and we send company to Hag Death for Sartas. The kin already talk, Mondom. You've heard them, and I've been told that it was partially the source of contention between Aldhelm and d'Mannberg. You can settle the dispute. You can also enhance your standing with the kin, especially if *you* are the one that goes."

"If I go?" Her hand moved away from Gyll's, touched his shoulder and trailed down his back. "Gyll, they all know that you were the one talking to Oldin. It'll simply say to them that Ulthane Gyll is still guiding the Hoorka, making sure that Thane Mondom does what's right."

Gyll could hear the pleading in her voice, the cry for his understanding. She wanted him to drop the subject before it created a rift between them. But he couldn't. It had inflamed him since he'd left Oldin. He wanted, and he wouldn't let Hoorka go without it.

"She had an ippicator," he said. "Alive."

"What?" Surprise lanced her voice, dragged her upright on the bedfield. "No ippicators have been seen—"

"A clone, Mondom. Oldin brought it out to show me that the Trading Families were on Neweden long before our ancestors. Some subtle point in her argument, yah? She thinks it demonstrates how the Alliance is just a fleeting organization in comparison to the Families."

Mondom moved on the bedfield, leaning away from Gyll and his fervor. "If Neweden learns that an ippicator has been cloned, then by all our gods, there'll be a jehad—both among the guilds who hold it sacred and toward all offworlders. That's a rank insult to our beliefs, a vile desecration—the ippicators belong to the afterlife. How could Oldin think—"

"She had it killed, after. I watched them put it in the

vaporizing field. She also promised that the tissue sample would be destroyed.''

"And you trust her?"

"Would it do any good if I didn't?"

"Still . . ."

"She simply wanted it as an example. Something to shock us out of complacency. You have to admit that it does that. She meant no insult."

Mondom stood, the bedfield rippling behind her. Gyll got to his feet a moment later. He reached out to touch her, but she drew back, shaking her head.

"Gyll, I love you," she said, "because I like the way you've pursued your dreams and tried to turn them into reality. Because you were so damned sure of yourself. And because when you thought you might have hurt Hoorka, when Aldhelm failed the contract on Gunnar and you had to stop him from breaking the code—well, then you took yourself away from leadership rather than risk harming your dream, your organization. Now you scare me, Gyll."

Light from the room's hoverlamp threw shadows over her face as she looked down at the floor, then up to Gyll. "Why are you suddenly so insistent? Don't you trust me to follow the guild's code? Don't you think that I want what you want—for Hoorka to become stronger and grow? You want to see Hoorka move offworld; it was *your* idea to contact the Alliance to pursue that goal. This damned Trader woman comes, fills your head with more dreams, and suddenly you want to abandon the route you've taken. Gyll, why in hell do you think you can trust her? Why do you think it's worth losing the ground we've gained?"

"I know it is, that's all." He frowned, angered by her anger. "Mondom, she's extending an offer, nothing more. It doesn't interfere with what we have with the Alliance, not yet. We lost nothing. All she asks now is for someone to look at the Trader structure, to bring information back to Hoorka so we can make a judgment. As for the Heritage offer, that's just to indicate the seriousness of her interest, and it's a better offer than you've gotten from d'Embry. The Alliance has done nothing to Guillene. What makes you think we can trust *them*?"

Mondom looked as if she were about to retort. Then the fire seemed to die in her. Her shoulders slumped; she stared down at the hard-packed dirt of the floor.

"Mondom," Gyll said. "I don't want to fight with you." He reached out to pull her to him, but she pushed aside his hands.

She went to her desk and fiddled with the flimsies there before swiveling in her floater to look back at him.

Her chin was up, defiant. Her mouth was a slash of tight lips.

"I'm Thane, Gyll. That title's supposed to give me the authority to control Hoorka's actions." Down, the chin. The lips flexed in a frown. "But the kin still see you as the real leader, despite that. You could undermine my authority in a moment. The kin would back you, almost every one of them—especially now that Sartas and Aldhelm are gone. Do this thing on Heritage if you must, Gyll. I won't try to use the shadow-thanedom you gave me to stop you. I can see the uselessness of that gesture."

She stopped, leaning back. She rubbed her eyes with thumb and forefinger, wearily. "Gyll, you're a frigging selfish person. You only care about yourself. You—made—Hoorka." Mondom lowered her voice in a parody of Gyll's tone. "That's your cry whenever something threatens. You may even be right in this. But I think you're just tired of the inactivity, maybe even tired of being Hoorka and all the killing and death that it brings with it—surely your last contracts have indicated that." She stopped and almost smiled. "You'd rather nurse that damned wort back to health than kill on contract, wouldn't you? You're tired of the slowness of the Alliance, and bored because you've removed yourself from the thaneship."

"That's not true, Mondom." Even to himself, the statement lacked conviction. He said it too softly, too slowly.

"It's not?" Mondom cocked her head. An idle hand rustled sheets on her desk. "This Trader woman's offered you a new challenge, and you're eager to take it—it's something new, another creation for you, neh?"

"I want to avenge Sartas. That's as far ahead as I'm thinking."

"You're sure of that? Then go ahead and do it, because I can't stop you."

"Mondom, if you don't want this, I won't go."

"Maybe you wouldn't, Gyll. Not this time, at least." She yawned suddenly, stretching. "Gods, I'm tired. Gyll, the day would come when you'd find another thing so important to you that you'd do it over my objections. It might as well be now. Go and tell Oldin that you'll go to Heritage. The rest . . . I'll think about it. But remember, Gyll, *you're* the one that will kill Guillene. I'll send no one else. If you don't want to kill, then tell Oldin no."

"You think I don't want the revenge?"

"I think you want the revenge. I'm just not so sure you'll like it." Mondom reached over the desk to press a contact on the wall. Her door opened. Beyond, the dark corridors of Underasgard were loud with kin.

"You're angry with me," Gyll said, but he could find no anger in her face.

"No," she said. Her voice sounded only weary. "But please go now, Gyll. I don't feel like arguing anymore, and I want to try to sleep."

Gyll didn't move. "I could stay . . ."

Mondom rubbed her temple with a hand; she smiled. "Later, perhaps. Gyll, I don't know how you feel right now, but I know I'm not in the mood."

"I won't go to Heritage. All you have to do is say it."

She shook her head. "You say you want it. Just remember this, Gyll. I'm selfish, too. If you try to fight me again, try to go over my authority—"

"I wasn't doing that now."

"Maybe you don't think so. But I'm still warning you, kin to kin, as a friend—I'll fight back next time. Hard, and as nasty as I need to be. Hoorka's been my life—I may not be its creator, like you, but to me, Hoorka is all. I'm Thane, and I intend to be Thane in more than words."

Gyll could find nothing more to say. Mondom leaned back once more, closing her eyes. Gyll walked into the corridor. The door closed behind him with a sinister finality.

The Regent d'Embry was relaxing in her office. A cup of tea steamed aromatically on her desk. The window was polarized black, the room lights were off but for a spotlight on the replica of d'Vellia's soundsculpture. The office was twilight, silent. D'Embry reclined on her floater, eyes closed, trying to forget the tedious drudgery of her day.

A bell chimed in the room. D'Embry groaned, muttering a curse that would have ensured a session with the morality-whip on her long-ago homeworld. "Leave me alone, Karl," she said to the room. "Handle it yourself. Show some initiative." She kept her eyes firmly and defiantly closed.

Again: a shivering of bright sound.

"Huard's cock—"

Her eyes opened. D'Embry groaned upright, took a sip of the cooling tea, and touched a contact that brought her com-unit down from the ceiling niche. The flat screen stared at her.

Another chiming, louder now.

Lips pursed in a scowl, she activated the screen. A wash of greenish illumination flooded the room. "This had better be good, Karl."

A whorling of light-motes resolved itself into a sallow and thin face. "I'm not so sure 'good' describes it, m'Dame, but it's something you'll want to see. Just a moment, and I'll switch you." His voice was high, excited. The screen dissolved into momentary chaos, then settled.

She saw.

Men and women in the uniform of Vingi's guards were moving through Dasta Burrough, a lassari sector. The view was jerky, dim, as if the camera operator was trying to keep his hoverholos near the center of the action but out of sight. The scene horrified d'Embry. The guards were working with quick and brutal efficiency, dragging lassari from their houses and taking them to a waiting flitter bearing the insignia of the Magistrate's Guild. Brutal: the guards used their crowd-prods liberally, without need, for the lassari were unarmed and sleep-confused. Screams punctuated the scenes. One guard (the camera zooming in) used his prod like a club. He swung, striking the head of the man he held by a twist of shirt-cloth. The lassari staggered from the blow, eyes rolling, hands up in futile defense. Blood streamed down the side of his face, soaking into the shirt.

The view suddenly shifted away.

"Karl, what in hell's going on?" D'Embry's voice was taut, her stomach coiled in a knot.

Karl's voice came over the scenes of carnage. "Dasta Burrough, m'Dame. From what I've been able to learn, the Li-Gallant sent his guards in to arrest suspected dissident lassari. He heard that this Renard was living in Dasta. It all happened suddenly—one of the monitor probes just happened to pick it up."

"Get me the Li-Gallant."

"I'm already trying, m'Dame."

A woman came stumbling from a darkened doorway into the street. There, a guardsman was using his crowd-prod on an unresisting man. The woman leapt on the back of the guardsman, beating with balled fists. The guard twisted, throwing the woman to the ground; she fell hard, and the sound of an activated vibroblade hissed in the speakers of the com-unit. The guardsman's arm—luminous vibrotip gleaming in the dark—rose and fell. The woman screamed.

D'Embry, stonily, watched.

Shift. An alley. In a pile of debris, a naked lassari lay. A guardswoman kicked him in the ribs, and the lassari's body shuddered from the impact. He did not otherwise move. A second guard watched, his crowd-prod holstered. Another kick . . .

Shift. A woman, lassari by the clothing, ran down a narrow lane. Her face was frightened, her disheveled hair hung in sweat-damp strands. Two guards ran after her. Then, around the corner ahead of her, three more guards appeared. The woman stopped, trapped, glancing about frantically. The guards laughed as they closed in around her.

Shift. The Li-Gallant. His thick face peered soberly out at d'Embry, a head and shoulder view. He wore a robe with metallic ribbons woven into it—they sparkled in the cloth. Behind him, an animo-painting swirled lazily. "Ahh, Regent d'Embry." He nodded. "I was surprised to receive the call from your staff—you keep late hours, m'Dame."

She had no patience for his amenities. "Li-Gallant"—her voice was trembling with reined anger; she strove to control it—"call off your guards."

His lower lip stuck out, the eyes narrowed. "You've been snooping, m'Dame. But I credit you—your sources are quick."

His uncaring banter drove her to fury. "*Damn* you, man!" she shouted. Her fist struck the desk. China rattled, tea sloshed. "What you're doing is violent and unnecessary. Call them off."

A slow shaking of his head. "What they're doing is *entirely* necessary for the good of all Neweden, Regent. We have a different set of rules here, after all. It demands an approach that varies from the one—"

She wanted to pick up the cup and throw it at the screen. His smugness mocked her. "I'm not calling you to discuss differences between Alliance worlds, Li-Gallant. As representative of Niffleheim, I'm telling you to stop this brutality."

"And I'm telling you"—the Li-Gallant seemed to lean back, as if reclining in a chair. The background focus shifted as the camera kept the face sharp—"that the Alliance has no authority in this. It's purely internal. It affects only Neweden and her people. As Li-Gallant, they are under my authority. This action is condoned by vote of the Assembly. I warn *you*, Regent. If you interfere, I'll lodge a very loud protest with Niffleheim Center. I'll also call for the Neweden Assembly to revoke our agreement with the Alliance. You know I now control the Assembly. I wonder who Niffleheim would back, Regent? You—an old woman obviously exceeding her authority and interfering in the affairs

of this little world? Or me—the governor of that little world,
merely doing as his society dictates?''

Vingi grinned. ''I've nothing more to say to you, Regent
d'Embry. Good night. Enjoy your pictures.''

His face dissolved in a flurry of light.

With a cry of inarticulate frustration, d'Embry picked up her
teacup. She held it in her hand, arm back, then paused. It took
more control than she thought she had, but she brought the arm
back down.

She drank.

The tea was cold.

11

The craft spread vaned fingers to the stars. Neweden wheeled
below, then suddenly behind, a fading ghost.

The bio-pilot chortled, a dribbling of spittle flying from his
lips, and craned his neck to glance at his passengers. ''Shit,'' he
said, noticing the chain of globules floating about him. He closed
his eyes a moment and an exhaust fan began to purr, pulling the
droplets away. The BP leaned back in the skeletal chair, the
umbilical cord of the ship's nervous system trailing from his
spinal sockets. He floated in free fall against the restraint of his
harness, one leg twitching spasmodically.

''Away and gone,'' he said. ''We're home again, Helgin.''

Gyll was impressed by the way Helgin interacted with the BP.
The Hoorka found the jerky, ungainly mannerisms embarrassing;
he did not like looking at the man, and yet he had to force
himself to avoid staring. Before they'd left Oldin's ship, the BP
had turned to find Gyll regarding him with an expression of
distaste; the man had merely smiled, as if used to that reaction.
Now, without the comfort of gravity, Gyll found that *he* was the
bumbler, the one with little coordination, and it bothered him
that the BP seemed to be understanding of Gyll's discomfiture.
Helgin, at least, had not seemed to be distressed by the spastic
motions of the BP. He was at ease, joking, acting much as
normal. Now, with Neweden hidden behind the cowl of their
engines, Helgin loosened his harness and shot across the cabin,
evidently luxuriating in the feel of weightlessness.

''By damn, Illtun, that was a cute maneuver past the Alliance

station. You're sure we weren't monitored? We could still do a
feint toward Longago and give them some misdirection. Siljun's
there; he'd back up our story.''

"Shit. You friggin' dwarves don't trust nobody." Illtun's head
jerked to one side, his left arm moved up, hand clenching, then
down again. "I promise you we weren't seen. Promise. I know
this ship and I know the mass-blinder. We were absolutely
transparent to their detectors."

"You're the pilot." Helgin bounced from a wall (Gyll wondered
how the circuits fixed there managed to continue working after
the abuse) and twisted in mid-cabin to face Gyll. "You like this,
Ulthane?"

Gyll vacillated between politeness and honesty, decided on
compromise. "I'm not sure," he said. He was fighting nausea
that had swept over him when an evasive move had put an
unusual amount of g-stress on the ship and its occupants. Gyll
didn't care for the grin on the dwarf's face—the Motsognir must
know what he felt like.

"I don't think Ulthane Gyll likes me, Helgin," Illtun said.
Gyll, startled, began a quick denial, but Illtun continued over his
protest. "It doesn't really matter, Ulthane. We BPs get fairly
thick skins from all the eyetracks. The ones I *do* mind are the
ones that decide to reshape your face because of their displeasure."

Illtun's face spasmed, a quick blinking of eyes. Gyll decided
that it was another symptom of the restructured nervous system.
He could not understand it any other way.

Helgin, now upside down to Gyll's orientation, frowned a
denial. "Neh, Illtun. The Hoorka isn't scowling at you—he's
just trying to control his stomach. Gods, Gyll, if you can stand
killing, you should be able to take this."

The banter bothered Gyll. He could feel his face redden in
response. Neweden reflexes: his hand strayed closer to the hilt of
his vibro, lost in the folds of his freely floating nightcloak and
further encumbered by the seat harness. "You joke too much,
Helgin," he said darkly, but the dwarf only burst into sudden
laughter.

"Gyll," Helgin said, his voice booming in the small cabin,
"you're a mudballer, a dirt-eater. Your training's been very
good, but it needs altering out here. The nightcloak—it's more
hindrance than help now, isn't it? I could take your weapon from
you, disable you with ease, if you wanted to fight. You have to
learn to quit responding with that damned Neweden pride, at
least in situations where you're at a disadvantage. It's only

because I like you and think you're intelligent enough to change that I say anything. Most world-bound asses aren't worth the effort. Up here, even Illtun—who looks so slow and ungainly under gravity—could do things beyond your abilities."

Illtun smiled, almost shyly, at Gyll. "It's not that tragic, sirrah. I'm quite used to the first-time stares, and I'm used to mudballers. If a BP goes out of the port on most worlds, he risks getting the shit beat out of him. Or worse. There's a lot of prejudice in the Alliance, a lot of blank adherence to their social structure. If you're on the bottom of that structure, it can be difficult."

"The Hoorka were once on the bottom. I changed that."

Illtun shrugged. His foot tapped the deck in erratic rhythm. "It's nice to be able to change things. Me, I work for the Oldins." He reached behind him to touch the umbilical of the ship. "I *am* the ship, out here. I can close my eyes and *be* the ship. No mudballer can match me with that. I kick, and the engines boot us along; flex my fingers, and the vanes swivel to catch the solars. I can be graceful with that metal body, if not my own. Watch," he said.

He closed his eyes—suddenly the port opposite Gyll was dizzy with star-trails, then all settled back again. "The Alliance made me from a nonfunctional being, a neurotic precatatonic, into something that works offworld. I'm grateful to 'em for that. But when they changed the brain stem and flipped the neural responses and fidgeted with my spine, they didn't make us acceptable to the mudballers. We're *still* mental defectives to them; cripples, half-humans. We ain't liked. You get used to it, but you never like it." Then he smiled again and seemed to laugh inwardly. "And I'm sorry for the lecture—it surfaces every once in a while, and you just have to suffer through it. Helgin knows."

Gyll didn't know how to respond. "Hoorka get stares, too. Every time we walk in Sterka."

"Still, your stares are at least veiled in respect," Illtun answered.

"Only because I strove to make it so."

Illtun smiled again. "So you tell me that the BPs need to do something to gain respect, to force it? No, Ulthane, sometimes there is no way to find a niche for yourself, and you have to go search for another place. You were lucky on Neweden. That might not happen anywhere else."

Illtun's good humor took the sting from his words. Gyll could not find it in himself to be angry with the man. As he tried to find a reply, Helgin spoke. The dwarf had one hand around an exposed pipe, his legs dangling in air. He seemed to recline on an invisible cushion. "The Hoorka didn't do well on Heritage."

That brought back the bright spot of anger in Gyll's mind—Guillene. Guillene had insulted Hoorka, and by insulting the guild, had insulted Gyll. The weapon that had killed Sartas had been aimed at all of them. "Hoorka will amend that mistake."

Helgin frowned. "Killing Guillene isn't going to solve anything."

"It will send a companion for Sartas to Hag Death. It will comfort his soul. It will calm my kin's rage."

"It will kill one man and do nothing to change the reasons Sartas was killed. You're too caught up in mythology and fate, Gyll, or at least you play that game."

"It's not a game to Neweden."

"And you'll never learn that Neweden isn't the universe."

Gyll spat his disgust, a guttural oath. "You think words can change—" he began, but a bell chimed on Illtun's console. The BP's head snapped up and he motioned to Helgin to take his seat. "No more useless arguing," Illtun said. "It's jumptime. Settle yourselves. I'll wake you on the other side."

He turned away from them. Deep in the bowels of the ship, thunder began to growl.

Frustration filled Gyll. He wanted to turn to Helgin and give vent to his resentment, to ask why—if Helgin felt this way—he would let Oldin send Hoorka to Heritage. But his head began to spin, as if he were suddenly dizzy. His eyes seemed to no longer work. He was being flailed by strands of pure color, torn by subsonic bellowing that grew ever louder. Gyll moaned, and as a yellow wash of tendrils snaked through the stars outside the port, all went dark.

He was still angry, but his ire had nothing to do with Guillene. Gyll had needed all his skills at silentstalk. There had been only one way into the confines of Park Hill—through the streets of Home. Even in the darkness of early morning, the avenues had not been deserted. He'd kept to the back ways, staying in shadow and simultaneously cursing his nightcloak for adding to the tropical heat and appreciating its dark cover. He was another fragment of night, moving through the grime and squalor of the outer sector. Helgin had urged him to use a light-shunter as additional camouflage or to at least dress like the rest of the populace, but Gyll had declined both options curtly. Dressing as a Heritage native would cause him difficulty once inside Park Hill, and the light-shunter would simply weigh him down. He'd gruffly reminded the Motsognir that Oldin had been willing to trust Hoorka expertise, and that the twentieth code-line stated that all cannot be anticipated: always take what is needed for the known hazards and trust skill and ingenuity for the rest. Extra equipment is extra hazard. Helgin had nodded in slow agreement, and Gyll had taken pleasure in reminding the dwarf that this was one of the code-lines that he and Oldin seemed so intent on having the Hoorka abandon. Helgin had merely bared his teeth in an unamused smile. "They catch you, Gyll, and the Diplos'll throw the Oldins from Alliance trade. Kaethe will find Grandsire FitzEvard manifestly not pleased, and his displeasure is never forgotten."

"It seems a terrible chance to take, then, on something that doesn't directly concern her."

"Don't worry," Helgin had replied. "She thinks she'll get something out of it, or she wouldn't have offered."

He made the transition from Home to Park Hill; filth to ornate cleanliness. He kept near the side of the road, ready to seek a hiding place if threatened, but Park Hill seemed caught in slumber. He pressed on, moving in the shadows.

He thought of Sartas and the torn body that had lain in the Cavern of the Dead: it had not even been recognizable as his kin-brother. And McWilms, still and silent in the antiseptic womb of the med-pad, covered with the crusted scabs of lacerations, the sheets empty where an arm should have been. *Guillene.* If he could keep the fury kindled, if he could see Sartas and McWilms when he stood in front of the man, it would be an easy kill, then. He'd do it gladly. *Another one to the Hag, another to join the dance that you began . . .*

The guards at Guillene's gates were simple: a hypodart of tranquilizer shot from the cover of nearby bushes—though Gyll garnered a few scratches even through his nightcloak; the thorns were sharp. Gyll hurried across the lane to the fallen men. There was a sharp buzzing in his ear, and he checked the snooper at his belt. A diode burned red—the gate was alarmed, and (swinging the snooper in an arc) the top of the fence. It took several seconds for the random field generator of the snooper to find a setting to blind the alarms. Finally, the diode went green and Gyll slipped inside, dragging the guards after him one by one. The gate closed behind him. *Soon, Sartas. Soon.*

Heritage's groundcover was pleasure, quiet and soft, hushing under his slippered feet. There were parts of Neweden where snagglegrass, crackling underfoot, was nearly as effective an alarm system as any electronic device. The snooper remained quiet, and Gyll could sense no other guards on the grounds as he crossed the lawn. It seemed ludicrously easy to him—the rich on Neweden swathed themselves in protection.

The house was dark but for a few windows on the third floor. The structure was built of native stone; it felt warm to his touch, still radiating the fierce heat of the day. Gyll slipped around the house, looking for a side entrance. A door: the snooper shrilled in his ear, and once again Gyll paused to let it find the combination of signals to open the door quietly. He heard the soft click of an inner lock and touched the door's contact. It yawned open. Gyll waited, sheltered in darkness, dartsling ready. No one came to investigate. He slipped inside.

It was quiet and cool. A sweet, smoky aroma hung in the air. He seemed to be in the kitchen; dishes were piled on a sonic washer, ovens lined the wall, a cup of mocha sat on the sideboard. Gyll looked closer at the cup. It steamed, still very hot. Someone was very near, then, or would be returning shortly. Either way, he had to move.

The third floor—he knew that must be the bedrooms. He needed to find the way up. The tense excitement of the hunt gripped him again. His mind clutched at the feeling, willing it to stay.

Gyll moved through a plush landscape. The house was filled with evidence of the company's money. The walls were friezed with animo-screens, all still and quiet now; the furniture was massive and glittering. He could see the umber gloss of malawood, the more expensive red-brown of teak. An old pipichord filled one wall with keyboards, pull-stops, and brass foliage. Lifianstone statues stood in static poses along a hall, a monstrous holotank filled the center of another room, chairs in disarray around it.

He found trouble only once—as he came to the top of the ramp leading to the second floor, he heard a voice just down the hall and the click of an opening door. He had no time—he froze, ready to fire a dart. A man—muscles in Gyll's belly relaxed as he saw that it was not Guillene—chuckled to himself as he entered the hallway. The man didn't look in Gyll's direction. Gyll watched him walk away, entering another door further along. The door shut behind him.

It seemed that Dame Fate watched Gyll. Nothing could go wrong. The feeling bothered Gyll. It all was too easy, too pat. At any moment he expected to be set upon; the back of his neck prickled under the collar of his nightcloak, but when he looked back, he saw nothing.

The snooper shrilled at him as he set foot on the third floor ramp: someone above. Gyll barely had time to move back before he heard footsteps and off-key whistling. Gyll put his back to the wall, dartsling readied. He watched the floor—*he'd told them a hundred times in practice sessions: if you're around a corner, the first part of a person you're likely to see is the foot or a hand. Watch the floor, watch the wall at about waist level—it will give you an extra half-second to react, and it may keep you alive.*

He saw the worn tip of a leather boot and stepped forward, already firing. The man had no chance. The hypodart spat, the man crumpled, and Gyll caught him before he reached the floor, lowering him quietly. He glanced at the face—not Guillene. He moved the man away from the ramp and his escape route, then darted cautiously up the ramp, listening.

Still nothing. This floor was smaller than the others—one large chamber in which he now stood, the far wall glimmering with ice-colors from which a cool breeze emanated. In the middle of the room, floaters were arranged around a large table. Two doors led off the room. The place looked and felt empty, but Gyll had the snooper survey it. Nothing. He went to the nearest door and thumbed the contact. It hissed open.

A kitchen. Gyll left the door open, moving to the next. He touched the contact, feeling the tenseness grip his stomach again. He knew already, before the door opened.

Yes. He looked into a bedroom dimly lit by a shuttered hoverlamp. On a bedfield of rumpled sheets, a man and a woman slept. As Gyll stepped into the room, the woman woke, staring at him with startled, sleep-rimmed eyes, her mouth just opening in the beginning of a query. She knuckled at her eyes, sitting up, pulling the sheet over her breasts.

The dart hit her then. The mouth closed, suddenly, and she fell back. Gyll let the door shut behind him and moved to the bed, but the man didn't awaken. He opened the shutters on the hoverlamp, letting the light fall on the man's face. A smear of wetness trailed from the mouth; he smiled in his dreams.

Guillene.

Gyll stared at him, assessing the man who had killed Sartas. *About my age, and that body hasn't seen much work. If he's cruel, it's a mental cruelty, and others do the work for him.*

Sartas, I hope you enjoy his company. Make him your slave before the Hag.

He let the snooper check the room, found two alarms and deactivated them. Then he pocketed the dartsling and slid his vibro from its sheath. He activated the weapon; the luminous tip darted out, trailing the wire. Its growl filled the room and woke Guillene.

The man turned in his sleep, moaning, and his eyes opened —blue-green, with flecks of brown. He saw Gyll. Guillene bolted upright, the bedfield rippling. The woman jounced with it, oblivious.

"Who the hell are you? Where is Cianta? I told him to . . ." Guillene seemed to see the vibro in Gyll's hand for the first time, and his voice faded to whisper. He glanced at the drugged woman slack-jawed beside him. "Mara?" he said. He did not touch her.

"She won't wake."

"You killed her?" For the first time, genuine fright showed in him; he looked as if he were about to scream. He slid away from the woman, as if the fact that she might be dead and that close to him frightened him more than the rest. Gyll knew then that he'd never had to see the results of his orders, never had to deal with the mess.

"She's done nothing to Hoorka," Gyll answered. "She's not dead. We don't kill the innocent if it can be helped." When Gyll named the Hoorka, Guillene had gasped, an involuntary intake of breath. He looked as if he were about to shout. Gyll put the vibro near his throat. "Don't yell, man. No one in the house will hear you; they're all like her."

"If you want valuables . . ."

"I simply wanted for you to be awake, so you can tell the Hag who was responsible." The vibro moved, menacing. Guillene leaned as far back from Gyll as the bedfield allowed. The sour odor of urine suddenly filled Gyll's nostrils. He looked down to see the sheets wet at Guillene's waist. His nose wrinkled in disgust.

"I can give you money, Hoorka. Far more than the contract." Guillene seemed not to notice that he had fouled himself. His voice was pitched high, he spoke too fast. "I'm worth nothing to you dead. Let me live, and I'll enrich your organization. It will do you more good in the long run."

Gyll didn't want to argue with the man. He tried to force himself into anger, and found that it had gone. "You're a poor trade for Sartas, man,'' he said. ''You don't deserve the quick death of the knife.'' *And words make a poor substitute for action. Remember Sartas; remember McWilms's face, the empty sleeve.* ''Dame Fate must want you. She made it easy for me.''

''Kill me, and nothing changes, Hoorka. It doesn't alter this world in the least. Moache will send someone else.''

''I don't care about this world.''

''They'll know who did this, Hoorka. The Alliance will seek your people out, because Moache will want them to do it. You can't hide your presence, and you'll just destroy your guild—that's the price of using your weapon.'' Guillene pressed his back against the wall. The dampened sheets dragged at him. He looked down at the vibro, not at Gyll, his chin pressing against his neck.

''Sartas's honor demands it.'' The scarlet rage had not left entirely. It was still there, masked by his disgust/pity for Guillene. He nurtured it in his mind as he would nurse a spark on tinder, willing it to grow, to leap into burning—to make the vibro move. *Stop the talk, man. Do what you wanted to do, what you told Mondom you must do.* ''This is for the Hoorka you killed and the apprentice you maimed. Tell Hag Death that Ulthane Gyll sent you to Her.''

''You don't even know that I did this.''

The man's bravado took Gyll aback. He let the vibro move away and heard the trembling breath of Guillene. ''Who else?'' Gyll spat. ''You'd go to the gods with a lie on your tongue?''

''Hoorka,'' Guillene said. His voice trembled. ''Your people killed de Sezimbra. His people would have had more reason for revenge.''

''*You* killed de Sezimbra. Not Hoorka.'' But the vibro didn't move.

Guillene seemed to take hope. The chin rose, the eyes met Gyll's for an instant, as if in a plea, but the voice was stronger. ''Hoorka, I give you my word. I'll spend what I have to and find the guilty ones, drag them to you with their confessions.''

Gyll knew the man lied. He could feel it in the words. He summoned up the image of Sartas's body. *That's what those lies bring,* he told himself.

Guillene still spoke, as if the voice could stop the thrust of vibro. ''Hoorka, things don't work the same on other worlds. You can't expect us to do as you would. Gods, man, if you Hoorka haven't learned that, then you're all fo—'' Guillene stopped. His eyes widened.

"Fools!" Rage flared, finally. "Is that what you say, man?"

The vibrotip circled before Guillene's face.

"Hoorka, please, you can't—"

"Insult Hoorka, and you insult me."

"You must understand—"

"Strike at Hoorka, and you've struck at me."

The vibro keened hungrily. Gyll's hand lunged forward, slashing across the throat.

The body fell sidewise, hung on the edge of the bedfield for a moment, then slid softly to the floor.

Staring down at Guillene, Gyll searched for the satisfaction he should feel in the death, the gratification. He felt very little. He went to the bed, grasped the woman under shoulders and knees and took her into the larger room. She would wake there—away from the blood-spattered bedroom and the stiffening corpse.

Then, frowning, he made his way from the house.

Aldhelm's body had lain the proscribed ten days in the Cavern of the Dead. Each day, as the sunstar touched the dawnrock with morning, an apprentice had added a scented log to the pile of wood that held the body, first anointing the log with the blood of kin. Ulthane Gyll, Thane Mondom, d'Mannberg, Bachier, and Serita had done the blood service—the first five days from a cut on the left hand, the second from the right. Chips of ippicator bone had been placed over the open eyes. Aldhelm's nightcloak had been pressed, the hem rewoven with gilt.

Now, as the dawnrock noted the passing of light, the Hoorka gathered. First came the jussar applicants with cloaks of red, then the apprentices with the normal black and gray uniform adorned by a scarlet sleeve, and finally the full kin. Their footsteps echoed among the stones. Glowtorches guttered fitfully in the hands of every tenth Hoorka, the erratic light throwing mad shadows to the roof. All passed once around the pyre, intoning the kin's chant to Hag Death. Cranmer, on a ledge above and to one side, busied himself recording the ceremony. The Hoorka rustled to a halt, arrayed before the pyre.

Gyll was moody, tired. He'd arrived at Sterka Port only a few hours before, with time only to plunge his vibro into ground near the dawnrock and then ready himself for Aldhelm's funeral. He had not been able to talk to Mondom, to tell her that Guillene was dead. Now he sat on the ground next to her, staring at the pyre and its silent burden, feeling the chill of Underasgard against his flesh. The scent of oil was heavy in the cavern,

mingling with the pungency of spices. Flame crackled beside
him as an apprentice came up and handed Mondom a torch. Gyll
glanced at Mondom. She seemed to feel the pressure of his gaze
and turned, smiling wanly. He touched her hand, almost as cool
as the rock it rested on. Her fingers interlaced his and pressed
gently. "I'm glad you're back in time," she said.

"It took longer than Helgin had thought. It wouldn't have
mattered. You're Thane. It's your task to see Aldhelm's rite done
properly."

"Still, this is better." The erratic torchlight made her face
waver, as if crossed by some unguessed emotion. She moved her
hand away, staring again at the pyre. "It's done, then?"

"Guillene's with the Hag."

"Have you told the kin?"

"Tomorrow. Tonight is for Aldhelm."

She only nodded, solemn. Smoke from her torch watered
Gyll's eyes. He leaned away from her.

*The torch Inglis held stank in Gyll's nostrils—or perhaps it
was Inglis himself. Gyll had found the cave system after an old
and drunken lassari had babbled of it in Sterka. He'd taken
Inglis with him to explore it. The caves, in Gyll's mind, might
make an excellent base for the group of lassari and jussar he'd
joined: thieves and murderers hiding from the wrath of the
Li-Gallant Perrin. Gyll had ideas for them—they had begun to
listen, grudgingly. Now Inglis stumbled over the broken floor of
the cavern and the torch came dangerously near Gyll's clothing.*

"Damn it, man. Watch where you're stepping."

*Inglis reared about, the torch whuffing through air. "Shut your
friggin' mouth, Gyll. Just because you've managed to get the
rest of 'em to listen don't mean you can order me around. Try
that again, and I'll shove this friggin' torch down your throat."*

*Gyll knew that the confrontation between he and Inglis had
been coming. The man had been undermining Gyll's growing
influence with the lassari band. Inglis had been one of the
leaders, ruling by grace of his size and feared brutality. Gyll
preferred to lead through discipline and intelligence, but these
were not traits Inglis understood or appreciated. The lassari had
been waiting to see which was the way of the future. Gyll could
think of no better place to settle it—the dark caverns, the rest of
the band waiting by the jagged mouth.*

*"Inglis," he said, wearily. "You've seen me fight—if you still
think you're better, then you're nothing but a fool."*

Inglis cursed and charged. The caverns echoed with their

conflict—it was short. Inglis knew only one tactic—a bearlike charge, a straightforward attack. Gyll dodged the first blow of Inglis's large fist, kicking the man as he lunged. As Inglis bent over in sudden agony, Gyll hammered at his neck with coupled hands. Inglis moaned, but did not go down. Gyll hit him again, and the man crumpled to the stones. Rock clunked dully under him, the torch guttered nearby.

In a few moments, Inglis groaned to his knees, as Gyll watched.

"Enough?" Gyll asked.

For his reply, Inglis yanked the dagger from his belt and charged once more. This time, Gyll had to break his arm. He picked up the dagger from the stones, held it at Inglis's throat from behind, one hand holding the chin up. The others of the band had by this time heard the fighting and entered. They stood around them like shadows, watching in silence.

"Enough?" Gyll asked again.

"You can beat me now, bastard, but I'll find you sometime," Inglis muttered through his teeth. He reached behind for Gyll, unwilling to yield.

Gyll pulled the dagger deep. Lifeblood splashed on the stones.

It was the first conflict in Underasgard betwen the lassari that would become the Hoorka.

Mondom had risen, handing the torch to Serita Iduna, who stood beside the pyre. From under her nightcloak, Mondom took out a dagger in a jeweled sheath—the Hoorka death-blade. It had once been a plain weapon, but now the blade was silvered, the hilt shone. She ascended the pyre—a rude stairway had been made in the logs—finally kneeling beside the body. Torchlight shone in her eyes; Gyll could see the tears gathered at the corners. He envied Mondom her grief. Searching inside himself, he felt very little. He could make excuses—he was still buoyed by the adrenaline of the Heritage trip, tired from the long day, but no . . . He'd tried to summon up the sorrow that he should feel, that he knew he *must* feel somewhere inside, but it had hidden itself. Yes, he felt emptiness, but that was an intellectual sensation. Mondom's bereavement was genuine. Gyll wondered what was wrong with himself.

Mondom lifted the dagger and kissed the blade, tears shining behind the bright metal. She touched the flat of the blade to Aldhelm's lips, then (her mouth taut, eyes half-closed and forcing the tears from under the lids) she plunged the dagger into Aldhelm's breast.

A sigh came from the massed kin.

Still kneeling, she let go the weapon. Hands at her sides, she began the invocation of She of the Five Limbs. The yellow-white hilt caught the torchlight. It shone, lustrous.

The sunstar was in Gyll's eyes—a bad position, but he couldn't move without making it obvious that he expected a fight. Kryll spat on the ground at Gyll's feet. "You can't do this, boy. I won't let you."

Gyll widened his stance, waiting. "No one can tell me what I can or can't do. If you people don't listen to me, we're going to stay lassari shit. I can make us guilded kin, but you're going to have to do things by my code."

Kryll laughed—yellowed teeth, cracked lips. "Man, you're a frigging idiot. Oh, a good fighter, I'll admit that, but you're a dreamer first. I've killed five men, two of 'em guilded kin. It may not have made me rich, but I'm better off than those idiots just dying in Dasta. We're comfortable out here, away from Sterka. Keep your damned stupidities to yourself."

"Kryll, if I have to kill you to get what I want, I'll do it. The Li-Gallant's guards'll even pay me for the body, neh?"

Kryll laughed again. He pulled an ugly, battered crowd-prod from the belt-loop at his waist. Gyll had seen him use it before. The prod had been altered, the limiting circuits taken out. It used the full charge of the battery with a touch. It charred the flesh, perhaps even killed. Kryll waved the weapon at Gyll. "You bother me too much, boy. C'mere, and I'll teach you what happens to lassari with dreams."

But quite another lesson was taught, and Kryll was not the professor but the student.

Mondom took the dagger from Aldhelm's breast and sheathed it again. She reached over the body and took the bone chips from the eyes. Though the body was too high-placed for him to see, Gyll knew that the eyes would be open, allowing the *j'nath,* the essence of the soul that is left behind when breath departs, to exit when the flames released it. Summoned by the invocation, She of the Five would take the *j'nath* and incorporate it into Herself. The ippicator chips were placed in Aldhelm's hands, an offering. Mondom bowed her head, rising to her feet. Spreading her arms wide, she intoned the benediction.

"Our brother Aldhelm goes to join She of the Five Limbs. Let all kin give praise."

With the others, Gyll repeated the response. "Let all give praise." The phrase echoed through the cavern.

"He will give Her the love of kin."

"Let all give praise."

"He will intercede with Her for Hoorka."

"Let all give praise."

The litany continued, phrase and response, for several minutes. Then Mondom lowered her hands. She bowed deeply to the body of Aldhelm and descended the pyre.

That kind of conversation always seemed to happen after lovemaking.

Darnell had cradled her head in his shoulder, sighing. Tangled, faintly damp hair sprawled his chest; the chill air of Underasgard cooled the sweat on his body. Gyll touched the headboard—covers obediently slid over them. "Thank you," Darnell said. She snuggled closer. "That's much better."

Gyll hmmmed agreement.

"I saw the uniforms. They're dark and somber." Her voice was sleepy, lazy. "You think they'll make much difference, Thane?"

"Yes." He was emphatic. His fingers kneaded her smooth-muscled back. "They'll give us an identity, a unity. I think it'll draw us closer, probably closer than the kin of most guilds."

"Some of the others don't like the fact that you didn't consult the rest before you made the decision."

"It was my decision to make. You have to grasp for what you think is right—whether it actually is or not—or you'll lose the leadership."

"And if the decision's wrong?"

"It doesn't matter. It's all in the act itself. You have to do what you think is right, regardless of consequences. Otherwise, you lose the respect of the rest; more importantly, you'll probably lose your respect for yourself. And that's worse."

"You sound as if you've thought out all the answers."

"I have. I'm Thane. I intend to stay Thane." He lay back, hand under head, relaxing. It was all going so well. Li-Gallant Perrin hadn't been able to ignore their application for guild status: the future of Hoorka would come to a vote in the Assembly within one phase of Sleipnir, and Gyll had talked with several of the rule-guild heads. It looked hopeful. He pulled Darnell closer, smiling. Yah, very well. He rested, content.

Serita handed the torch back to Mondom. The flame dimmed, then flared. Shadows slid over Mondom's face. She looked at Gyll. "Ulthane," she said, "will you send Aldhelm on? I think he would prefer it."

Gyll nodded, rising to his feet. He shook sooty dirt from his nightcloak and walked over to Mondom, taking the torch from her. He wanted to hug her—the face was so tragic, so hurt. Tears had left faint tracks on her cheeks. Mondom stepped away from him, going to join the silent kin; Gyll turned to the pyre. The aroma of sandalwood and oil was heavy. He looked up at the body. "Aldhelm"—a whisper—"I wouldn't have it this way. I'm sorry. I wish we could have remained friends, kin-brother."

He touched the flame to the base of the pyre. Nothing happened for a moment, then a small flame appeared, wavered, and surged. Crackling, hissing; the fire leaped from log to log, climbing. The buffeting heat drove Gyll back while the eternal night of Underasgard was banished from the cavern. The smell of smoke and oil filled the room. Gyll knew that the dark cloud of Aldhelm's funeral would now be rising from the vents of natural chimneys in the room, a fuming from the slopes above Underasgard's mouth. The wind would smear the soot and ash across the sky.

In reverse order of their entrance, the Hoorka filed from the room. Gyll, standing beside Mondom, touched her arm. She smiled sadly at him; Gyll pulled her to him with one arm. She touched her head to his shoulder. Through the pall of smoke, Gyll could see Cranmer—coughing and sneezing—getting ready to vacate his perch.

Their turn came. Gyll squeezed Mondom, then walked ahead of her from the Cavern of the Dead. At their backs, logs collapsed in on each other. A frantic gathering of sparks danced their way to the roof.

12

An excerpt from the acousidots of Sondall-Cadhurst Cranmer. The following transcript is from one of the earliest recordings of the Hoorka dots. The subject, Redac Allin, was one of the original Hoorka, a member of the lassari thugs taken by the young Gyll Hermond. The dot was quoted by Cranmer in the first treatise on the Hoorka, Social Homogenization: The Hoorka in Neweden Society. *(Niffleheim Journal of Archeo-Sociology,* Marcus 245, *pp.1389–1457.) Cranmer, in his notes, recorded that he wished to do a later full-holo interview with Allin, but the man*

*was slain a few weeks later during a contract. His passing was
not particularly mourned, even by the Hoorka-kin.*

EXCERPT FROM THE DOT OF 11.16.211:

"Sirrah Allin, you were one of the original Hoorka."

"Yah. I can remember when Gyll—the Thane—came to us."

"What did the band do before the Thane organized you as a
guild?"

"I did the same's I did after. I killed. Only difference was that
I didn't take the person's money. Sometimes the old way was
better—we didn't need no contract."

"But you were lassari then. Isn't the kinship better?"

"Yah, I suppose. Ain't much choice when you're lassari:
steal, do the shitwork kin throw at you, or starve. Good choices,
neh? I stole. Got more that way, got to stick knives in kin."

"You didn't have to kill, did you? I mean, there was no
compelling reason for you to do so. From what I understand,
most of your band refrained from that, if for no other reason than
the fact that the guilded kin pursue murderers far more than
thieves. You were an exception."

"The ones the Hag eats don't talk. That's how half the suckers
get caught and lose their hands. Killing keeps 'em quiet. It's
safer to kill."

"Did you enjoy it, find it pleasurable?"

(A longish pause.) "You look at me like I'm some kind of
specimen, scholar."

"I meant no offense. I'm interested in your feelings. I've
heard it said that you don't find your task as Hoorka at all, ahh,
distasteful."

"You could find out. I'd arrange a demonstration for you. The
Thane could get other scholars later."

(There is a nervous rustling of flimsies. Cranmer clears his
throat.) "Ahh, that won't be necessary."

"Too bad. I tell you, scholar, I don't mind the killing. Not at
all. People will go to the Hag anyway—maybe she'll like me
better when my time comes, neh? After all, I send her so
many . . . It's better now, with the run. It gives it a thrill, like a
hunt. The bastards might get away from you unless you're
careful, if you ain't good. The killing, the last part—I don't
mind it at all. Does that bother you, little man?"

"No." *(A remark that might be made here—Cranmer was
never known as a man given to foolish bravery. Given that, his
following remarks can only be attributed to errant imprudence.)*

"But some might think that it's an indication of some, ahh, mental misalignment. The Alliance—well, if you were on Niffleheim, you'd've been wiped."

"Ain't on Niffleheim, are we? And on Neweden, you can't insult kin and expect to be untouched."

"It wasn't an insult. It was just a statement."

"So I'm not even smart enough to know the difference? Scholar, you wag your tongue too much. Let me take it out for you."

(The next few minutes on the dot are quite confused. There is a scuffling of feet, chairs clatter to stone, and Cranmer shouts for the Thane. There is the sound of a struggle, a yelp in pain in Cranmer's voice, and a muffled exclamation. The recorder is—possibly—knocked to the ground, for the next sound is Cranmer.)

"Hello? Oh, good. It still words. Thank you, Thane. I . . . well . . ."

"You're not much of a fighter, Sond. You'd better get that cut seen to. Allin, you'll apologize to Cranmer, and you'll keep your temper in Underasgard."

"Your scholar insulted me, Thane. I had the right—"

"The scholar's not from Neweden. He doesn't yet understand us. Man, do I have to treat you like a child? Go to my rooms and wait for me." (The sound of the door opening and closing.)

"Thane, I didn't mean to cause trouble. I should have been more careful in what I said to him."

"We all have to learn, Sond. But I'd suggest you learn Neweden ways or learn to fight. Preferably both."

"Karl, get Oldin. Now."

"Surely, m'Dame, but it will take a few minutes."

"Just do it."

D'Embry quivered with fury. She could not stop the trembling of the thin hand she held out in front of her. Muttering a curse, she gave up the effort.

Damn that scheming bitch!

She wanted no more calls like the last. It had come from Diplo Center on Heritage. Heritage's Regent, Kav Long (she remembered him as a vaguely competent secretary doing menial tasks when she'd last visited Niffleheim) had been curt and scornful.

"I thought you had Neweden under control, d'Embry," Long had said, with no preamble.

"I do." She'd been puzzled and irritated with the morning's interruption.

Long had laughed without amusement, his face creased by static—the transmission was none too good; something in the Einsteinian jump always did that. "Guillene was killed last night, d'Embry. It couldn't have been more than one or two assassins. They entered Moache grounds, disabled several guards and the household staff, and killed the man in his bed. Very neatly: the throat was slit. He was dead too damn long before we got there, too—the brain'd deteriorated beyond the point of saving. Some of your frigging assassins got loose." The blond face quavered, lost in electronic storming.

She had protested, but the vague suspicion that Long was right already had formed in her mind. "That's impossible. Listen, you young fool, the Hoorka haven't any craft capable of it, and Sterka Port is tight—I can guarantee that. Guillene wasn't exactly loved by the Moache employees or by de Sezimbra's associates, was he? I'd suggest you look closer to home, Long. You can get assassins on any world."

He'd exhaled in disgust. "I'll admit that. I'll admit that vibros are common enough, too, but let's be realistic. It wasn't anybody here—none of them would be that good. That leaves your black and gray wonders. Moache Mining is upset." He laughed nervously, and d'Embry realized at that instant where his anger originated. "Hell, they're a lot more than just upset. They've already bypassed the Center here and gone straight to Niffleheim. You know they're going to listen there. Moache's got the money to make 'em do it. You goofed, m'Dame. Niffleheim'll have your head." A pause, a snarling of static. "Mine, too."

Kav Long cut the contact.

Oldin. It had to be through Oldin.

"M'Dame, I have Oldin."

"Good," she snapped. "Karl, I want you to go through the records of all the satellite net stations. See if you can find the slightest indication that a Trader craft might have left Neweden space. And do it quickly."

"Yah, m'Dame."

D'Embry took a deep breath, running her hands through her thin, white hair. She settled herself in her floater, arranged the ippicator necklace on her blouse. A vein-laced hand reached out, touched the contact on her desk.

The screen of the com-link pulsed light and settled. Kaethe Oldin smiled beatifically out at her. Oldin's eyebrows were today slivers of platinum, shimmering. Half the face was in cosmetic shadow. The glossed mouth moved. "M'Dame d'Embry, what can I do for you?"

"You sent a Hoorka to Heritage, Trader Oldin. You allowed Guillene to be killed."

Eyebrows, glittering, rose in surprise. Her head half-turned, but the gaze was fixed on d'Embry. "That would be a violation of the Trader-Alliance pact, Regent. Certainly you don't think me stupid enough to ruin my business here by running a ferry service for assassins? The Hoorka can hire Alliance vessels, and Grandsire FitzEvard would have my head if I lost revenue."

"Let's not play games, Trader Oldin." *She's good at it—just the right expressions, the correct stance between indignant surprise and amusement. If I didn't know it had to be her . . .* "I'm awfully tired of games."

"Games, Regent? Are you making a formal accusation, then? If so, I demand my right to refute the 'proof' of misconduct." Again, the smile, infuriating. "If you're not making the accusation, then I think you're mistaken as to who's playing a game."

D'Embry forced down a retort: she breathed once, slowly, knotting her hands together. "Trader Oldin, the Hoorka have no interstellar craft. No Alliance-registered ships have gone to Heritage in the last few days—I've checked. You are the only possibility left."

"Has the orbital net noted one of the boats from *Peregrine* leaving for anywhere but Sterka Port?"

"No," d'Embry admitted ruefully. "But what one person can design, another can find a way around. Believe me, Trader, I've no delusions as to your capabilities."

"I thank you for the compliment, m'Dame, but I still suggest you owe me an apology." Oldin said it sweetly, a sugared voice.

"Ulthane Gyll has been to *Peregrine,* Trader. The first time was only for a few hours. He went again two days ago; he didn't return until yesterday evening."

"That constitutes no crime, Regent. As you know, I've used the Hoorka myself. I wanted Ulthane Gyll to see the ship, to see the goods we had. Then I asked him to stay overnight. He was kind enough to accept my offer. I find him quite charming, actually."

"Trader Oldin, this is a serious matter." D'Embry's voice was rising. She forced herself back into the icy demeanor she affected before her staff. *Calm, calm. You're falling right into the bitch's hands. That's exactly what she wants from you—anger and the loss of control. She's most likely recording the conversation.*

"I realize that you consider the situation serious, Regent. Is Moache Mining putting pressure on you? I would wager that Niffleheim called and wanted a scapegoat produced to drag before the Directors, and it's your job to find one or be used yourself. I can understand your anxiety to place the blame on the Trading Families, m'Dame. I'd be doing the same were I in your position. People have spat on us for centuries: the Alliance, the Free Worlds, Huard. Why change now—we're convenient gypsies, there and gone again."

"You plead your case eloquently, Trader. One would think you've given it much thought. Did you know you'd need to defend yourself?" She wanted Oldin, wanted that ship out of Neweden space.

"What of the other guilds, m'Dame?" Oldin continued as if she hadn't heard d'Embry. "Some of them are rich enough to have bought or hired the needed ship—silence can be bought, too. Maybe they ferried Hoorka in hopes of future favors. Or maybe one of your Alliance ships logged a false destination code. Or maybe Guillene was killed by one of his own." Behind Oldin, some out-of-focus person bustled past, carrying something that looked halfway between snail and dog. Oldin glanced at him, snapped an unheard order, then turned back to d'Embry. "My log is available to you, Regent. Call and ask for our pilot or the Motsognir Helgin. We can send it to you within a day or so."

"I *do* want that log, Trader. I can tell you that now. I want it by noon."

"Regent, it will take—"

"Noon, Trader. A failure to comply will indicate that you are not willing to cooperate with the local authority. That can result in your expulsion from Neweden space. That's in the pact, too." D'Embry allowed herself to enjoy the look of irritation that crossed Oldin's face, wiping away the smug half-smile. The Regent was certain that the log would show exactly what Oldin intended it to say, even with the lack of notice: there would be no record of a *Peregrine* boat leaving Neweden orbit. D'Embry wouldn't prove anything, but if it caused Oldin *any* discomfiture, she found it worthwhile. Somewhere inside, a small voice chastised her—*you're getting petty, old woman, hurting back because you've been hurt.* And the answer: *yah, doesn't it feel good?*

Oldin seemed to begin a statement, then swallowed the word

with a twitch of her mouth. She stared at d'Embry. "Regent, I protest—"

"You may protest as much as you like," d'Embry said. "As Regent, I'll give your protestations the attention they deserve. Just be sure that your log reaches me in the next few hours. By noon. That's all, Trader Oldin."

With a sense of childish enjoyment, d'Embry snapped the contact. The petulant face of Oldin disappeared in static. The screen went black.

Ulthane Gyll looked at the silent, expectant faces around him and put a foot up on the stool's seat. Most of the full kin were there, seated or standing around the table. Only Thane Mondom was absent. That caused him pain. She'd said that she would not come—*this is your show,* she'd told him, *not mine. It's not pettiness on my part, Gyll. But I didn't want it. Not the way it was done.* He had tried to convince himself that her absence would not make a difference.

"Guillene is dead," he said simply, without preamble. "I killed him. She of the Five has fed on his blood."

Gyll was surprised at the amount of satisfaction he heard in his voice. He'd not thought he would feel that way; it had taken him so much effort to will the blade to move. But now that it was done . . .

The kin said nothing for a long moment, though Gyll could see smiles on some of the faces, nods of pleased relief. The debt to a kin-brother was settled. Serita said it for them all, a throaty few words, half-whispered. "Good. Then it's over."

"Did he die easily, Ulthane," d'Mannberg asked.

Gyll shrugged. "He died," he said.

D'Mannberg's thick hands clenched. "He knew it was Hoorka?"

"I knew that he'd been informed of the bloodfeud, and I didn't kill from hiding. He was awake. He knew."

"And who gave you the ride?" Bachier, down the table. "Certainly not the Regent?"

"Neh." *Certainly not, and it's why Mondom was wrong in this. The Regent would never have let her do it.* "I talked to Trader Oldin—it was due to her generosity. And that's not information to go outside the kin, either. Nor is this: I've talked to Oldin about other possibilities for Hoorka." He didn't know why he said that; he'd not intended to discuss Oldin's offering publicly, not until he and Mondom had arrived at a decision. He pulled his nightcloak around him, wondering if it hadn't been a mistake.

"Offworld?" Serita's voice held a cautious note, a negative query that puzzled Gyll. "The offworld contracts have caused us nothing but trouble, Ulthane. Maybe Hoorka should stay on Neweden, where we're understood." She looked at him with steady green eyes.

Her words doubly startled Gyll; they were identical to the argument Aldhelm had given him. *Is Aldhelm coming back to haunt me, like the rest of the dead ones that get in my dreams?* "Hoorka must expand," he began, automatically. "That had always been my intent. Neweden was to be our beginning, our home, but never the totality of our existence. That's Thane Mondom's feelings, too."

"We know that, Ulthane. Most of us agreed with you." Bachier again. He shifted in his seat, nervously. "We probably still do, to an extent. But Sartas and McWilms . . . The situation has made *me* think it over again, I know. We've enough problems right here on Neweden: the Li-Gallant and Gunnar, the lassari killing Eorl and bothering all guilded kin." Bachier shook his head. "I'm not saying anything definite, Ulthane. But *maybe* we should ask ourselves whether Neweden should be enough for us. Maybe we should postpone our dreams for a while and make sure we're stable here."

Others about the room nodded. A murmur of agreement rumbled around the table.

Gyll pulled back suddenly, the boot that had been on the stool stamping earth. The nightcloak swirled. He could feel anger building inside him and he wanted to leave, before it burst out in front of kin. "That's a damned poor way of thinking." As he watched, Bachier's face went scarlet. *Careful, you fool.* "I'm sorry, Bachier, but I can't agree with that at all. *I* would not be satisfied with Neweden. I expected us to go offworld one day, even though the code was designed for this world. Opportunities await us—we shouldn't be afraid to grasp at them."

"It's not that we're being fearful laggards." D'Mannberg's booming voice pulled Gyll's head around. "And we're not trying to change Hoorka policy. We're just asking if maybe the time isn't right."

"To the Hag with time!" Gyll shouted the words. He strode to the far wall of the cavern, turning on his toes to face them again. "If we do that, Sartas has died for nothing, and McWilms is suffering for a whim. Are you all so afraid of the Hag that you'd cocoon yourselves on this one world?''

"Ulthane—'' d'Mannberg began.

"No! Listen to me.'' Gyll halted the protest with a raised forefinger. "We have to be able to admit mistakes. That much I can agree with. The Alliance may not be the best way for us to pursue our goals. Maybe we need to examine client worlds more carefully. But Hoorka *will* go offworld. Through the Regent or some other way. We aspire, or we die. I won't see the Hoorka become like the ippicator.''

"We can understand how you feel,'' Serita said.

"Can you? Damn it, I *made* Hoorka. I killed to be sure it was molded the way I wanted it to be. I fought the prejudices of Neweden for it. I gave up the thaneship, but Hoorka is still my creation. I won't see it die. And to stay on Neweden is to accept a slow death.''

Gyll strode to the mouth of the cavern. He looked back at the assassins. "I won't have it,'' he said.

13

Gyll couldn't decipher Mondom's mood. She seemed caught on some intangible interface between frantic gaiety and quiet moodiness. Something worked at the muscles of her drawn face—a pensiveness he couldn't understand.

She was sitting at her desk floater when he entered the room, intent on the flimsies there, a hoverlamp casting a dark image of her head on the cavern wall. She looked up at the sound of the door. Seeing Gyll, she smiled with an odd enthusiasm. She rose and went to him, taking his hands. "Well, Gyll?''

"I told them,'' he said. He didn't return the pressure of her hands. She held them a moment longer, then went to the bedfield and sat. She patted the covers. "Here. Sit with me.''

It was the opening he needed, he thought as he sat beside her. A chance to explain his feelings, to vent all the uncertainties and come to a final understanding. He no longer wanted to go on the way they had, always circling each other and never settling anything. He sat, trying to find a beginning. "The reaction was odd, Mondom. They didn't say what I thought would be said.''

"McWilms is coming back to the caverns,'' she said, interrupting

him. Her eyes were wide, too wide, as if she were frightened.
Still, the voice was calm and steady. "They'll release him
tomorrow. I talked with him over the com. He'll still need a
portable med-pack, and it'll be some time before the arm bud
grows well enough for him to begin using it, but he's anxious to
be in Underasgard again. He wanted to talk to you, Gyll. He
wants to know about Guillene, how it happened, everything."

"He knows the man's dead, doesn't he?"

"Yah, but he wants it told to him, in all the detail. He's very
bitter, Gyll, very angry." She picked at the cloth of the bedsheet,
then smoothed it down again.

"Does he blame Hoorka, like the rest? Does he think it was
all a tragic mistake?" He couldn't keep his own spite from his
voice.

"No." Her eyes questioned him. "He's very anxious for his
initiation into full kinship, if that's what you mean. He doesn't
blame Hoorka for what happened. What he is angry about is the
Alliance, the way they handled it."

"Oldin told me that they wouldn't handle it well."

Mondom broke in hurriedly, before he could say more. Gyll
could see the nervous smile, the restless eyes, the quick movements of her hands. Though he let her talk, he knew it to be an
avoidance. *Oldin's the key—that's the subject she's steering you
around. She doesn't want to argue. But it will just be harder
later.* "Well, McWilms doesn't want us to abandon the work
we've done," she said. She faced him, one leg on the bed, one
on the floor. Her hands sought his once more, clasped them to
her knee. "That's the good part. He doesn't feel that Hoorka
should stay on Neweden. I thought that the kin might react that
way—and your face is too open to have hidden it from me. I can
guess at what they told you. But they all admire you, Gyll.
You're the creator. McWilms is still sure of Hoorka's goals. The
rest of them will return to that way of thinking, in a few days or
weeks. Ahh, Gyll, don't look so damned hurt."

She pulled him to her—he didn't resist, didn't help. Arms
around chest, she hugged him; after a moment, Gyll put his arms
around her and returned the embrace. They kissed, softly, then
she laid her head on his shoulder. "Gyll, I don't want to fight.
Not tonight. I've hated it, every time." Her voice was a rough
whisper in his ear.

"You don't want to be Thane?" He spoke into the fragrance
of her hair.

He could feel her head shake—a short movement. "I'm not

giving that up, Gyll; neh. But I also don't want it to drive a
wedge between the two of us.''

"Mondom—" he began. Emotions warred: to tell her that he
had already made a decision in his own mind, to hold it back lest
he ruin the moment—the intimacy had become rarer between
them of late. "Mondom," he said again.

"Hush, love. Not now." Her mouth sought his, open. She
leaned back, pulling him down on her. He felt her hands slip
under the folds of his nightcloak, tug at his shirt. Warm, her
fingers kneaded his back and ran the hills of his spine. She
hugged him fiercely.

Aroused despite himself, he responded. He kissed her, as if
that gave denial to his doubts. The interior debate dissolved in
heat. He fumbled with the clasps of her blouse, and she laughed
under his mouth at his clumsiness. "Here, let me help."

"Quiet," he told her. "I can manage."

Cloth fell away, whispering.

Afterward, they lay in each other's arms. Mondom's breath
was cool on his face as he lazily stroked the damp smoothness of
her side, fingers tracing the lines of her body. As he reached her
waist, she quickly rolled away, muscles rippling under his hand.
"That tickles," she said, grinning.

"You didn't think so a few minutes ago." He touched her
again; she moved further back, then rolled into him, nipping at
his shoulder.

"Hey! That hurts, woman."

"You didn't think so a few minutes ago."

Gyll laughed, rubbing his shoulder. "Consider the point made."
He stroked her again, this time with more pressure. "Better?"
he asked.

She snuggled against him in answer.

They lay that way for several minutes, simply enjoying the
closeness, the dark, cool silence around them. Gyll's hand
moved. They kissed—long, slow, gentle—then lay back again.
Gyll found himself more aware than ever of the separation their
clashing prides had caused. He found himself wishing that they
could have returned to this long ago.

"You're thinking," Mondom said, a contralto accusation.

"I'm not allowed? And how did you know?"

"Your hand stopped. You're lying there with your eyes focused on the ceiling, open. You've entirely ceased to notice me,

yet nothing's intruded on us—the distraction has to be inside. Now, what are you thinking?''

He thought of delaying, of temporizing, then knew that even that hesitation had spoken for him. ''I wanted to tell you before,'' he said. ''So you'll have to forgive my waiting.''

On her side, head on hand, she waited.

''I think—I *know,* rather—what I want to do, for both your sake and mine,'' he continued. The words were slow at first, hesitant, but came faster and more definite as he went on. Mondom watched him as he spoke, her gaze never letting his eyes wander. ''That's what I've been ruminating over for the past several days. You need time, love, time without my interference so that the kin accept you wholly as Thane. I know you've felt it—a slowness when they take orders from you, a belligerence from some of them; Aldhelm was certainly that way.''

Sorrow tugged at the corners of her mouth at his mention of Aldhelm, then she frowned. ''All you're doing with this preamble is giving your words a sugarcoating, Gyll. I'm all grown up. If it's going to be bitter, just say it.'' Her stare challenged him. He couldn't evade it. He said nothing for a moment, gathering the words in his mind. Then he nodded, sighed.

''Yah, you're right.'' He took a breath, touching her, as if by contact he could make her take the phrases as he wished them to be taken. ''I want to go with Oldin. They'll be leaving in a few weeks. I want to spend a few months investigating the Trading Families; see what FitzEvard Oldin is holding for the Hoorka, see if we can be mutually helpful to each other. And that will leave you as the only authority here. It'll get me out of your way so that the kin don't go past you to me.''

''The kin have never 'gone past me.''' Her voice mocked him. ''It's just you and me, Gyll. We fight more than any of the rest of the kin.'' She glanced back at his hand, atop her waist. Slowly, he removed it.

''If that's the case, Mondom, then maybe we just need the time apart.''

''If you feel that way, all you have to do is say so. You don't have to go running off with this Oldin woman. Underasgard is big enough.''

So quickly from affection to argument: she had not moved, but Gyll could feel a growing distance between them. He chastised himself. *You knew it, you knew it . . .* ''Mondom, you're my friend, my lover, my only real confidant among the kin. Do you think I'd give that up so lightly?''

"I don't think you want to give *any*thing up, Gyll. Not me, not Neweden, not Oldin, not the Alliance, not—especially not—your leadership of Hoorka. I think you've found that you've made a mistake, giving up the thaneship."

He didn't try to deny it. "All I want to do is explore a possible new avenue for Hoorka, for my—*our*—kin. It doesn't violate any of our present agreements with the Li-Gallant or the Alliance, and it may give us a new avenue for expansion. It's just me and a few months, Mondom; that's all we're talking about. The Hoorka can spare that much."

Her laughter scraped at his composure. "With Aldhelm, Renier, Sartas, and Eorl dead? With McWilms hurt? With the kin's morale at low ebb? Gods, Gyll . . . The rotation's already too tight."

"Then one more out of it won't matter. And my work's been mediocre of late—that was everyone's complaint, even yours. I'll admit it." He could hear the bitterness creeping into his voice, the pitch moving higher and louder. He forced himself into calmness again; he tried to sound rational. "The kin can spare me. Both you and d'Mannberg are better teachers than I for the apprentices, and a quicker rotation will only hone the skills of Hoorka. We can use the practice room less."

"It's amazing how convincing you can be when you want something, Gyll." Mondom growled in disgust, deep in her throat. She rolled off the bedrield to her feet, whistling on a hoverlamp. Golden light threw harsh shadows across her body—under the disheveled hair, under the small breasts, across one leg. She half-turned from him, gazing into nether space. Her head shook, then she turned back to him. Her eyes were narrowed, hard; her face was pinched and somehow ugly.

"No," she said. "No. I don't like the idea. And Gyll . . . I want you to leave me now. Don't talk anymore. Just take your clothes and go back to your room. Go pet your wort."

"Mondom—"

"No!" She turned her back to him, facing the desk, the cold stone of the wall. "Just go."

She would say nothing else.

Helgin lounged against the side of the shuttle's landing gear. The gear was both dirty and oily; it smudged the sleeve of the tunic he wore. He scratched at his beard with a crooked forefinger and glanced at Gyll. Around them, the port made busy noises.

"She's not on *Peregrine,* Hoorka. She had business in Sterka, someone to see. I don't know when she'll be back, and I doubt that she'll be in the mood for visitors. Oh, she'll pretend it, but she's a poor actress."

Gyll didn't let his disappointment show. He nodded. "There wasn't anything specific . . . I just wanted to talk with her . . ." He felt vaguely foolish. He hadn't wanted to stay in Underasgard after the argument with Mondom and had come to the port on a whim. He'd gone to his rooms after leaving her, fed and cuddled the wort for a time, then left. It hadn't been until he reached Sterka that he realized where he was going. He'd gone through port security and out onto the field after seeing the shuttle in its dock.

"Well, she talks well enough. I'll grant that." Helgin moved against the gear. Grime smeared his back. "And she'd probably not mind talking with you, usually. But her real weakness is for short men with beards." He leered under the lush foliage of facial hair.

"Helgin, I don't know how to take you. I tell you again: You'd die on Neweden."

"You can pretend that if you like." The dwarf lurched upright. He stretched out his arms, seemed to see the dirt marbling the fabric for the first time, and grimaced. He rubbed at it. "You want to come inside? It's warmer."

Gyll shrugged. They entered the shuttle, went to the small lounge. Helgin walked over to an ornate chest sitting on the room's table and opened it. In a bed of bluish velvet, glass clinked. "Want a drink, Gyll? I've some brandy from Desolate that is better than fair."

Gyll stood, hesitant, but Helgin had already begun pouring. He handed one of the glasses to Gyll. The pungent odor wrinkled Gyll's nose; he sniffed, swirled the liquor. Helgin watched.

"Yah, that's the proper way—it doesn't do you a damn bit of good, but it looks nice," Helgin said. "Have a seat. You look distressed."

Gyll frowned, not sure whether he should be annoyed or flattered at the dwarf's concern. He watched the brandy move in the glass. "You talk too openly, Motsognir."

"Are you going to be stuffy again, Hoorka? You need to learn that people who have an affection for you aren't likely to jump behind your defenses and leave your ego in rubble. Either that, or you need to conceal your face better. And if that insults you, then so be it. Gods, I get tired of you Newedeners."

"I'm sure they're none too pleased with you," Gyll replied.

Helgin grinned. It was infectious. After a moment, Gyll could only smile back. Shaking his head, he sat in the nearest floater. Helgin sat across from him. "I don't understand you, Helgin. If you were one of my people, if you were guilded kin, then we'd have been in more than one fight over your atrocious lack of manners."

"And I'd've won most of them, which wouldn't have proved anything or have bettered those manners." Helgin drained his glass in a gulp. He grimaced, then smacked his lips and reached for the bottle.

"Is that the way you were taught to drink a brandy?" Gyll shuddered in sympathy.

"Ahh, you see, that's where you're wrong again. That *is* the way to drink a brandy on Desolate—quickly, before the sun takes it or dust settles on it or somebody tries to take it away. It's all in your cultural set." He poured. "Why'd you want to see Oldin?"

Gyll rotated the stem of the glass between thumb and forefinger; he took a sip. The brandy warmed its way down his throat. "Mondom and I talked again," he said at last. "Actually, we had a bit of a disagreement. She doesn't see any value in having Hoorka go with the Trading Families."

Helgin downed the second glass with an abrupt motion. He wiped at his lips with the back of his hand. "And where does that leave you?"

"I don't know," Gyll admitted. He sipped again, relishing the fiery tartness of the liquor.

"Do *you* see a value in it?"

"Yah." He said it easily, surprising himself.

"Then there's no problem. You go." The dwarf leaned back, then reached forward again for the bottle. Gyll could see a streak of oily filth on the floater's back. Helgin looked at the remainder of the brandy appraisingly, then set it down again.

"You don't understand, Helgin. It's not that easy. She *is* Thane. I've no authority over her; I gave all that up. She's the leader of my kin. She's also my lover, my friend. I risk losing all that. And she may well be right—it could all be a waste of time. Kaethe's simply vague about the possibilities, and in any event it's not her but her grandsire that would make any decision."

"Gods, you people make everything so complicated for yourselves." Helgin rose from his floater. He paced the room, pulling at his beard. "Everyone makes their decisions based on their fears. You're afraid of Mondom, so you chain yourself to Neweden. Your Li-Gallant's afraid to lose his power, so he raids the helpless lassari to demonstrate his capabilities. D'Embry's afraid of Niffleheim, and Kaethe—she's afraid of FitzEvard. All the choices predicated on fear, never on hope."

"What are you afraid of, Motsognir?" Gyll tugged at his nightcloak; he set the brandy glass on the arm of the floater. "All you do is talk."

"Nothing here frightens me."

"Then you don't know Neweden very well."

Helgin nodded. He halted his aimless wandering of the room and stood in front of Gyll. Gyll couldn't decide whether the dwarf was irritated; he glowered under the bristling of eyebrows, but he seemed to always glower.

"I know Neweden better than you might think, Gyll," Helgin said. "Better than maybe yourself. What event has occupied the minds of guilded kin for the last several months?"

"The killing of Gunnar, I suppose." Gyll could not fathom where Helgin was heading.

"Do you know who killed him?"

Lines deepened in Gyll's forehead. He leaned forward in his floater, feeling his stomach tensing. "You claim to have that knowledge, Motsognir?"

Helgin nodded; his beard moved on his soiled tunic. "Beyond any doubt."

Gyll could only think of Aldhelm, of the way he'd looked, transfixed on d'Mannberg's foil, the pain etched on his face. *Leave the Hag-kin alone. Let him rest.* "I've no interest in that."

"I couldn't tell you, in any case. And knowing wouldn't change any of the results. I'm pleased you don't ask. That's an advance in your perceptions."

"And all you've done is brag again, without having proved a thing." Gyll snorted disgust. "And you spout sophistry like a university professor. You're a deep man, Helgin, for one so short."

"Then let me tell you something else." Helgin reached for the brandy with deliberate nonchalance. He poured himself another glassful, watching Gyll. Gyll sat in what he hoped was an attitude of stolid unconcern. He was growing tired of the Motsognir's posturing. Helgin looked as if he were about to drink, then lowered the glass slightly. His dark eyes regarded Gyll over the rim. "You *need* to go with Kaethe, Gyll. She makes noises like she's very interested in whether you do so or not, but in reality I tell you that it doesn't really much matter to her. It can't, because she has to do what FitzEvard wishes. But you *need* the

Trading Families, if you really are concerned with the survival of
Hoorka. Neweden doesn't yet realize it, but Gunnar's death is a
watershed. Neweden was slowly changing, but his death has
tipped the balance. With Gunnar gone, with Potok in exile and
his rule-guild in disgrace, Vingi has a free hand, and he's not
clever enough to use it well. Neweden is going to undergo a
wracking change and the Hoorka—if they want survival—are
going to need as many options as they can gather.''

"That may or may not be, but Mondom doesn't want it. And I
only have your word that this 'change' will occur. That doesn't
mean much, does it?''

There was silence for a moment. Gyll stroked the bowl of his
brandy glass. He glanced up, but Helgin was peering into the
depths of his own dark liquid as if some answer were hidden
there. Then, with that same casual toss, the dwarf drank. His
eyes closed for a second, then he threw the glass aside. It
shattered in a corner.

"Get up," he said.

Gyll hesitated, uncertain as to the Motsognir's intention. The
knot of tension in his stomach returned. He rose, slowly, looking
down at the dwarf.

"Get out your vibro."

"Helgin—"

"Get it out," Helgin growled, hands on hips. A sandalled foot
scuffed at the floor impatiently.

Gyll moved his nightcloak aside with a practiced swing,
unsheathing the vibro in the same movement. He held it before
the dwarf, unactivated. The Motsognir nodded, then stepped
back. He spread his hands apart, crouching.

"Turn it on and come at me."

"Helgin, I don't—"

"*Do* it."

Nearly, he did not. Almost, he turned and walked away. But
the dwarf started a mirthless laugh as Gyll's hand dropped, and
that brought the vibro back up. Gyll touched the stud on the hilt
and the vibrowire slicked out to dagger length: threatening, for
unlike the foils, the dagger could not be adjusted to a lesser
setting. Its low murmur shivered in his hand. Gyll saw that
Helgin's attention was now focused on the weapon. "It's not
going to prove anything, Helgin."

"Don't worry, Hoorka. You're not going to touch me. You're
too old and too fat for that. Look at your waist—you're out of
shape. Try it."

"You're a fool."

"Then let me be one. I'll prove it otherwise. Come at me, or does even this kind of challenge frighten you?"

Gyll wasn't angry. The taunts were too transparent for that. He was only puzzled. Yet he did move forward, letting his instincts guide him but still holding back: he did not want to harm the dwarf. Helgin backed away as Gyll advanced, then suddenly rolled and kicked in one gliding motion. Gyll winced as Helgin's foot caught his wrist, moving the vibro aside and nearly tearing it from his hand. Instinct ruled: he jabbed at the Motsognir, but the dwarf was too quick. The vibro sliced air, and Helgin was past and on his feet again before Gyll could turn.

"You see, Hoorka. You're not nearly as good as you like to think." Still in that low crouch, Helgin sneered. His teeth gleamed in lamplight, mocking.

Gyll said nothing, but now he too set his balance lower, the vibro moving before him in a small, tight circle. He closed cautiously, backing the dwarf to the wall, not letting him slip past. Helgin swept out an arm, cuffing at Gyll's knife hand. Gyll cut at the hand, and Helgin came at him, a blur of motion, shouting. Gyll felt pain lance his forearm as Helgin struck him; grunting, he slashed, felt the vibro touch, and then Helgin hit him again. He couldn't hold the vibro this time—he heard it clatter away from him.

They faced each other, breathing heavily. Beneath torn cloth, a jagged line of blood showed on Helgin's arm. Gyll stared at it, and in that hesitation, Helgin could have attacked or dove for the vibro. He did neither. The Motsognir abruptly straightened. He began the usual grin, but midway it was inverted into grimace. He touched his injured arm gingerly, looked at the blood on his finger as if he could deny its existence. "Well," he growled.

"I'm sorry, Helgin." Gyll shook his head. "You ... goaded me. I didn't mean ..."

"Yah. Don't worry, Hoorka. I'll live. And I could have still taken you. You gave me too much time, and you've a lot to learn about using your hands and feet as weapons. If you want proof ..." Again, Helgin went into that crouch, but Gyll shook his head once more.

"I don't want to fight you."

Helgin stared at Gyll.

"Let's call it even," Gyll continued. "You disarmed me, and, yah, I'll even admit you're far better than I would have thought, and I wouldn't want to face you on even terms. I don't consider you a braggart any longer."

Helgin nodded, pursing his thick lips. He scratched at his beard. "You don't like killing, do you?"

Gyll forced down irritation. "I don't like unnecessary bloodletting. That's all."

"Ahh." Helgin said nothing more. Rubbing his arm, he strode past Gyll back to his floater. Gyll went to where the vibro lay, picked it up, and sheathed it again. He sat.

"If both you and I were fools," Helgin said, "that little exhibition would prove that I've always spoken the truth to you. But I don't consider you a fool—you can think what you want about the rest. But . . . I repeat, Gyll, you need to go with Oldin."

Gyll did not want to return to that subject. "You need your arm attended to."

Helgin glanced down. Blood had soaked into the raveled edges of cloth. "It's a scratch. And you're avoiding the statement."

"I can't do much about it. You say it's for the sake of Hoorka. Fine. But if I go against Mondom, then I've done quite a bit to harm Hoorka myself, just by that act. Either way, I seem to lose. And if I'm here, at least I have a chance to give her advice."

Helgin made a disgusted sound. "You need to learn another lesson, Gyll. Worlds and politics don't matter. It's the individuals involved in them. You need to worry about yourself first. A little healthy selfishness never hurt anyone."

"I'm done talking about it."

A dour head shake; Helgin leaned forward, poured Gyll more brandy, then sat back holding the bottle. "Then we'll talk about something else. Have you ever seen rockfoam from Karm's Hole? It puts a polished ippicator bone to shame . . ."

They were still talking about nothing when Kaethe returned to the shuttle a few hours later.

14

An excerpt from the acousidots of Sondall-Cadhurst Cranmer. The following was a very informal recording—much like some of the others, it was most likely done without Gyll Hermond's knowledge or consent. The "Ramulf" spoken of appears in the Neweden Chronicles as a minor thief executed on 9.19.214—

evidently some discussion of this was used by Cranmer as a device to probe Hermond.

EXCERPT FROM THE DOT OF 9.20.214:

"... but you have to realize, Sond, that Ramulf is—eh, *was*—just a friggin' lassari. Man, you can't expect better from the kinless."

"They're just people like the rest, Thane. The fact that you're part of a guild doesn't alter your basic personality."

"You say that, but I notice that you tend to avoid lassari, too."

"I would have thought you'd be more sympathetic toward them."

"Hmm? Explain yourself, scholar."

"As I understand it, your family was lassari. Your father . . ."

"My *true-father*—" (Here Gyll pauses, as if pressing home a point) "—was lassari, yah. But that relationship, true-father to biological son, doesn't have much importance on Neweden. Once you've reached puberty, you're jussar and free to find guild-kin. My true-father and my true-mother died lassari—I don't hide that fact from anyone because it doesn't bring any shame to me. If he'd had even a spark of creativity . . . but his mind didn't work that way. Understand: he was an offworlder; trained to kill, yah, but narrow-minded and stupid. He didn't have the cultural set for Neweden. I grew up here—Neweden is ingrained in me. My true-father was dirt, a common thief. I'm glad he bothered to train me as he did, but I'd still spit in his face if he were alive. He's lassari. I could synthesize his training, his skills, and I saw that I could devise something out of it that would be viable here."

"Your true-father was executed?"

"Sent to the Hag unguilded and without honor, as he deserved. It doesn't hurt to say that, Cranmer. Neweden isn't and shouldn't be kind to murderers—it's the foulest thing to do when you can declare bloodfeud and retain your honor and your vengeance. Man, I'm not kidding you—if I met my true-father tomorrow I'd prick him with my blade, and it wouldn't be a fast death."

"Hell, Thane, the Hoorka slay, what—fifty, sixty people a standard? I know your objection, too, so don't say it. You've no personal grudge against those people; you don't even know them. Even *I* might be able to kill someone who'd provoked me a great deal, but I doubt that I could go out and kill without provocation—do it for pay."

"In a war you'd be killing, and doing it for pay. Cranmer, you ought to think before you talk."

"Still, I have to persist. The Hoorka aren't at war."

"Hag's ass, Cranmer. Then why do you bother with us? You can find an assassin on a hundred worlds, but you chose to look at the Hoorka—if you didn't think us different, you wouldn't bother."

"Do you enjoy your work?"

(Here there is a long pause. Hermond seems to be about to reply, then stops in mid-syllable.) "I don't enjoy it, scholar. I also don't necessarily dislike it. It's what I've been trained for, and it's all subject to the gods' wishes."

"That's all? Thane, I think I know you better."

(A breath-sigh.) "And you won't rest until I say more . . ."

(Laughter. But it is only Cranmer's gaiety that is heard.)

"Fine, Şond. I'll tell you something, then, but if it ever goes past this room, if it's ever whispered to anyone else, I'll have you given to the Hag in pieces. At times, every once in a while, I wonder if I'd do this again, if I'd create the Hoorka. And I ask myself if all the souls I've sent to the Hag aren't going to be waiting for me when it's my turn."

Long before they could be seen, the presence of the Dead was announced. First, a faint and distant chant like the sound of a muffled chorus; then, as the soughing chant became louder and more distinct, the acrid smell of the too-sweet incense invaded the air. Nostrils wrinkled, heads began to turn . . .

The procession of the Dead snaked through the outer streets of Sterka toward the ornate arch that signified the boundary of Neweden's capital. They ignored the fine, soaking mist the morning had brought.

There, near the Avenue of Taverns, a band of jussar had gathered under the weathershield of the Inn of Seven Ogres. This was the group's daily ritual, however confined by the weather— the flaunting of their carefree status, neither kin nor kinless, a loud display of self. They wore little despite the chill drizzle; the day had the promise of summer's heat and the clouds near the horizon looked broken, a possible herald of late sun. Fluoro-patterns swirled on bare chests, around the nexus of nipples; chains of heavy, dull links draped over the right shoulders and wrapped twice around the waists. On their wide belts, sheathed vibros were prominent. The jussar jostled one another (the inn-master looking out in disgust but not having the heart to cast the youths out into the rain) and annoyed the passersby. They made their comments with a caution native to them: jussar were tolerated past the point of other guild-kin—and certainly beyond the constricted limits of lassari—but they were by no means inviolate. Despite the patience shown them, jussar died as often as kin in insult-born arguments.

The slow tidal swell of the Hag's chant came to them, mixed with the subsonic drone of the port's machinery and the assorted waking-sounds of Sterka. They laughed. The Dead were easy prey on a miserable day, a harmless butt for jest and gibe. As the procession came into view down the long expanse of the avenue, the jussar strolled out onto the wet pavement, splashing each other, cursing, laughing. They arranged themselves in a ragged double line, a gauntlet through which the Dead would have to pass. The Dead paid them no attention, continuing the march with eyes focused ahead or half-shut, their mouths moving in the endless mantra. The jussar harried them, shouting insults, pushing against them, the boys fondling obscenely the female Dead, the girls taunting the men with bare breasts and suggestive touches.

They received little reaction, but it was a pleasant enough diversion.

Until . . .

One of the jussar, mouth open in a giggling shout, stumbled up against a Dead One—a burly man who looked as if he might once have been a laborer or mercenary. The man's torn shirt revealed the squared firmness of taut musculature. He staggered back as the jussar shoved against him to regain his balance, but the Dead One retained his footing with a deft movement. The jussar, still giggling, pushed at the man again, easily, half-turning away as he did so, obviously expecting no resistance.

The Dead One did as none of the Dead had done before: he reached out with a meaty hand, clamped fingers on the jussar's shoulder, pulling him back. "Hey!" the jussar said, angrily, as he turned, but the Dead One's fist stopped his words. The boy held his nose in pain and surprise, blood trickling from one nostril and over the fingers. For a moment, the tableau held, the jussar sniffing in consternation, the Dead One with his hand still fisted at his side, his composure shattered and his mouth slack with surprise. The chant-bell the Dead One held in his other hand dropped to the pavement with a dull clunking.

The jussar, with a scream of rage, hauled the man from the Dead's procession. The rest of the Dead walked on, seemingly uninterested in their fellow's plight. The group of youths surrounded him, leering; he made no further resistance, head down, hands at sides. The jussar closed about him. Fists rose and fell, the whine of a vibro shrilled. They beat him bloody and senseless, leaving him in the puddles of the street.

The Dead, uncaring, went through the arch and away from Sterka. They would seek Hag Death elsewhere.

The Regent d'Embry laced her fingers together on her bare desk top. The fingers were alternately blue and red—bodytint shimmered at the interface of color.

"I'm glad all of you were able to be here on such short notice," she said. "This business could have been conducted over com-units, but I prefer the more personal contact."

The two Hoorka seated across from her looked everywhere but at the Regent. Kaethe Oldin, cloaked in a heavy and glaring-orange cape, had her back to the rest of them, intent on the d'Vellia soundsculpture in the corner of the room. D'Embry was slightly puzzled by the attitude of the Hoorka. All her reports had said that Gyll and Mondom were quite close, lovers, yet the two were seemingly at odds: it showed in the way the Ulthane leaned away from Mondom, in the covert glances the woman sent toward him. D'Embry shrugged mentally. She felt *good,* for once; she would allow none of this to bother her, not a tiff between the Hoorka, not the presence of Oldin, not the dreary rain that pattered on her window. She'd not realized just how much the annoyance of Oldin had permeated her moods.

"You're kicking me off Neweden." Kaethe spoke without turning from the sculpture. As the others glanced at her—d'Embry with a sudden, unbidden scowl—Kaethe touched the artwork with an appreciative forefinger. She took a step toward the desk. Under the metallic arch of her eyebrows, her face revealed no distress. "It doesn't matter greatly to me, Regent. I've been thrown out before. You're by no means the first to do so; the Families are quite used to it. How long do I have?"

D'Embry determined once more that she would not let Oldin antagonize her. She regarded the woman blandly—no one noticed the whitening of flesh under the bodytint as her hands clenched together more firmly. "Since you've anticipated me so well, I won't bother with niceties, Trader Oldin. I want *Peregrine* and you and all your paraphernalia out of orbit and heading away tomorrow."

Oldin glanced toward Gyll. D'Embry saw the contact and

wondered at it. Mondom too looked at Gyll. "By the terms of
the pact"—Kaethe returned her attention to d'Embry—"I've a
right to know why you're taking this action." She stepped
forward again, so that the full cape touched the edge of d'Embry's
desk. The cloth was distressingly bright; d'Embry found the
color hideous and most unflattering to Oldin's skin.

"For our part, I wonder why you've asked the Hoorka here,"
Mondom said.

"Your guild is peripherally involved in this, and I've other
business to discuss after Trader Oldin has left. However, if you
want to leave until we've concluded this..."

"No, Thane Mondom, by all means stay. It'll be an education
for you." Oldin smiled, but there was little friendliness in the
gesture. Still, of the four, she alone appeared relaxed, neither
uncomfortable nor impatient. Oldin glanced about, reached down
to extrude a hump-chair from the floor, and seated herself heavily
and too quickly. "I'll never accustom myself to this much
gravity," she said. She arranged the cape loosely around her.
"Set out your case, Regent."

"Very well." D'Embry turned cold gray eyes to Oldin. "First,
there is the matter of two voided guarantees on items purchased
by Neweden citizens."

"That's petty, Regent." Oldin dismissed the point with a wave
of her hand. "That can easily be rectified."

"I don't doubt that, Trader. But there is also the Hoorka
contract you signed against Cade Gies. In itself, I can do nothing
about that, as much as I find it distasteful. But... in his work for
the Alliance, Gies had access to the Center terminals. We've
discovered that he had abused that privilege, having illegally
obtained records from the archives. There was some attempt at
deception, but the man was rather clumsy, and his access-code
has been traced. We've searched his office and rooms thoroughly,
but have been unable to find the printouts of that information he
acquired. We also have found that Gies 'purchased' several
expensive Trader items—they were in his rooms. He could not
possibly have afforded them on his salary."

"I see your implications, Regent—you needn't go any further
with this. I have heard no proof that I'm in any degree responsible for the alleged espionage."

Oldin leaned forward in her seat. Elbow on thigh, she cupped
her chin in her hand. With the same faint mocking smile, she
waited. "And what else, Regent?" she asked.

"There's another matter, which may or may not be directly related to the first: the death of Sirrah Guillene on Heritage."

D'Embry, anticipating, saw the glance between the two Hoorka. It confirmed her suspicions—the Hoorka were involved in Guillene's murder. She felt no anger. From what she had heard of Heritage and Moache's practices there, Guillene was not someone that would be greatly mourned. Still, it irritated her that Mondom and Gyll would have circumvented her authority in that manner.

Oldin slouched back in the chair. "That's just rancor on your part, Regent. I know Niffleheim's been screaming about that one, and I think you've been listening to your own paranoia."

Damn the woman. So frigging smug . . . The thoughts surged, and d'Embry choked them down, trying to retain the good humor, the anticipation of success. "Ulthane Gyll was ferried up to *Peregrine* the day Guillene died. He was there for quite some time."

"That's not exactly an offense." Oldin glanced at Gyll, the smile widened. D'Embry watched Mondom watching Gyll.

"Yet you have to admit that it arouses suspicions," she said. "I've no delusions about the Families' wiles—you could have easily slipped past our monitors."

"Proof, Regent?"

D'Embry shrugged. "I'll admit that I have very little at the moment. Still, I've forwarded a record of my order to Niffleheim. I asked you here so that you're legally informed and to see if you wish to have a court examination to determine the justification of the eviction order. By the pact. Do you want it, Trader? I assure you that if you say yes, I'll have my people begin digging, very hard. I think we both know what will be found."

"There's nothing to find, Regent. Believe me. I guarantee it." For a brief second, their eyes met, locked in interior battle. Then Oldin's lips lifted in her mocking smirk, and she leaned back. "But *Peregrine* was leaving soon in any event. Our sales have slowed, and your port charges aren't cheap. I'd already told Ulthane Gyll of that intention. Having you bring together the courtmasters and arranging for my defense would take up more time than I'd planned to spend on Neweden. It's simply not worth the trouble, Regent. I'll obey your damned order." With a groan of exertion, she stood. The cape settled around her knees. "Which means that I've much to arrange. Is that all, then, Regent?"

"Almost, Trader Oldin. I've heard that you may have extended an invitation to Hoorka, some offer."

Oldin pursed her lips, nodding. "Good, good. Your sources are excellent, and I compliment you, Regent. I'll have to check the tongues of some of my crew. But...any agreement between the Hoorka and Family Oldin is only my business and theirs."

D'Embry looked from Oldin to the Hoorka. Mondom stared into a blank corner of the office. Gyll examined his callused hands. "Oldin's right," he said. "It's not the concern of the Alliance."

"As long as the Hoorka are based on Neweden, *every*thing the Hoorka do affects the Alliance." D'Embry's voice had the inflections of a teacher scolding a child. It snapped Gyll's head up. His mouth was a tight line, but he said nothing.

"You see, Ulthane—the Alliance always works on bluster and force." Oldin, near the door, grinned back at them. "They try so hard to make you fear them, so that you do what they say and don't upset their nice, safe, little boundaries."

"Trader Oldin, if you wish to see force, keep *Peregrine* in orbit after tomorrow." Softly.

Oldin shook her head. A brief coruscation, her eyebrows caught light. "It's not worth it, Regent. I'd love to be the one to teach you a lesson about overestimation of abilities, but it'll have to be postponed for now. Grandsire would be upset if I endangered the pact without his permission. You played out the scenario nicely, though, timed it just right. It will look like you succeeded in getting rid of me, when all you had to do was wait a few more weeks. I'm certain it'll look good on your record. Niffleheim can say to Moache, see, we got rid of the nasty troublemakers."

"For a woman with much to get ready, you talk a lot."

Again, that eternal smile. "I'll be going now. Ulthane, Thane; whatever she says to you, remember that what we've spoken about is still valid. Don't make a decision just because you're scared of jeopardizing your standing with the Alliance. They're a dying breed. They'll soon join the ippicators and the Hag like all the rest."

Oldin slapped at the door control, swept through, and strode into the corridors of Center.

D'Embry watched the door sigh closed. She'd not moved from her position. The hands were still in an attitude of reverence on the desk, the spine was erect against the straight-backed floater. "That wasn't a scene I wished the two of you to see."

Mondom shrugged. She brushed at the shoulder of her nightcloak. "How does it affect Hoorka? That's all I care about."

"Did you send someone to Heritage?"

"We'd declared bloodfeud against Guillene, m'Dame. All we wanted was his death, in any manner it could be accomplished. If someone else did the deed before us, it really doesn't matter. Guillene's Hag-kin now, and we don't speak of him."

"You haven't answered the question."

Silence.

After a moment, d'Embry exhaled heavily, closing her eyes. She unclenched her hands, her posture sagged. The movement aged her. She tapped at the desk with a finger the color of ice. "I don't know where this leaves us, Thane, Ulthane. Niffleheim was upset with the entire Heritage affair—the Hoorka work well enough for Neweden, but Heritage . . ."

"Which means what, Regent?" Mondom asked the question.

"It means that there has to be some reevaluation, an examination of Hoorka and the Alliance."

"But you're not restricting us to Neweden again?"

"I didn't say that, Thane."

"What *are* you saying?" Gyll broke in. He was tired, tired of the evasion, tired of the semantic games he'd seen played here this morning. He'd rather be out in the drizzle and clouds, or back in Underasgard—to have time to think.

D'Embry smiled faintly. "I'm sorry, Ulthane. You'll have to forgive an old woman her whims. I'll try to be more direct. I do feel that the Hoorka can still find a place in the Alliance. But I think we—you and Thane Mondom and I—need to examine the offworld contracts more carefully, with an eye toward the compatibility of social structures. For the time being, I'm going to hold all contracts in abeyance, until I've had the opportunity to study this more."

"But we'll eventually have offworld work?" Mondom.

"I would think so."

Mondom looked at Gyll. He was unable to decipher her expression. It seemed to waver between triumph and uncertainty.

"In that case, you may consider the Hoorka to have dropped any thought of working with the Trading Families."

D'Embry nodded. "That's good, Thane. I wouldn't have liked the other options open to me."

Gyll could only seethe, silent, in frustration.

The thin, cold drizzle glazed the expanse of Sterka Port. The rain-slicked surface darkly mirrored the ships on their pads, the spires and conveyors that fed and relieved them. Further back were the huddled buildings of the city, looking miserable under the mist and low clouds.

Gyll turned from the window and handed his identification to the impassive gate-ward. "I'm boarding the *Peregrine* shuttle," he said.

The ward nodded, glancing at Gyll, the full pack over the Hoorka's shoulder, the bumblewort in its traveling cage. He rustled the flimsies in pretended scrutiny. "You know *Peregrine*'s asked for clearance to leave orbit." The sentence fell halfway between declaration and query.

"I know," Gyll replied. He gave his attention to the view outside the window again.

It had not been a pleasant day. He and Mondom had begun arguing from the moment they'd left d'Embry's offices. It was a quiet disagreement, marked by an exaggerated politeness that bothered him more than any violent confrontation. The apprentice driving their flitter had kept his eyes discreetly averted, but Gyll knew that the ears had been busy. The gossip would spread through Underasgard as soon as his shift was done. Mondom had left him at Tri-Guild Square, saying that she had errands to run. Gyll knew the excuse was to avoid continuing the discussion in her rooms where the civilized pretense could be dropped. And he knew that her position was now set in stone, hardened by her fear of losing authority as Thane. She would not bend.

He'd begun packing as soon as he returned to his rooms. He took very little beyond a few essentials, amazed at what he felt he could do without for the few months he would be with Oldin. He could have given the wort to Cranmer for the duration, but he indulged a whim and shrank the field-cage down to traveling size. A few months . . . and then he would know whether the Families were worth further expenditure of energy. He told himself that Mondom's anger would be softened by time.

And he told himself that he wasn't simply avoiding Mondom by doing it in this manner. He left a short note for her in her com-unit; it would have to be enough.

The ward snapped shut the paper-case with a grunt. "You'll need to be quick, then. You'll only have a few hours before she leaves."

He nodded—the ward did not have to know that he didn't intend to return before *Peregrine* left. Gyll started toward the field entrance.

"Gyll!"

The shout turned him. Down the corridor stood Mondom,

breathing rapidly as if after a long run. Port workers and passengers moved aside, away from the Hoorka woman with anger on her face, her nightcloak back to reveal the dagger at her belt. Gyll watched her approach, waiting, willing himself to stay calm. The wort moved in the cage, curling itself in a corner. Mondom stopped a few meters away, hands on hips, frowning. The gate-ward began to come forward and demand her papers, but Mondom quelled him with a look.

"Ulthane," she said. Her voice was dangerously quiet. "I hope you're not taking the shuttle. I hope it was just an airing for the wort." Over her dark eyes, lines deepened.

He shrugged helplessly. "I'm sorry, Mondom."

"*Thane* Mondom, Ulthane. You left Underasgard without my permission. You break your own code—obedience to the Thane is paramount."

"I told you what I intended." Then, after a pause: "Thane. We've gone over it too many times. I'm doing this for the good of your own authority and for Hoorka. That's not exactly deserving of censure."

"You're doing it for yourself first. I know you that well, Gyll." For a moment, the harshness softened, the lines of her face smoothing. Gyll thought she might smile, that they might hug and depart still friends. But her stance had not altered, and if her fingers clenched uneasily, they still strayed near the hilt of her dagger. Her eyebrows lowered, the corners of her mouth twisted down. "I didn't want it to come to a confrontation, Gyll, but you seem to want to force it. Fine. As Thane, as kin-lord of your guild, I'm telling you to return to Underasgard. We'll talk there, try to settle our differences—maybe we need to split the guild, start another guildhome on Illi or the Waste, with you Thane of one. I don't know, but we can find some way to assuage your boredom, your ennui. But first you have to come back."

Almost, he stepped toward her. He swayed. Then his resolution hardened. "I can't."

"You mean you won't."

Again, he shrugged. There seemed to be nothing else to do. He stared at Mondom, willing her to back down, but she would not—she returned his gaze flatly. Gyll shifted the pack on his shoulder, hefted the wort's cage in his right hand, wiped at the sweat on his forehead. The gate-ward examined papers to one side. Passersby stared curiously at the two, sidling past and giving the Hoorka as much space as possible in the corridor.

"Mondom, you know how I feel about you. I really don't want to hurt you. That's partly why I want to go with the Families."

Her face spoke disbelief.

"I don't want to hurt myself, either," he continued. "It's better this way. When I come back, much of the pain'll be gone. We'll both be surer of ourselves, more confident of our positions." He waited for her to answer, half-wanting her to say something to convince him to stay, half-impatient to leave. His fingers drummed the strap of the pack. When she said nothing, he finally turned away. Through the windows of the port, he could see the Trader shuttle. Under the spidery bulk, a figure lounged near the lift: Helgin.

"You can't go as Hoorka, Gyll."

He stopped.

"I mean that, Gyll." Her voice wavered on the edge of breaking. Her defiance was brittle; he knew he could break it with a word. Her gaze fluttered, away and back. "If you go, you do so unguilded. Lassari, not Hoorka-kin. And you won't be welcome to return."

"You can't mean that."

"I do, Gyll. I mean it more than anything else I've ever said to you."

He could see a trembling in her lower lip, but he knew her better than to think it vulnerability. Emotion, yes; she might give in to tears when this was over and she was alone, but he could sense no weakness in her resolve now. He wanted to touch her, to pull her to him, but he knew he could not—she wouldn't allow it. *It would make you look silly, old fool. It's over between you.*

"You'll change your mind," he said. "When I come back."

"No." Chin lifting, she defied him. "Stay or go; it's your decision, Gyll. I'm long past thinking I can change your mind or force you into acceptance with logic or bribes or love. You insist on doing everything alone. Fine. But you're not going as Hoorka, and if you step on that ship, you may as well stay with the Families forever. You've Hoorka property on you. I've come to reclaim it."

"*What?*" Surprise lashed him into irritation. He nearly bellowed the word. People nearby halted in mid-stride. "I *made* the guild, woman. I got us everything we share."

"And now you've cast yourself from the kin. Your nightcloak, the guild holoclasp, that vibro: they all belong to Hoorka. I'll let you have the wort's cage, but I want the rest, Gyll." Her fingers caressed the dagger's hilt. "I'm as stubborn as you. Or is the Ulthane a thief as well as lassari?"

Her eyes were suddenly arid, the verging tears gone. Even the gate-ward, an offworlder, could sense the head of the conflict. He put his back to a wall, eyes wide. Muttering, those watching skittered away. Gyll was startled by Mondom's quick vehemence, the casual use of the impersonal mode to insult him. He grimaced, lips drawn back. He set the wort's cage on the floor, let the pack fall unheeded. He set his legs apart, a fighting stance. For a long moment, they regarded each other, balanced between fury and defiance.

That's Mondom, not some contracted victim, not an enemy. Gyll's restless hand touched the smooth leather of his vibro sheath. *You've not liked taking blood—do you want hers so badly?*

"I mean it, Gyll."

The rage left him. He couldn't do this, couldn't let the conflict become physical. *You forced it, old man. Be satisfied with it.* Slowly, Gyll forced himself to calmness. He unclasped the nightcloak from his shoulders, swinging the heavy cloth around and letting it drop around his feet. Then, hurrying as if he wanted the task done, he unbuckled the sheath-belt with the Hoorka insignia and let vibro and belt drop on top of the cloak. He stared down at the pile.

He felt very naked.

"Is this the way you want it?" he asked.

She shook her head, slowly, sadly. She let her nightcloak fall around her shoulder, reached back to pull the hood up so that her face was shadowed. All he could see was the glinting of her pupils. "No, Gyll. It's the way *you* wanted it."

"That's very facile." He could not stop the words from sounding bitter.

A shrug.

"Your feelings will change, Mondom. You'll miss me, miss the advice and help I can give you. You'll need it, when the Li-Gallant tries to control the guild's way, when d'Embry procrastinates on her promises." He bent down to retrieve the pack; it slid over his shoulder easily without the encumbrance of the nightcloak. He picked up the wort's cage. Outside the window, above its rain-image, the shuttle still waited.

To the side, the ward began rustling paper once more.

"I won't say that you're wrong, Gyll. But there's a lot of scars that have to heal. I don't think I'll change my decision."

Mondom stepped forward, bent to take the cloak and vibro. Holding them in her arm, she looked at Gyll. He could not guess at what she might be feeling under the mask of gray and black cloth. They were close enough to touch, but then she pivoted and began walking away. Gyll watched her leave, thinking with every step that she would stop for another word, another chance at reconciliation.

She reached an intersecting hallway and turned left.

Gyll was suddenly aware of the gaggle of people, offworlders and Newedeners, staring at him. He forced himself into aloofness. *Feel the emotions, yes, but keep them hidden. You have to feel, but don't let the others see it unless they are your kin.* The old code. The Hoorka lore he'd created.

Except that now he had no kin.

Gyll moved away from the onlookers and Neweden. He walked out into the damp embrace of the sky.

Helgin, seeing his approach, waved.

ABOUT THE AUTHOR

STEPHEN LEIGH has been selling short stories to SF magazines (*Analog, Asimov's, Destinies*) since 1976. Although he has a Bachelor's degree in Fine Art and Art Education, he makes his living as a bass guitarist and singer for a couple of rock groups. He is married to Denise Parsley Leigh, who is an activist in SF fandom, and they presently live in Cincinnati, OH. His previous book about Neweden was SLOW FALL TO DAWN, which was one of the first novels on the 1981 Locus Recommended Reading List.

A powerful new novel
by one of the most brilliant
and evocative writers of our time.

NEVERYÓNA
by Samuel R. Delany

For Pryn, a young girl who flees the village of Ellamon on the back of a dragon, Neveryóna is a shining symbol, just out of reach. Her search leads her to the exotic port city of Kolhari, where she walks with Gorgik the Liberator as he schemes against the Court of Eagles. It brings her to the house of Madame Keyne, a wealthy merchant woman trapped by her own desires. And it sends Pryn on a journey with a circle of strange stars, seeking a mad queen's golden treasure and an answer to the riddle of a city beyond the edges of imagination.

Buy *NEVERYÓNA*, on sale March 15, 1983, wherever Bantam paperbacks are sold or use this handy coupon for ordering: